# THE K

## Other books by Julia Clarke

Between You and Me
Chasing Rainbows
Summertime Blues
You Lose Some, You Win Some
The Other Alice

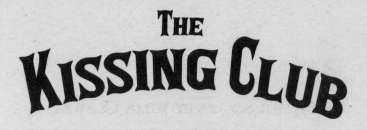

# THE KISSING CLUB

BY JULIA CLARKE

# OXFORD
## UNIVERSITY PRESS

Great Clarendon Street, Oxford OX2 6DP

Oxford University Press is a department of the University of Oxford.
It furthers the University's objective of excellence in research, scholarship,
and education by publishing worldwide in

Oxford   New York

Auckland   Cape Town   Dar es Salaam   Hong Kong   Karachi
Kuala Lumpur   Madrid   Melbourne   Mexico City   Nairobi
New Delhi   Shanghai   Taipei   Toronto

With offices in

Argentina   Austria   Brazil   Chile   Czech Republic   France   Greece
Guatemala   Hungary   Italy   Japan   Poland   Portugal   Singapore
South Korea   Switzerland   Thailand   Turkey   Ukraine   Vietnam

Oxford is a registered trade mark of Oxford University Press
in the UK and in certain other countries

British Library Cataloguing in Publication Data

Data available

ISBN-13: 978-0-19-275416-5

1 3 5 7 9 10 8 6 4 2

Printed in Great Britain by Cox and Wyman Ltd, Reading, Berkshire

Paper used in the production of this book is a natural,
recyclable product made from wood grown in sustainable forests.

The manufacturing process conforms to the enviromental
regulations of the country of origin.

'Success has many fathers, but failure is an orphan.'
Proverb


To all the wonderful people who were kind
to me when I was an orphan.
This book is for you.

# PRELUDE

When I was fourteen I joined the 'Kissing Club'. I became a professional virgin and also gave up telling lies. The first bit was pretty easy—the second was pretty hard . . . But I'd better start at the beginning—if I am going to tell the truth about what happened.

OK, so, now . . . this is the totally true story. Promise. It was Easter. I had gone to the USA to stay with my pen pal—Augusta. Augusta and I had been friends since her dad worked at the American military base that had been built on the moors high above our village. When Augusta arrived at our small local school she was instantly unpopular. She was too loud, too pushy, she wore weird clothes and spoke funny . . . you know the kind of thing. And the harder she tried to join in and make people like her, the harder they ignored her. I too was a bit of an outsider (my parents were from Leeds so we were incomers). But at least I spoke with a Yorkshire accent, wore clothes from ASDA, knew how to whisper, and didn't say I was going to 'the bathroom' when I wanted a wee.

Anyway, although Augusta was quite a bit older than me, none of the kids of her age would speak to her and I suppose that's why we palled up. But, for whatever reason, we started spending time together and soon become inseparable at school. I imagine I was a bit weird at that age anyway, so we made a good pair.

Being friends with Augusta was the start of my double life as a compulsive liar. Augusta was my best friend at school—we didn't socialize outside. Maybe this was because of the age difference between us, maybe because she lived up at the military base and they didn't like visitors. This suited me because my two other best friends (Florence and Sienna) went to a private school in Harrogate so we met up only at weekends. It was as if I lived in two separate worlds and I could play god and organize them any way I wanted. So at weekends I told stories about me and Augusta (and Augusta's amazing life) and during the week I told Augusta strange and marvellous tales about my Saturday and Sunday exploits and my crazy companions.

I fell into a very easy game of telling tall stories and it was completely addictive. And even when Augusta's dad got posted back to the States I still didn't stop. When Augusta got home we emailed and snail-mailed each other all the time and sent each other photos and presents. And it was just so comforting to write to Augusta about all the things which I wished were happening in my life—instead of all the boring stuff that was reality. And I didn't even have the lingering worry that my two worlds might at some point collide and

I would be found out. My imagination went into overdrive. Sometimes, now, I feel physically sick when I think of the ridiculous stories I used to spin. But falsehood was like a web that held me fast. The more I made up the more I had to make up. The lies grew and grew until they had a life force of their own. If I hadn't enjoyed it so much it would have been scary.

To make it worse, Augusta was a very appreciative audience: she lapped up all the intricate plots and unnecessary details like a thirsty kitten with a saucer of cream. We traded emails like a diary. Sometimes it was as if Augusta knew more about me than I knew about myself. The fantasies went straight from my brain into the computer and sometimes I hardly knew I'd written them.

We used to wish all the time that we could meet up, but Augusta went to summer camp every year like a religion and my parents couldn't afford holidays in the USA. But finally, at fourteen I was old enough to go on my own. I was hopelessly overexcited for months beforehand and for the first week of my stay.

It is so clear in my memory the evening I came down to earth and became a normal person (or at least as normal as I can get). Augusta had said we would go to a meeting in a church hall. Now church hall meant only one thing to me: the dark smelly annex attached to the village school that was used for jumble sales and PE lessons. Our church hall had dusty floors, ragged velveteen curtains and smelt of wet raincoats, sweaty feet, and old clothes. So my nose wrinkled at the very idea of spending a whole evening in one—it sounded a grim idea, especially when all I wanted to do was go to the shopping mall, hang out in a café drinking smoothies, and look at all the scrummy clothes in the stores.

I should have known that an *American* church hall would be different. The church was huge, angular, and modern with a gigantic stainless steel spire that could have doubled up as a space rocket. It was surrounded by acres of immaculate flood-lit gardens and a completely crazy number of neon signs. There was enough light pollution radiating from the site to keep a small African country in electricity for a year. I was well impressed.

'Wow!' I said.

'We're going to a "Kissing Club" meeting. I've been keeping it as a surprise for you. You're going to meet Wesley,' Augusta said dreamily.

'Wow!' I said again. Augusta liked secrets (and was good at keeping them). I think it was her defence against the barrage of disinformation which I deluged her with. She just couldn't compete in the story stakes so she kept quiet about anything of interest and revealed it crumb by crumb—like a sleek complacent mouse with a secret hoard of cheese shavings.

'So who is this Wesley, then?' I asked casually.

'You'll see . . . ' Augusta said, and she gave me one of her sly, dark-eyed, glances. Lucky, lucky Augusta, who as well as having rich, wonderfully-indulgent parents, was also very beautiful, with glossy midnight hair and upswept black eyes. She had matured early and stood head and shoulders above me. I felt like some kind of inferior species as I stood knock-kneed and pale-skinned next to her curvaceous body and bronzed limbs. At sixteen she looked like a very young Catherine Zeta Jones. Looking back it's no wonder I couldn't compete with her and had to make up fairy stories.

The inside of the church hall gleamed and dazzled like a Christmas Grotto. The floor was hi-shine parquet and the walls were so sparkling white you really needed sunglasses to look at them. The whole place smelt amazing with a woody, citrus fragrance—a bit like bath cleaner, but nicer. There was a big curved stage that was set up for a slide show. And above the stage was a colourful banner that said: *The Kissing Club—a vow for life.*

Augusta dragged me down to sit on the front row. 'I want to be as near to Wesley as possible,' she breathed into my ear.

'What's going to happen?' I asked.

'Well, I've been coming for like weeks, but it is OK for you to come. I told Wesley I wanted to bring you and he said we were going to résumé and then have a guest speaker and you would be able to pick everything up.'

'Is it a Bible class?' I asked a bit suspiciously. I hadn't been brought up a heathen. My parents always insisted we went to the village church for feast days and random visits. But going to church was as much a cultural and social event as a religious one. I found Augusta's family hard work where godly matters were concerned. I was embarrassed by the way they talked about Jesus as if he was a close family friend and felt slightly threatened by Augusta's habit of reading the Bible *every* day.

'No, it's not a Bible class . . . But it's real important,' Augusta said with emotion.

The two front rows of seats filled up: mainly teenage girls but also a few boys. Augusta and I chewed gum. She daydreamed and I noticed what everyone was wearing. Augusta thought my preoccupation with clothes was overly weird and accused me of being hypercritical when I tried to discuss people's fashion sense. I'd got the impression that Americans consider it rude to comment on what people are wearing. So I kept my opinion on the merits of crop pants and polka dots to myself.

First the lights dimmed so it was like being in a proper theatre. Then a spotlight opened up on the curtain at the back of the stage. Next to me Augusta swayed slightly. Her face was enraptured, her lower lip drooping with anticipation as if we were going to have celestial brownies and ice cream. But when the curtain parted and music began in a swell I lost interest in Augusta. I watched enthralled as a beautiful boy walked to the front of the stage and up onto the podium and held his arms out to us.

He was totally gorgeous. God must have mixed up a special palette because I have never before, or since, seen anyone with such exquisite colouring. His skin was the softest cappuccino beige and his curly hair was darkest nut brown. He was fine-boned, almost languidly fragile, and unmistakably African-American.

'That is Wesley . . . ' Augusta breathed into my ear; even her whisper was reverent.

I shivered and sighed in reply and she squeezed my arm as if to say, 'I know . . . '

I would have liked to whisper back: 'Why is he wearing those awful clothes?' But it would have been sacrilegious in the face of Augusta's devotion. But to be *so* beautiful and to be kitted out in a grey shirt, maroon skinny tie, and shiny black trousers hurt my eyes! He looked as if he was wearing some kind of weird retro school uniform.

It was just as well that Wesley was so beautiful and I was taken up with planning what colours and clothes would look good on him because the meeting was an awful shock to my system.

First of all Wesley stood there in front of us, radiating loveliness, and gave us a bit of a pep talk about relationships, which was fine. He talked about love and commitment and every time he said the word 'love' Augusta sighed.

But then he made us get into groups. Me and Augusta were with two girls—Lois and Lauren—and they had the biggest braces in the world and were wearing identical clothes (so I wondered if they were clones). The other person in our group was a boy called Hal. He had a crew cut and acne and was so shy he wouldn't even look at us.

And the games we played in the first part of the programme were gross. It was like being taken through the rules of some really sick reality TV programme. First we played the spitting game. This involved each of us spitting into a glass of water and then offering it around to the rest of the group and asking them to drink it. Let me tell you there were no takers for any glass of water with a big blob of snotty spit floating in it like a jellyfish. (And some of the stuff that came out of Lois's and Lauren's braces had to be seen to be believed! Their glasses of water could have kept a couple of goldfish alive for weeks.)

Of course we all got really over-excited and hysterical when we played this game. And we screeched and yucked for all we were worth and said we wouldn't drink any of the glasses of water—even if we were stuck in the Sahara for weeks and were dying.

Finally—when we'd all expressed our feelings very clearly—Wesley made us all sit and listen to him. He explained, slowly and carefully (as if we were infants), that when we passed our glass of water to the rest of the group and asked them to drink it we were asking them to share our body fluids. (Or in Lois's and Lauren's case the remains of their dinner, although tactfully he didn't mention this.) Wesley went on to explain that sharing body fluids is what you did when you had sex. He went into some fairly graphic descriptions of how this occurred. And everyone was very quiet after he had finished speaking and sat and stared down at their glass of water in an embarrassed kind of way. It was a total relief when we were allowed to troop into the kitchen and pour the spitty water down the sink.

Then—having got rid of our glasses—we did a dice rolling game. We were still in the same group and to my surprise Hal was really competitive and got excited when he threw a double six. But it didn't do him any good at all! There were no winners in this game. It didn't matter which number you turned up, the prize was always something terrible.

I got a sexually transmitted infection three times in a row, and my face burned like an inferno. And Augusta got pregnant twice, and only got herpes on her third throw, which I thought was totally unfair as having a baby or two and a cold sore seemed loads nicer than getting three really horrible diseases (especially as Wesley went through the symptoms of what I'd got in detail, which was mortifying and totally embarrassing).

Eventually we'd all had three turns and we'd all lost out in the game of chance. Wesley turned to us and smiled sympathetically: 'Just remember—every time you have sex it's like throwing the dice, it's a gamble, and the outcomes are serious,' he said.

After that little bummer we had cookies and a drink and it was time for the guest speaker. We all sat and waited and Wesley led this utterly beautiful girl out onto the stage and up on to the podium. She had unbelievably gorgeous pinky golden hair that curled down over her shoulders like a silken waterfall.

'Oh-my-goodness-what-colour-is-her-hair?' I whispered to Augusta.

'Strawberry-blonde . . . ' Augusta mouthed back to me.

'Wow . . . ' I said. I had never felt so drab. My childhood fairness had darkened over the years to dull mouse: the colour of a hamster if you wanted to be precise about it. Hamster-blonde did not compete with strawberry-blonde in the glamour stakes. I suddenly wanted to be strawberry-blonde more than I wanted to live.

Wesley introduced Miss Strawberry Blonde as 'Loretta-Mae Eddison'. And I wondered in a moment of bitterness why my parents hadn't given me a wonderful double-barrelled Christian name instead of calling me dull old Emily. And I don't even have a nice middle name as I was called Jean after my Granny Sutton.

Loretta-Mae smiled at us—showing perfect American teeth—and began her talk. Her opening sentence electrified me. This was partly to do with the fact that me and Augusta were sitting right in the middle of the front row so when Loretta-Mae smiled and looked at the audience it was as if she was staring into my eyes and talking straight to me. But it wasn't just that—it was also what she said.

'Truth is the most important basis for any relationship,' she said slowly. She had a wonderful drawling

10

accent and the words truth and relationship hit me like a couple of well-aimed snowballs, causing a ricochet of sensation down my neck.

'Without truth there can be no trust. And without trust there can be no love. I truly believe that. And that is why I am here today to talk to all you young people. So I'm gonna start with truth . . . I'm gonna tell you people the truth. Because the truth is so important . . . '

I shifted uneasily in my seat and to my dismay Augusta gave me a sideways look and the merest hint of a snigger. In her eyes, in a flash, I saw a glimpse of accusation, amusement, and pity. And I realized (in a moment of profound and complete humiliation) that Augusta hadn't been taken in by my exaggerations, fibs, and downright untruths over the years. Not all of them, anyway. I imagined her, and her parents, laughing quietly at my excesses and forgiving me with Christian charity for my ridiculous behaviour. They would, doubtless, pray for me. I was very likely the emotional equivalent of the little boy in Africa whom they had 'adopted' through their church group and who they now supported through school. They sent him money for clothes, books, and pens because he was dirt poor. And they extended forgiveness, friendship, and hospitality to me because I was a misfit and a liar.

I swallowed hard, trying to get my head around this terrible revelation. And all the time Loretta-Mae was talking and showing slides up on the screen. And what she was saying was pretty shocking too.

'When I was thirteen I started running around with boys,' she intoned huskily. And up on the screen came a photograph of Loretta-Mae at thirteen. She looked as cute and wholesome as a home-baked apple pie. Her gorgeous hair was in bunches and her smile was wide and open.

'At sixteen years of age I started having sex with a boy . . . We tried to use protection. But we were children playing adult games and it wasn't easy for us to be responsible.'

At sixteen years of age Loretta-Mae looked like a film star with tumbling curls and mascara darkening her pale lashes.

'At just seventeen I got pregnant . . . I went to a clinic in the city and had my baby aborted. My parents said it was for the best and that I needed to get an education and I believed them.'

Loretta-Mae at seventeen was painfully thin. Her vibrant hair was pulled back in a ponytail and even though she smiled into the camera her eyes looked sad.

'At twenty I met and married Talbot; he was the love of my life. I didn't tell him about the boys I'd run around with, or the sex I had when I was sixteen, or that I'd been pregnant. I told myself it didn't matter. All that counted was the present and our future together.'

Loretta-Mae flashed up some really amazing wedding photos. Augusta and I were open-mouthed with admiration and awe. Loretta-Mae wore the most beautiful white-lace dress that clung to her slender body like mountain mist at sunrise. Talbot looked like a film star too: dark hair, white teeth, and a tux.

Loretta-Mae paused and glanced back at the final photo. There they were—the happy couple—frozen for posterity. They were smiling, confetti was falling, and Loretta-Mae's magical hair was held back from her face by a little tiara as if she were a princess. It looked like an advert for something wonderful.

Loretta-Mae's voice was flat with pain as she said, 'My wedding was a sham. I shouldn't have been wearing that white dress. I was not worthy of the virginity that it symbolized. I lied to myself, to my parents, to the minister, to the congregation and—by omission— to a good man. And I paid for it. Believe me . . . '

The slide disappeared. The screen was dark. Loretta-Mae stared into my eyes and said, 'No one could understand why we couldn't conceive the child we wanted so much. Then a doctor told me and Talbot the bad news. I'd had an infection after the termination. I'd never get pregnant. And it split us up. It was the lack of truth that Talbot could not stand, not the fact that we would never have a child of our own.'

Next to me Augusta sobbed aloud—and I had tears in my eyes.

'I have been lucky.' Loretta-Mae flashed up a new picture. She was arm in arm with a man; he had silver hair and a kind face. There were two boys standing with them, adolescent lads, gangly and awkward as young goslings.

13

'After Talbot divorced me I met Albert at a church meeting. He was a widower with two young sons. I told him the truth about myself and now we are married. I have two wonderful stepsons . . . ' Loretta-Mae held out her hands to us. 'God has been good to me,' she said. And two little tears, small as diamonds, slid from her eyes and trickled down her cheeks.

It was after that I signed the pledge. Wesley said I should think about it longer, consider for a while. But I was determined. Loretta-Mae had made a big impression on me. I wanted to be a virgin on the day I married. I vowed I wouldn't do more than kiss until I was a bride. So I paid my dollars and I got a silver ring to wear.

I also made a pact with myself that from that day forward I would tell the truth. And for a while it was easier than I would have believed possible. After years of having to remember endless details of the worlds I had created it was a relief to just concentrate on reality. I felt like a juggler who had been manically keeping plates spinning on sticks who finally had been allowed to stop. I was liberated by the simplicity of my life.

And I found being a member of the Kissing Club liberating too. It didn't matter that I couldn't go to meetings or get together with other girls who were in the club. I actually liked being one of a kind. It gave me a sense of being special, different. That appealed to me. And I didn't find it hard to keep the promise I'd made. In fact I thought it was always going to be very, very easy. I planned my wedding day and I designed wedding dresses (endlessly). In my head I invented a whole 'happy ever after' life that would be my future. I lived a dream. And, for a while, I was a happy fool.

# CHAPTER ONE

Today I told my parents I am pregnant. I told them it was a virgin birth. I didn't know what else to say. I could hardly tell them the truth, could I? After I'd said it I realized what a completely crazy thing it was to have uttered. I would have liked to laugh to take away the puzzled, strained look on their faces. But instead—just like when I was a naughty child telling fibs—I elaborated:

'It was my birthday. There was a big thunderstorm. Do you remember? And when the lightning came down from the sky an angel came down too and told me I would have a baby. I think it will be a boy. I'm almost certain that is what she said . . . ' I paused for a moment, as if going through the conversation again in my head: which was an extremely phoney thing to do because, of course, I was making it all up on the spur of the moment.

For a split second I faltered—I nearly said, 'I'm sorry, that was a load of poo. Forget I said that.' But I couldn't. I was too caught up in the story. I'd managed, since joining the Kissing Club, not to tell proper lies. And being truthful had made me feel good about myself, because my parents have always been really strict about things like truth and honesty, and I always wanted to please them (even when I wasn't able to do so).

This sudden eruption of lying was the first time for years that I had told a great big, obvious, deliberate untruth straight out like that. (Although, of course, I'd carried on telling the usual little white lies to avoid hurting people's feelings.)

But suddenly, terrifyingly, telling a proper lie was back again like a seriously addictive vice. As if making up fantasy was a snort of some unbelievable drug that hooks you immediately, and never ever lets you get away. So that even after years of being clean, you get the taste, just one tiny taste, and you're back—a junky once again.

I took a deep breath and rejoiced in the comfort of it. It just felt so much better than the truth. It was like having a warm bath instead of a cold shower. It was like ice cream on a hot day. It was like freedom from pain.

Despite all that, part of me (my conscience, I guess), was shocked at how easily all those lies had gushed out from me—and spoken with such sincerity too! I suppose it's because I would have liked it to be true. I would have given anything for it to be true. It would be wonderful if an angel really had come and told me about the baby . . . If conceiving really had been a magical, wonderful, once-in-a-lifetime-I'll-never-forget-it-because-it-was-so-special-type-moment.

What was scary was that once I'd started with the stupid story of the virgin birth I found I couldn't stop. It was just so easy and it felt so disturbingly good. For the first time in ages I felt as if I was in control of something.

With the precision of a con-artist I smiled at my parents and added: 'Although I shouldn't say "she" should I? I should just say "angel"—because strictly speaking angels don't have a sex, do they? I mean they are neutral.' There was a long pause. 'Or I should say they are hermaphrodites, that's the correct term, isn't it?' I added that very precisely—as if getting everything right was really important to me.

After I'd said that there was complete and utter silence from them. The ticking of the clock on the wall sounded like a giant heart. And outside I could hear the crows cawing and calling to each other from the chestnut trees at the bottom of the garden.

I was silent too. I just stared at the food on the table, desperation growing inside me like a tidal surge. We always eat in the kitchen on Saturday lunchtime and for breakfast. My parents are quite robotic and habitual and so our lives follow very set patterns. They are totally well organized. So Saturday lunchtimes we have a barbeque out on the patio if the weather is kind or a barbeque-type meal cooked in the kitchen if it isn't.

Today, as it is a cold and blustery October day with a hint of winter in the wind, we sat in the kitchen. My mother had cooked really scrummy lamb chops, roasted to a crisp in a hot oven, with vegetables that had been rolled around in the lamb fat and browned. Also, as a side dish, we had a wonderful vegetable rice with little baby prawns and sweetcorn mixed in.

Two minutes after conception I'd felt hungry and I haven't been able to stop eating ever since. I have doubled in size over the last four months—and all of me is now so fat that no one has ever thought to ask about the bulge above my waistband. It could be caused by greed or pregnancy or even some kind of awful terminal disease which makes you overeat until you explode.

I don't know why I chose that moment to tell them. I could have kept quiet for a bit longer. I could have thought about what to do—asked someone for advice—or sat my parents down and talked to them sensibly and seriously. Instead, saying that about the angel made it seem as if I was mucking about. They looked down at the food on their plates. They didn't believe me. They thought it was some kind of sick joke.

For a moment I wondered if I really had told them such a complete load of crap. My brain seems to have turned to mush these days so maybe it was all a hallucination. I have become bovine—all I think about these days is sleeping and eating. And being back at school and talking sensibly to people has been impossibly hard.

But, unfortunately, I could tell from the length of the silence, and their crestfallen faces, that I really had spoken. I had told them the truth (well, part of the truth anyway) and I suppose I'd done it because I wanted them to know. That must have been the reason. If I really analyse my feelings then a bit of me is hurt that they haven't worked it out for themselves like weeks ago. I mean we are a family—we are meant to be close. And here I am, so changed that I don't recognize myself, and my parents didn't seem to have spotted a thing.

I suppose I have been waiting, almost holding my breath, for my mother to work out what is happening, has happened, to me. I couldn't quite believe that she hadn't registered that I don't drink coffee any more but crave hot chocolate, that I can't eat anything but fruit for breakfast, but pig out after ten in the morning on as much carb as I can get my hands on. Why has she not noticed that for elevenses I can eat half a loaf of bread, toasted and layered with jam and cream cheese, and still be ready for lunch? Why hasn't she put two and two together and come up with a big fat FOUR—to match her big fat pregnant daughter?

How ironic that it should be food—the big obsession in my life at the moment—that finally brought it out into the open and made me tell! Because today, as I heaped my plate with peppers, courgettes, mushrooms, and as much of the lovely rice as I could balance onto the serving spoon, my mother said gently, 'I should go a little easy on the rice if I were you, Emily. It's full of calories. Why don't you fill up on some salad?'

Silently my father handed me the salad bowl. I reached over and took hold of it. My mouth was actually quite wet with saliva because the smell of the meal was making my taste buds melt and my stomach was screaming out that it needed food and fast. I reached into the salad bowl and picked up a baby tomato. It was greenish and firm, just the way I like them. I popped it into my mouth, crushing it greedily with my teeth.

'Tongs,' my mother said, her tone reproving, as she held the implement out to me. 'Don't use your fingers, please.'

'Sorry,' I mumbled. 'I'm hungry.'

'We can see that,' my father said with a grin; he was trying to be lighthearted. He shot my mother a glance (which they didn't think I saw); it was as if he was asking her not to be hard on me.

And it was then that I said it: 'Actually—I'm hungry because I'm pregnant. I'm eating for two.'

And that bit at least was true. I should have left it there, let the idea bed in—waited for the questions— instead of telling that story about the angel. As it was, as soon as I had finished with my virgin birth saga I began to eat (I was so desperate for food I would have killed anyone who tried to take that plate away from me). And all the while my parents sat in stunned silence, looking down at their plates, making a pretence of eating, while I—with a degree of heartlessness which shocked me—gnawed at my chop bones like a ravenous dog. Not even the shock and anxiety radiating from my parents like earth tremors could affect my appetite.

Eventually I finished. I suppressed a burp as I wiped my mouth. 'Thank you that was lovely,' I said gratefully. I looked at my mother's plate with concern. Her chops were untouched.

'Can I have your chops—it's such a shame to waste them, isn't it?' Before she had a chance to reply I reached over and speared them with my fork.

My mother looked as if she might cry. 'I think we'll have coffee in the conservatory,' she said, her voice very faint, not much more than a whisper.

'Nothing for me, thanks. I might have some ice cream when I've finished up here,' I said, without looking up from my plate of food.

They didn't answer and I carried on eating. Out of the corner of my eye I watched them: my mother pouring hot water onto the filters, my father fetching cream and laying out a tray with mugs and sugar. When it was all ready my father carried the tray, with hands that were not quite steady, and they left the room without a word. I heard the doors between the kitchen and the conservatory close and the low hum of their voices.

I paused before I ate the last of the vegetable rice straight out of the bowl, and wondered in a moment of sharp pity what would be the worst problem for them: a daughter who has an eating disorder, a daughter who has a personality defect resulting in hallucinations and religious mania, or a daughter who is pregnant.

Unfortunately, at the present time, I expect they are seriously worried that they have a daughter with all three.

# CHAPTER TWO

As I pull on my duffle coat and leave the house I think about how being a triplet was the beginning of my troubles. Although at the time I thought it was the very best thing that ever happened to me.

Thinking about the triplets makes me sad because this baby is one thing which I have not been able to share with them. It is my particular secret and it has set me apart. And, ironically, until the night of the visit from the angel (or my biggest mistake ever) depending on which version I am telling, I was the one who was craziest about being a triplet. It has always been really important to me. Too important maybe . . . But I was lonely before it happened. And I never realized until I wasn't lonely any more.

I am very much an only child. My mother is fond of recounting how she planned her career break to have me. How much it cost her in terms of promotion etc. I also know how hard she and my father have worked for our standard of living: the house in the country, holidays, nice clothes, and good food. I always knew that I would never have a little brother or sister. My mother was always firm and kind, but quite definite about it—just like she was about not having a dog or a cat. 'I work full time. We are out of the house all day. It wouldn't be fair.'

The day I met the twins and became a triplet stands out from the rest of my childhood like a fairy tale. There was the leaving of our old house, a narrow terrace in the centre of the city, and the journey out to the green space of the countryside. I must have visited the country before that day, but I can't remember it. It was as if that day was the very first time. Maybe it was all so special it wiped out older, dustier memories of rainy days or not very enjoyable visits. Because that day the sun shone and the world seemed to glow with excitement as we followed the furniture van.

I had not seen the house before moving day. Because of that I think my parents expected me to be desperate to race around and explore, afire with curiosity about it—but I wasn't. I knew it had a garden and I would have my own room. I wasn't familiar with gardens. I didn't know what to expect. And I already had my own room.

Truth was I was actually a bit upset about leaving Leeds. I liked my school where I had a best friend called Molly. I liked living around the corner from my grandparents who collected me from school and looked after me until my mother finished work.

My parents grumbled endlessly about the city: traffic, graffiti, litter, yobs in the park, and syringes in the sandpit. I didn't understand what upset them. But I had got a strong idea from them that living in the city

24

was somehow dirty and living in the country would be clean. I was in for a big shock!

But luckily, before the realization had dawned on me that the countryside (for all the pretty green colours) is a place full of filth, sex, and violence, I had fallen in love with the twins. I was so totally smitten that I would have willingly lived anywhere on Planet Earth where I could be a triplet.

I saw the twins as soon as we arrived. Our new home was a modern detached square-box of a house set at the end of a cul-de-sac. And they were standing on the pavement at the side of our driveway, staring wide-eyed at the removal van.

'There it is, Emily, Number Six, Hunter's Beck, our new house. What do you think?' my mother said excitedly. But I was too busy looking at the two girls to be interested in a mere house. They were eerily similar even though one was slightly taller than the other. They wore jeans and T-shirts and they both had blonde hair tied up in ponytails. I wondered about their ages, I wondered if they would like me, I wondered if they would play with me. And suddenly I wanted them to be friends with me so much it hurt like a tummy ache.

'It looks like a welcoming committee is here to meet you, Emily,' said my father, glancing at the girls and then back at me with a smile. 'With a bit of luck you'll have someone to play with.'

'You'll soon make lots of lovely friends at your new school,' my mother added quickly—as if something about the girls had not taken her fancy.

'They look nice,' I said longingly, putting my thumb into my mouth for a moment of comfort, and staring at the girls while trying to pretend that I wasn't looking in their direction.

'Go and talk to them while we put the kettle on and make the removal men a cup of tea. Then we'll show you around the house,' my father said encouragingly.

'Don't you want to see your new bedroom first?' my mother asked, rather surprised.

'Go and say hello. If you disappear into the house straightaway they may think you're a snob,' my father said wisely.

'I'll go and say hello,' I said bravely.

I hopped out of the car and made my way over to the girls. 'My name is Em'ly. This is my new house,' I said, waving a hand in the direction of Number Six.

'I'm Florence and this is Sienna. And that is our house.' The taller of the girls waved a hand dismissively towards a house at the other end of the road. 'How old are you?' she added.

'Seven.'

'When is your birthday?'

'June twenty-first.'

'It never is . . . ' Florence said loudly. Then she turned to Sienna and they both shook their heads in puzzled disbelief.

'It is too,' I said weakly. No one had ever quarrelled with me over my birth date before. I felt undone, undermined. I wished I had been born on some other day or that I'd refused to answer their questions and kept my birthday a secret.

The girls stared at me with large puzzled blue eyes for what seemed like ages. Then they exchanged meaningful glances and shrugged their shoulders—after that they giggled together for a while. I was fascinated by the way that they communicated without words and gawped at them with my mouth open.

At last Florence decided to enlighten me. 'June twenty-first is *our* birthday,' she said excitedly. 'We're twins,' she added importantly.

'Twins!' I said, breathless with envy. I was also knocked out by the coincidence of them having the same birthday as me—and encouraged by the fact that they were both smiling at me. 'How lucky can you get—to be twins,' I added.

And I suddenly knew in a moment of stomach churning despair that the thing I wanted most in the world (even more than a baby brother or sister or a kitten or a puppy) was to have a twin sister. I was beyond jealousy—I was simply awestruck by their fortunate destiny.

'Yes,' Florence said importantly. 'We are lucky, aren't we?' She preened herself for a moment, shaking her ponytail back and looking at her sister as if consulting a mirror. Then she turned her attention back to me and added kindly, 'You know something. You look like us.'

'Do I?' I said with astonishment. I suppose, when I thought about it, I did. My hair was blondish. My eyes were blue. So were theirs. We all had the uniformity of childhood in our clear round faces and upturned noses. Molly (my best friend in Leeds) had hair the colour of beetroot and a face covered in freckles. I certainly didn't look like her. But now, by some wonderful cosmic coincidence, I looked like the twins. And then Sienna said, in her quiet lisping way, as she pulled at Florence's hand:

'We could be triplets, you know . . . '

'YES!' Florence shouted. 'We'll be triplets! Do you want to?' she said to me.

'Can I?' I asked. At that moment I was so surprised by the very idea of being a triplet that I found it difficult to really imagine what it would be like. But I could sense from Sienna's gentle smile and Florence's enthusiastic grin that I was being offered something really special.

'Thank you very much . . . ' I said humbly.

'Yeah, well, we have the same birthday, so we should be triplets,' Florence announced bossily. 'Come on. We'll show you our Wendy house. We're going to have tea in there. We'll ask if you can too. You have to do things together if you're triplets and always look after each other.'

And that's what we did. We stuck together like glue. And once we had decided that we really were triplets we even changed our names, like some kind of weird reverse christening. I suppose what really happened was that when the three of us were playing together it was just too cumbersome to use our full names all the time. Anyway, to me it seemed really special that within days we were calling each other Flo, Si, and Em.

I have been so lost in my memories that without even knowing it I find I have walked the length of the main street and stopped at No. 2 Bridge Cottages. I can see Mrs Patton waving to me from the front room window. I make my way up the pathway—carefully avoiding the garden ornaments, plant pots, and gnomes. The front door opens a crack when I reach it and Mrs Patton peers out.

'Are you going out walking, dear?' Mrs Patton asks, above the high excited sound of barking.

'Yes I am. Would Peaches like to come out to play?'

Mrs Patton laughs. She likes it when I talk about Peaches as if she is a child. I have invented a whole imaginary world for Peaches and sometimes I share it with Mrs Patton. It is our main topic of conversation. Mrs Patton's old, she's a widow and lives alone. She's interested in the WI, the local church, knitting, and her grandchildren. I'm studying for A levels and am into fashion, films, books, and music. Therefore our worlds do not collide. We probably wouldn't have more than two words to say to each other if it wasn't for the parallel universe which I have carefully constructed for Peaches. This fantasy world that Peaches and I inhabit amuses Mrs Patton no end—and it amuses me. I haven't told anyone else about it—not even the twins; other people (apart from Mrs Patton) might think me seriously dotty. Maybe I am, because the truth is that some days Peaches seems like the best friend I have.

'Of course she would like to go out. You are so kind. She loves going walkies with you.'

'She'll need her tartan coat—the wind is chilly,' I say, thrusting my hands more deeply into my duffle coat pockets. 'I've got a spare hanky and a cough sweet for her though,' I add. 'And we'll play ring-a-ring-a-roses and tag, so she won't get cold. I always let her win at tag, that's why it's her favourite game.'

Mrs Patton says, 'Come in for a minute while I get her ready.'

'It's OK. I'm fine out here,' I reply quickly. I feel as if I need fresh air and exercise after the bizarre lunch-time conversation with my parents. And anyway, Mrs Patton's cottage sometimes makes me feel really sad. It's just so full of stuff. Pictures crowd the walls and ill-matching furniture jostles for space. And the ornaments! Every surface is piled high. And it's really random—there are twisted Fimo shapes and awkward first attempts at pottery that her grandchildren have made at school and they are heaped up alongside antique china, vases, jugs, teapots, crystal glasses, and some rather beautiful old silver. It's like an enormous car boot sale. And I suppose the one advantage is that any burglar would have a complete nervous break-down trying to sort out what was actually valuable from utter rubbish.

One day Mrs Patton must have noticed me staring at a shelf that was groaning because she said with a little laugh: 'All my life is here in this house, you know, dear. That's why I shall never be able to leave it, even though it really is too big now for just me and Peaches.'

It set me to thinking about our house—which is minimalist. My mother is allergic to anything which needs dusting. If our life is in our house then we travel light and leave no traces. And all I have to show what my life contains is a wardrobe that has only the clothes that fit me (according to my mother hoarding clothes that are too small is a hanging offence) and a bookcase/CD rack which has to be culled at least once a year and the rejects relocated to a charity shop.

Sometimes, in Mrs Patton's overfull little house, I feel somehow naked and abandoned. In pride of place in the sitting room, on a special glass shelf, are the first ballet shoes of all the granddaughters who dance. They have been dipped and preserved for ever: and there must be lots of gracefully talented granddaughters because every year there seems to be a new pair of tiny shoes. The little girls are also performers and take exams, so upstairs, in Mrs Patton's spare room, there is a clothes rail covered in a clean sheet where all their stage costumes and pretty dancing dresses are kept for posterity.

'I don't suppose they'll ever want them again. But I like to keep them anyway,' Mrs Patton said comfortingly to me, when she showed me the little tutus, gauzy skirts, and pretend fairy wings. 'They might come in useful sometime,' she added wistfully. Which frankly seemed a fairly tragic kind of wish to me, as there aren't too many opportunities in life to use miniature wings and tiny tutus, are there?

31

The front door opens—wide this time. 'Her tartan coat needs washing. I've put her into her pink one,' Mrs Patton says, handing Peaches over to me.

'I won't let her get muddy, promise.' I bury my face in the soft fur on the top of Peaches's head and whisper loudly, 'Got to be a good girl and stay away from puddles. Or you and me will be in trouble.'

Mrs Patton's face crinkles. She hands me several plastic bags: 'There's some biscuits for Peaches and some chocolate for you.'

'See you later,' I call, as I march down the path with Peaches tucked firmly under my arm. I always pretend that I walk Peaches up to the village green, keeping politely to the edge and avoiding the cricket pitch in the centre, because this is what Mrs Patton does when she goes for a walk.

But I don't do that—ever. Instead, most days, Peaches and I slip across the mill yard and take the dangerous path next to the river and follow it as it meanders downhill to the reservoir. Sometimes we walk all the way around the reservoir and come back on the far side of the water, hiking through scrubby woods and crossing on a narrow swing bridge that sways hypnotically on a windy day. Mrs Patton would die a thousand deaths if she could see us. I also regularly sneak home and wash Peaches in our shower (my mother would die a thousand deaths if she knew that). Mrs Patton often comments that I have kept Peaches nicely and she seems to come back cleaner than when she went out—and I just smile serenely in reply.

Today I am chased by a black demon of a mood that snaps at my heels like a mad dog. I need to do something to erase the memory of lunchtime with my parents. So I take by far the most risky route—a walk fraught with memories and danger.

Instead of cutting through the mill yard and heading downstream, through the safety of the familiar fields and woods, I head upstream. I feel like a Native American scout heading into enemy territory. Because going upstream not only takes me across rough moorland, but also through an overgrown wood that is dark as a forest with towering pines. And then, when I've hiked through that wilderness, I will arrive at the boundary of Nell Acre—the biggest house in the village.

From the footpath I will be able to see the roofs, the chimneys, the gardens of the house. I will be able to smell if there is a bonfire blazing in the garden. I might be able to hear the roar of a car engine from the driveway. Sometimes in the summer, if you loiter on the path next to the river, it is possible to smell the barbeque at Nell Acre and hear music and voices from the garden. If you are really nosy (like me and the twins) it is also possible to peer through the hedge and catch a glimpse of perfect people in designer clothes, hear their laughter and the clink of glasses, and know that a party is in full swing.

I know that going anywhere near Nell Acre will make me unhappy. I suppose I feel I need to be tortured or made to suffer for the awful way I told my parents about the baby. And that is why I set off as if pursued by a vengeful ghost. Peaches is excited. She is wriggling in my arms. As soon as we are off the road and onto the moor I set her down and take off the pink coat.

'There you are, Peaches. You don't need your coat on. You run around and keep warm like a gypsy dog. And don't worry about getting dirty,' I add encouragingly. 'It'll wash off.'

She races around me in circles, barking her thanks. I love the fact that when I get Peaches out to wild places she turns into a wolf bitch and isn't a lap dog at all. There are a few straggles of sheep grazing on the moor. She rushes them and makes them bolt. I call her and she runs to me, tail wagging. I could almost swear that she is grinning.

'Don't do that, please, darling,' I say, like an over-indulgent mother. 'This is their home. Manners, please, Peaches.'

She eyes the sheep regretfully and then rushes into the heather and disturbs a grouse that screams like a cat and flies clumsily away.

'He's a bit too big for you, Peaches,' I call. 'Come on—let's see what we can find in the woods.'

I chatter to her as we walk. It is all for me—to calm my nerves—not for her. She is too busy following scent trails and running with the wind in her curls to care about my conversation. Anyway, Mrs Patton talks to her all the time; she is probably bored stiff with human company.

# CHAPTER THREE

The dog hits us like a missile. One minute me and Peaches are trotting along next to the river minding our own business. The next minute it's as if we are being targeted by enemy fire: under attack from a fury of golden gleaming fur and raucous barking—and there is no time for evasive action.

Peaches screams like a little banshee. She isn't at all brave where other dogs are concerned and she doesn't bother to growl or do any of the normal dog-type things. Sex appeal or aggression are simply not on her agenda. Instead she goes into victim mode. She collapses into a pathetic mat of writhing apricot curls and squeals. This abject pose and crazy noise sends the other dog bonkers. It goes into a frenzy of barking, jumping, and pawing. Peaches screams again, and I realize suddenly that I have joined in. Peaches and I are both squealing like piglets being murdered. And even though I can see this noise is making the dog even more excited I can't stop—because the dog has got its nose under Peaches's little belly and is throwing her up into the air. And then Peaches is flying through the air like a beanie baby dog. And I feel as if I am being strangled by the sounds coming out of my throat.

The dog—I can see now that it is a huge oversized retriever—is in the river. Peaches is in the river. And I am in the river too. Water is filling my wellies so they are like concrete boots but I don't care. I am desperate to get to Peaches before the dog does. Inspired by terror I rip off one of my gloves and throw it into the middle of the river. 'FETCH!' I shout like a mad person. The retriever barks and splashes off—doing goofy dog-paddle to get to this treasure before it sinks. I hurl the other glove even further out, sending with it a vile wish that the dog might choke on it and be swept away to an untimely but fully-justified death.

While the hell-hound's back is turned I wade further out into the murky water of the river. It is the colour of bad tea and cold as death. I feel the chill creeping to my thighs as I scoop Peaches up in my arms. I am crying, sobbing, and effing and blinding so hard that I don't realize that someone else is in the water with me.

It is Corey Thomas from Nell Acre. And there aren't many people in the world I want to see less than him. I curse my bad luck, my appalling timing. I curse him for being on the footpath and for having a stupid dog. I am so full of despair that if it wasn't for Peaches I might throw myself into the middle of the river, where the current swirls in a dangerous eddy, and end it all. My life never seemed so bleak.

He holds out his hands. 'Give the dog to me. Let me

help,' he says. But I shake my head and refuse to let go of her.

'I'm really sorry. Are you OK?' he says. 'Let me take it. Don't go in any deeper will you . . . ' he adds in a concerned voice.

'Drop dead, you moron!' I shriek at him. 'It's all your fault! You and your bloody dangerous dog! It attacked us and threw her in the river . . . '

He moves forward and gets hold of my arm. 'Let me get you out of the water. Then you can shout at me all you like,' he says. I can feel the ripples of cold water rising up my legs. My wellies are pink and cute and hardly reach the middle of my calf. They are now totally submerged and I feel as if I am stuck in quicksand.

I would like to shrug Corey Thomas off and swear at him some more but I am not really sure if I can get out of the river without help and Peaches and I are both shivering with cold and shock.

'I can't move!' I say despairingly to him.

He gets his hands under my armpits and hauls me across to the bank and up onto the path as if I am some great aquatic mammal that has been beached by a storm. For someone so thin he is surprisingly strong. I lean against a tree and try to control my sobs. My wellies have vanished and Corey looks down at my socks and groans.

'Jeez. I'm sorry. You are in a mess. Do you want me to try to get your boots out of the water for you?'

'Eff off,' I say, scowling at him. Then, with shaking

frozen hands, I unfasten my coat and get Peaches inside—nestling her tiny soaking body next to my dry jumper. 'I don't care about my sodding boots. I'm worried about Peaches. She hates getting wet, she always wears a little mac when it's raining.' My voice is rising hysterically and I can't stop it. 'She has soft fur it gets . . . it gets waterlogged . . . And I don't know if she got hurt when she was thrown into the water. She's only small and she has fragile little chicken bones . . . '

I have to stop then. I am crying hard like a tiny child having a tantrum. My mouth is open and tears and snot are running in warm rivulets down my face. I raise my sleeve and try to wipe them away, realizing that it is safer to be angry and swear at him than to cry.

'I'm sorry. But let me help you now. Come up to the house. It's only two minutes away,' he cajoles. 'There's no one home but me. Get down, Kizzy!' he snaps at the dog, which is leaping up at him, both my gloves held in its mouth like a trophy.

He clips a lead on the monster and turns to me. 'Come on,' he urges. 'You can't walk all the way back to the village without boots, can you? Come up to the house. Please.'

'All right,' I say. And I use my sleeve on my nose again and follow him reluctantly. I can feel the dank wetness from Peaches seeping through my jumper and turning my bra into an icy band. I am jittering with cold. I would probably follow the devil himself for the chance to get Peaches and myself warm and dry.

'You're sure that no one else will be there, aren't you?' I mutter.

He doesn't look at me as he replies. 'No one will be back for hours. Come on.'

By the time we reach the house everything is a blur. We leave the retriever in the utility room. Most of the river water has drained off me, but I am aware of my damp socks making footprints on the immaculate stone floors and cream carpets as we trail through the kitchen and up the stairs.

'Give the pooch to me. I'll get her washed,' Corey says.

Through chattering teeth I start to give him instructions about the exact temperature of the water and to be sure to have towels all ready, but he interrupts me: 'Thanks. But I think I know how to bath a dog. And if I'm stuck I'll use my imagination.'

He shows me into a guest room. The en-suite bathroom has a shower, a bath, and a pile of fluffy towels. 'I'll find you some clothes and leave them on the bed.'

'But do Peaches first, won't you?' I say, as I hand her over to him.

'Yes, I will,' he says patiently. 'Then I'll make you a hot drink. Tea or coffee?'

'Tea. I can't drink coffee at the moment . . . ' I mutter.

He gives me an inscrutable look and leaves without a word. I run a bath, strip off my wet clothes, and lower myself into the warm water. Corey Thomas has been kind to me and I should feel grateful. But I don't.

I just feel chippy and irritable. I would like to swear at him about his horrible dog until the air is purple and ripe with foulness. I don't want to be here in this house. I am so full of pain suddenly that tears spring into my eyes and begin to drip down my cheeks.

We (the triplets) never liked Corey from the first day he and his family moved to the village. Now it seems a bit irrational and cruel but I suppose the first reason was that he was a boy—and a boy who was the same age as us.

The summer the Thomas family arrived we were all twelve—which meant that we triplets, with our long blondish hair and tanned limbs, looked like glorious budding young women. And Corey Thomas, with his sparrow legs and delicate face, looked like a puny undersized geek. We girls were trim as young greyhounds with developing breasts and downy armpits— whereas he was six inches shorter with a face smooth as a dark cherub's and a soppy fringe of hair that skimmed his black eyebrows. He was still a little boy— he looked about nine—whereas we thought we were sharp as icicles and, when tarted up, could easily pass for fifteen.

The second reason we disliked him was that he didn't look like his brother. And this *was* so totally irrational and cruel of us that the memory almost makes me blush with shame. I hold my breath and submerge my head in the bath until my chest hurts. How shallow we were! Not even being only twelve could excuse the hysteria with which we greeted Brett Thomas.

Brett Thomas looks like a reincarnation of the legendary James Dean. It was me that told the twins that. I even found a picture to prove it. He's not tall, but blond and cute, and even at fifteen he behaved as if he was the epitome of cool.

He loves himself. He knows he is good-looking. And people warm to him. Not just pubescent girls but old ladies, men, other boys. He is totally charming. And Mr Thomas is the same. He looks like James Dean too, only older and a bit jowly. And people like him too.

But people don't like Corey Thomas. He is the cuckoo in the nest—the outsider—with his dark eyes and silences and way of looking at people that is thought to be rude. 'What an odd little boy,' was the accepted comment about him when he arrived. Not that he has ever done anything that you could put your finger on. It is more that he doesn't make any kind of effort and this is in marked contrast to Brett who is always unfailingly polite to men and subtly flirtatious with women. Brett even flirted—in a very jokey way—with us triplets from day one. And in return we gave him our undying adoration.

I lather up my hair and rinse it. And then I concentrate on getting the river mud out of my toenails. I determine that I will not think about anything but getting warm and dry and looking after Peaches. Remembering, or attempting to contemplate the past, is far too dangerous. And I can't afford it at the moment.

In the bedroom I find a mug of tea and a pile of

clothes: T-shirts, sweatshirts, and tracky bottoms. I find some things that fit me (kind of). I look at myself in the mirror and wonder why my bump looks bigger in baggy clothes than it does in tight tops. I drink the tea and wish for biscuits or better still a nice Danish pastry.

I wander down to the kitchen, mug in hand, desperate for food. Lunch seems part of another lifetime. I feel as if I might expire from starvation if I don't get some kind of nourishment soon.

Peaches is running around the kitchen, wagging her tail and yapping. She looks wonderful. I put my mug down on the table and pick her up for a cuddle.

'You've made a good job of bathing her,' I say grudgingly to Corey, without actually looking at him. I snuffle my nose into her fur. 'Yum, she smells of coconut . . . good enough to eat. By the way do you have any food? I'm starving.'

I risk a glance at him. He stares at me for a moment and then smiles. 'What would you like? Have a look in the freezer and help yourself. Make yourself at home, please.'

'OK,' I say. I am embarrassed because I have been thinking such hateful things about him. And now he's being thoughtful and polite and really rather sweet and I know I should thank him but I can't find the words.

I find crumpets and fruit bread and begin to make toast. At the same time I make more tea. Corey sits at the table and watches me.

'Would you like some toast?' I ask him.

'Thanks,' he says. 'I'm sorry about the dog jumping on you like that.'

'Is the brute yours?' I ask.

'No, Brett bought her for Lara. Some kind of baby-substitute-bonding exercise, I suppose. He's really serious about Lara. And Lara was fine when Kizzy was a tiny cutesy puppy. But now she's a huge shitting monster Lara has really gone off the idea of having a dog. Most of the time Kizzy gets left here and I look after her.'

'Really?' I say, through a mouthful of crumpet.

'Do you remember Lara?' he asks. 'She was at the party in the summer. She's the unnaturally blonde girl with loads of make-up, nails like talons, and a fake tan. She was giving Brett the run around that night. She dumps him at regular intervals. I think that's what keeps him so keen.'

'Do you have any jam?' I ask vaguely, as I reach for some more toast.

He stares at me for a moment and then disappears off to find jam. I spread it thickly on my toast and we eat in silence for a while. I savour the relief and pleasure of feeling full again. If I get too hungry I start to feel sick and that is awful. I munch in silence trying not to think about anything but the food.

Peaches has curled up on my lap and gone to sleep. She is exhausted.

'I'll find you some shoes. Lara's left some here. Hopefully there's something suitable from her "country girl phase" that lasted all of two weeks,' Corey says.

43

I'm not sure how I feel about wearing Lara's shoes—even if they happen to fit. But I can't walk back in bare feet.

He goes out of the room. I put Peaches down by the side of a big Aga and look in the fridge. There's some gorgeous stuff in there and I quite fancy a Greek yogurt but it seems a bit rude to just help myself. I close the door quickly to avoid temptation.

Corey comes back into the kitchen with a pair of lace-up boots. They are rather lovely pink Timberlands and they look unworn.

'These are a size six,' he says.

'I'm a five,' I say.

'I bought a pair of thick socks just in case,' he says. The socks are also pink and unworn.

'Thanks, and thanks for the clothes and the food and bathing Peaches. You could have just run away and left us.'

'I wouldn't have done that,' he says. He is staring at me again. I am leaning back against the Aga enjoying the warmth on my back. And as his eyes travel over me I am suddenly very aware of the great curves of my swollen breasts thrusting up against the tracksuit top and bulge of my belly beneath them. In the past I'd always been rather envious of the twins, who have always had much bigger boobs than me. Now I'm being paid out for the sin of envy because mine are monstrous—like a snowy mountain range, the breast equivalent of the Himalayas—and every day, I swear to God, they get bigger. By the time I give birth I suspect

44

I will look like an old milker drooping into the farmyard with teats nearly touching the ground. And I am standing in front of Corey Thomas in a T-shirt and top and I feel naked.

I stand up straight and pull self-consciously at the tracksuit top, because I can see by the way his eyes are transfixed that he is thinking about my breasts too.

He manages finally to tear his gaze away from me. I see him swallow and rub his fingers across his brow. Then he looks up and meets my eyes: 'Emily, are you going to have a baby?' he asks very quietly.

I turn my back on him, and pretend to be studying the top of the Aga. I am actually really choked. Tears prickle in my eyes and there is a lump in my throat. I can't believe that, out of all the people in the world, he is the one who has looked at me and worked out what is going on.

I nod and mumble: 'Yes, I am . . . '

'Don't cry,' he says. And he moves across and stands next to me. He hesitates for a moment and then puts his arm tentatively around my shoulders.

'Have you told anyone?' he asks quietly, as he looks into my face.

'I told my parents today.' Then for some bizarre reason I find myself confessing to him: 'I said it was a virgin birth and that an angel came down to see me.' I stop, startled. Then I gulp down tears, and wipe my eyes on my sleeve.

'OK,' he says slowly. 'That sounds like a really

sensible way to go about it. I bet that made them feel a whole load better.'

I elbow him away. 'Oh, shut up. What did you expect me to tell them?'

He shrugs. 'Sorry. It just doesn't seem helpful to wind them up. I should imagine they're upset. Have you told the father yet?'

'No . . . '

'Don't you think maybe you should? I mean—don't you feel he has a right to know? We're not just sperm donors.'

'Oh, shut up! Don't get all politically correct with me and start talking about men's rights,' I snarl at him in sudden fury.

'I'm sorry,' he says. 'It's just I'd want to know if it was my baby.'

'Well, it isn't your baby, is it,' I say, a tad spitefully. 'And I don't think it's worth telling him.'

'Emily . . . you do know who the father is, don't you?' he says. His voice is suddenly full of concern and the smooth skin of his forehead is creased in a frown.

'Yes,' I mutter. 'I know . . . ' I pull on my coat, and then I sit down on one of the kitchen chairs and begin to pull on the pink socks and shoes.

'Would you like me to walk down with you?' he asks kindly, as if I am very old or an invalid.

'No, I don't want you to walk down with me,' I say rudely. The truth is I've got a terrible hormone rush and I really want to be on my own and have a good cry.

'OK, but if there's anything I can do . . . '

'There's nothing you can do, thanks,' I say abruptly.

'OK,' he says again. We walk through the house and to the front door in silence. He holds the door open for me. I hurry through—after the warmth of the house the cold air makes me catch my breath. And I use this as an excuse not to speak to him again but just to walk quickly down the gravel driveway.

At the end of the drive, before the curve of the road takes me out of sight, I turn. He is still standing at the front door, staring after me. His face is blank, his dark eyes shadowed. I wish I'd made him swear not to tell anyone about the baby. I hesitate, wondering if I should walk back and make him promise not to breathe a word. But even while I am thinking this I see him turn on his heel, go back into the house and close the door. And suddenly it seems impossible for me to go back and knock on that door or speak to him again. Instead I walk quickly through the fading autumn light, cradling Peaches inside my coat.

# CHAPTER FOUR

I have another bath when I get home and huddle over the gas fire in the sitting room. But the chill from the river and from Corey's dark stare seems to have got right inside me, seeping into my bones and vital organs. I wonder if the baby, floating in its little sac of fluid, is chilly, and my arms instinctively wrap around my belly as I contemplate this idea.

Now I have spoken about the baby it is becoming more real to me. Before I was in a dreamlike state but now the words have been spoken it is starting to seem like reality. I have told my parents (kind of) and Corey knows. Admitting the truth has been like planting a seed—gradually the idea is taking root, showing shoots, gaining a hold on my mind. A baby. I am going to have a baby. I know I should think about all the practical stuff, like how do I go to university and fulfil my potential with a baby? But I can't think about that now. For the time being it is enough that I can acknowledge the fact of the baby and admit it to myself and to others—I shall take it one step at a time.

My mother comes home early. The front door opens with a thud and I hear her in the kitchen unloading shopping. The amount of noise my mother makes is directly related to her stress levels. At the moment it is like having a thunderbolt trapped in the house. She is marching up and down the hall like an Orc preparing to do battle. I am tempted to sneak up to my room and pretend to be busy reading but the lure of food is too strong. I have been nibbling raisins and Brazil nuts since I got in, but I am already anticipating supper and wondering what we will have. I am also wondering if she has bought anything I could pig out on until our evening meal is ready. I am thinking doughnuts, I am thinking shortbread, I am thinking pain au chocolat, and I am eager as a hungry puppy as I stumble into the kitchen.

My mother is working in true military fashion. The table is stacked with the shopping. I look it over like a disappointed antique dealer at a particularly scruffy car boot sale. It is a pretty dismal load of shopping. There's lots of salad, some steak, and a whole array of cans called 'Slim Zeal'.

I pick a can up and handle it carefully. It is asparagus flavour, it can be consumed cold or warm, and contains the nutrients of a whole meal in a can. The thought of cold asparagus-flavoured gunk kills my appetite for a second and I feel my mouth purse up in a moment of disgust.

The labels on the other cans don't set my taste buds tingling either. There's chocolate and something called neutral. What the hell is 'neutral' meant to taste of? I try to imagine something that tastes of nothing and can't come up with anything apart from maybe porridge without salt or sugar—but at least that has texture. But a neutral drink that you have instead of a meal—yuck—it would slip down your throat and you wouldn't even know you'd had it. That would be my idea of hell as I crave nourishment and comfort food in equal measure. I am just about to ask my mother if we can have a pudding with custard (I'm pretty sure there's an apple crumble in the freezer) when she starts talking.

'I thought I'd try to lose a bit of weight, you know, before Christmas. It's just the pounds have been stealing up on me. Every time I buy new clothes they have to be a bit bigger. If not a larger size then a style that's more roomy—you know what I mean. I'm starting to feel middle-aged. A middle-aged woman with middle-aged spread . . . I thought you might like to try a healthy eating diet with me . . . '

Without looking at me she reaches into her handbag and pulls out a leaflet for a slimming club. 'And I thought we could try this. We could go together once a week or even once a month if you would prefer. It would be fun . . . and we'll get some new scales . . . ' she says this with great enthusiasm, as if getting new scales would be some kind of treat.

I glance at the leaflet as I put down the can of neutral Slim Zeal which I've been studying. I don't really know what to say. All I can think about is proper food and what we are going to have for supper. Everything else in the world seems irrelevant to that burningly important question.

'I'm pleased you're confident enough not to worry about your weight,' my mother says firmly. I am getting the feeling she's been rehearsing what to say to me on the way home in the car. 'I've worried sometimes about the twins. So obsessed with their figures and scared to put on an extra pound. It's not good. I went through a stage of puppy fat when I was seventeen. You just have to go with the flow. I'm glad you're not in a mope about your weight . . . ' She stops frozen in mid sentence. She looks across at me. Her face is puckered. It takes me a minute to realize that she is so tired her eyes are drooping. She looks like a caricature of her normal self. 'You're not in a mope about your weight, are you, Emily?'

'No,' I say carefully. 'I'm not in a mope about my weight.' There is a beat of silence. Then I add: 'What are we having for supper, can I help get it ready?' I stand up a bit straighter, willing the baby to move over towards my spine and not protrude so much. Standing tall and pulling my shoulders back makes my monstrous boobs stick out even further but there's not a lot I can do about them.

'Why are you wearing that awful tracksuit?' my mother asks. The pretence is gone. She looks and sounds anguished. The tracksuit makes me look enormous, I know it does. I look like a big, grey, baggy elephant-girl. I tighten all my muscles and hold my stomach in. It's quite an effort.

'I went for a walk and got cold and muddy, so I had a bath,' I mutter.

'I'll make us a salad . . . ' my mother says. I can feel her eyes on me and her expression is hurt. 'I'm fine. I can manage fine . . . ' she adds.

She wants me out of the kitchen. The sight of me is like hot pins in her eyes. And I want to be out of the kitchen too. You can hold your stomach in for only so long when you are pregnant . . . I make for the door.

'What do you think about the slimming club, Emily?' she says to my retreating back.

'Yeah, fine, whatever,' I say brightly. The chill from earlier in the day has spread to my brain now. I can't face any hassle. I just want to be warm and fed.

I keep a low profile for the rest of the half-term week. I smile and gulp down a Slim Zeal with each meal and eat enough salad to keep a colony of rabbits happy for a year.

My parents are like tightrope walkers with each other and with me. Their eyes are fixed, glazed with concentration as they look straight ahead. It is as if they are terrified to look up or down or to the side, for fear of losing balance and falling into an abyss. They talk in staccato sentences—only communicating what is absolutely necessary. And as for me—I hoard food in my room to quell the nausea and hunger pangs and I walk Peaches for miles and wash her carefully before taking her home. And I don't go anywhere near Nell Acre because I have developed a curious and unreasonable dread of seeing Corey Thomas.

I don't see the twins until their first week back at

school. They go to a private girl's school. I go to the local comprehensive. But it's a ritual that we meet up when they are delivered home on a Friday in the school minibus.

They are looking fabulous. They have been staying in their parent's timeshare in Majorca and ten days in the sun has highlighted their hair and tanned their faces. We sit around their kitchen table, drinking hot chocolate and talking, and I feel like a ghost triplet— the one that is disappearing into greyness and mist.

I tell them about the Slim Zeal and make them laugh. Then I say: 'Of course it's all a waste of time. I shall get fatter before I get thinner.'

'Is that a riddle?' Sienna asks smiling.

'Why don't you get an exercise bike?' Flo says, looking at me critically. 'That's a good way to lose a few pounds and get a flat stomach.'

I shrug. 'Maybe . . . ' I say.

'Are you all right, Em?' Sienna says gently. 'You seem . . . ' There is a long silence in the kitchen. The cold tap is dripping. Things like that drive Flo mad; she jumps to her feet and turns it off.

'Are you searching for the right word?' I ask. 'Discarding "fat", "moody", "scruffy", and "difficult" in case they cause offence?'

'Oh, don't be soft,' Flo says. 'You're none of those things. You have put on a few pounds, but so would I if I scoffed like you. Do you realize that you've eaten half a packet of Jaffa cakes and two apples since we've been sitting here?'

'Have I?' I say in surprise, and they burst out laughing.

'That's the ultimate comfort eating. You don't even know you're doing it,' Flo says in her usual bossy tone. 'You need to get a grip. I think you need a boyfriend. What about that guy in your English group who you fancied last year?'

'Who?' I say. Fancying boys seems part of another lifetime.

'Russ. The one with the dark hair—you talked about him lots,' Si fills me in.

'I don't remember . . . ' I say lamely. 'Anyway, I don't need a boyfriend. Believe me.'

'I think you do,' Flo says.

Si, always sensitive, looks into my face and says, 'Don't tease her, Flo.'

'I'm not teasing her.'

'Look. I don't need a bloody boyfriend,' I say. 'In fact, it's the last thing in the world I need. If you must know I'm pregnant.'

There have been only a very few times in all the years that we have been the triplets that I have held centre stage. Normally I am the quiet one, the triplet who listens and nods, who follows where the twins lead. But, just for an instant, they are both staring at me and I have their total and undivided attention. I just wish it was for something other than this particular bit of news.

'You can't possibly be . . . ' Sienna says, and she looks as if she might cry.

'It's utterly impossible. You've never had a serious boyfriend,' Florence adds, her voice rising with emotion. 'You've never really been interested in boys . . . too busy being in love with Brett Thomas . . . and you joined that Kissing Club thing and signed a pledge. You're still wearing that gorgeous ring your parents bought you . . . to celebrate the fact that you promise to abstain from sex until you marry,' she recites. And she reaches across and touches the ring as if to remind us all what it symbolizes. She and Si have always been a bit envious of my ring. I look down at it now—a narrow white-gold band with a tiny ruby—bought to replace the inscribed silver ring that Mum said looked like something out of a cracker. We are all staring at it—and it seems to me that the stone gleams like a tiny droplet of glistening blood.

'Don't muck about, please, Em . . . ' Si says anxiously to me.

'I'm not mucking about,' I mumble, reaching for another Jaffa cake.

'How can you be pregnant?' Si says. Then she adds quickly, 'Oh, Emily! You're not trying to tell us that something awful has happened to you! That you've been forced or raped or something terrible like that?'

'No . . . I was a willing partner,' I whisper ruefully. The memory of my willingness comes back to haunt me in a sudden rush and my face heats spontaneously. 'It wasn't anything like that, honest. I wasn't even drunk . . . ' I mutter miserably.

'Well, for crying out loud, 'fess up and tell us what

happened?' Flo says. 'Tell us everything, now,' she adds firmly.

When Flo commands Sienna and I deliver—she has always been leader of the triplets, in charge completely. I take a deep breath.

'It was casual sex,' I say very slowly. 'And it really is as sordid and hurtful and soul-destroying as people say it is. And I did it and now I'm pregnant.' And then I get a hormone rush and burst into tears.

Their voices are loud and urgent. It's just as well we are alone in the house. There is a volley of questions.

'Tell us who it was?'

'Is it someone we know?'

'Where did you do it?'

'How many times?'

'Surely not just once?'

'No one gets pregnant doing it just once!'

'Of course you can get pregnant the first time! Just shut up, will you!'

'Why did you sleep with him?'

'Where on earth did you go?'

'What was it like?'

'For goodness' sake. Tell!'

The twins seem to forget sometimes that there are two of them speaking. I have wondered if they don't hear the other twin's voice or something spooky like that. Now being interrogated in stereo freaks me out. I put my hands over my ears and say: 'I can't tell you anything more than that . . . '

'You must,' Flo says urgently. 'It's bad to keep things

to yourself. This is why you're comfort eating. You must tell us everything.'

'I think you should,' Si adds. 'You'll feel loads better.'

'How do you know,' I say mulishly. I can't remember ever standing up to them before, or arguing with them, or not doing exactly what I was told to do when I was told to do it.

'Because me and Flo share everything, and tell each other everything, and we always feel better afterwards,' Si says reasonably.

'That's because you really are twins. You're sisters. But I don't have a sister, do I? It's all just pretend, isn't it? We're not really triplets. You're twins and I am just poor, sad, singleton Emily. I sometimes think I just have pretend relationships with everyone,' I add miserably.

I see a glance pass between the twins—a clear unspoken communication. A wave of utter loneliness and desolation sweeps over me. Then Flo comes and kneels at my feet. She puts her arms around my hulking body and presses her face against mine. I breathe in the warm female scent of her. Pregnancy has made my sense of smell so sensitive I can distinguish the sharp lemony aroma of her shampoo, her strawberry perfume, and the warm tea-laced fragrance of her breath.

Flo says: 'You can get it sorted out you know, Em. And we could help you. There're places you can go and people who know what to do. There's no shame or blame attached. No one needs to know—if that's how you want it to be. You don't have to tell your parents or our parents. We could go down to London if you like. Si and I would come with you, so you wouldn't be on your own. And we could stay with our auntie, she's really great. She'd help all she can, I know she would. She works in a really tough school in Balham and she knows all about this sort of trouble, I can tell you.'

I shake my head. 'It's too late for anything like that . . . ' I mumble.

'Of course it's not . . . ' Flo says urgently. I feel both the twins staring hard at me as if trying to divine from my girth exactly how pregnant I am.

'It'll be all right. It will be all right,' I say, as I shake myself free from Flo and stand up. I am suddenly bone-weary and hungry for some proper food. I want to go home and make myself some cheese and tomatoes on toast. Then I want to snuggle under my duvet and read *Tess of the D'Urbervilles* and cheer myself up. It takes up too much energy to talk to people—I am tired of the emotional tension between me and the twins. I want to get away from them. I stifle a yawn. I see another glance pass between them.

Flo looks at me directly and says rather sternly: 'This isn't just one of your stories, is it, Emily? You aren't just having us on?'

Sienna makes a little noise, a strangled sigh or a gasp, as if shocked by her sister's insensitivity and plain speaking. If Si had wanted to ask me if I was telling a big porky pie she would have put it much more kindly than that.

I look at them rather blankly.

'You know Em doesn't tell stories any more . . . It was just a phase. You know that . . . ' Sienna says quickly. 'If Em says she's pregnant then I believe her,' she adds bravely. The glances passing between the twins are like crossfire. I yawn again. It matters not a jot to me whether they believe me or not. Time will tell. The truth will out. All the old clichés will come true.

'I'm like the little boy who cried "Wolf",' I say calmly. 'The trouble with spending part of your childhood being a compulsive liar is that when you do start to tell the truth no one believes you. Anyway, thanks for listening.'

'But is it true?' Flo asks, giving me one of her most hawkish direct looks.

I shrug. I know I am being irritating. It must be years of never answering back or taking the initiative when I was a triplet. Now I have the upper hand I can't stop. 'Make your own minds up,' I say.

# Chapter Five

On Monday I get a formal docket requesting me to go to Mr Anthony's office at the end of school. Mr Anthony is in charge of the special education unit. He has been writing me anguished notes since the beginning of the year asking why I haven't been going to the classes I volunteered to assist with. All these mentoring and pastoral duties go down on our UCAS forms and for that reason alone I should have been attending. Although I actually feel worse about letting Mr Anthony down because I know that he relies on help from sixth formers to get around all the kids who need one-to-one care. Helping him was always a highlight of my week and I've missed going. But I have just been too tired and unfocused to get there or even write a note of explanation to him.

When I arrive at his office he beckons me in and then closes the door on stampeding herds of first years that are leaving school in a cloud of dust as if they are wildebeest on a migration route. He unfastens the window as wide as it will go and leans into the opening taking gulps of the cold afternoon air.

'Thank goodness this day is nearly over,' he says

wearily. I don't think I am meant to answer. I think he is actually talking to himself. Anyway, I am very relieved that he has opened the window, because the room stinks of unwashed bodies and mouldy school uniforms. And I might have had to make an excuse and leave if he hadn't taken the initiative and let some air in, because bad smells make me feel nauseous very quickly these days.

I pop a mint into my mouth and enjoy the draught from the window. Mr Anthony is the kindest of men and he has an endless stream of unfortunates who make a beeline for his door. He is the saviour of the oppressed, the bullied, the weak of heart and mind, the profligate and the needy. It is well known in school that anyone in trouble can knock on his door and get sympathy and justice.

Mr Anthony is different to other teachers. He seems to know everyone and everything about them: not just their names and what form they are in, but personal stuff like who their brothers and sisters are (even if they have different surnames) and all about their grannies that have died and what they are interested in. He's a real people person. He has a heart as big as the world and needy kids gravitate to him because of it. And all the poor little dollops that have been in to see him today must have had BO.

When Mr Anthony started at the school I was in Year 7. And all the girls (apart from the weirdos who wanted to be goths) had mega crushes on him because he was so young and good looking. Now, when he

61

turns to face me, I register with shock that he looks exhausted: there are dark rings under his lovely blue eyes, his skin looks grey, his gorgeous blond hair needs washing, and his shirt collar is rolling up in a way that indicates that it has not been ironed.

When he got married he broke the hearts of an entire generation of Year 7 and 8 girls (who had hoped he would wait for them). And now I ask myself why his wife doesn't look after him better. I've seen her at school functions. She's a pretty little dark-haired nursery nurse. They make a blinding couple. I can't understand why she's neglecting him. If he was mine I'd iron every sock and handkerchief in his wardrobe and tuck him up into bed early with mugs of cocoa.

'Are you all right, sir?' I blurt out before I can stop myself. I don't like to see him looking so old and worn out. He's a saint and I feel that God (and his wife) should look after him better.

He runs his hands across his forehead and hides his face from me. 'To be honest, things are a bit difficult at the moment,' he mutters. Then he shakes his head and says, 'But enough of that—Emily—I've asked to see you because I'm concerned about you.' He looks at me very directly—his blue eyes looking straight into mine—and I catch a glimpse of the old Mr Anthony behind the weariness. He glances down at the papers on his desk.

'I've asked Mrs Asquith for copies of your tutor's report sheets and they all tell the same story: course work not handed in, poor attendance, lack of concentration and co-operation. Emily, you are one of the school's top achievers. Your GCSE results were excellent. So what has gone wrong?' He frowns swiftly and then straightens his face. 'Also, you haven't kept to your commitments within my department. I've been meaning to speak to you about it, but I thought it might be pressure of work. What's happened, Emily? Last year you didn't miss a single week and now this year—nothing, and not even an attempt at an apology or explanation. I thought you built up a really strong rapport with your group. I was going to give you more responsibility because the children you worked with had grown to trust you. And now you've let them down. They miss you—and so do I,' he adds gently.

Honestly, he's such an unbelievably nice guy. Even when he's telling you off he still makes you feel as if he cares about you and you are special.

I shrug and look away as I say, 'I'm sorry. I've been tired.'

He looks concerned. 'Aren't you well? You look . . . ' he stops and stares at me.

I shrug again. It's warm in his office—even with the window open. The radiator thermostat must have got stuck on high. I undo my duffle coat and then take it off. 'I'm sorry,' I say lamely. 'I was going to write to you but I didn't get around to it.' I fold my coat carefully in my lap and stare down at it.

'I know there's a lot of stress at this point in your school career. But you have to work on your time management and pace yourself. I can help you with that, Emily. Or Mrs Asquith will give you any help she can. But you do have to ask. You have to talk to people. We're not clairvoyants. Now,' he turns away from me and reaches for his diary, 'how about making an appointment to see me or Mrs Asquith later this week and talk everything through? It's not too late to make up the lost sessions with my department so your record of achievement isn't affected. Especially as you've been ill . . . By the way,' he adds kindly, 'have you been tested for ME? The Epstein Barr virus causes ME and glandular fever and it's very common among your age group.'

'The kissing disease,' I say. 'You get it from too much snogging.' I don't know why I am trying to embarrass him. I am in a rebellious mood. School has this affect on me nowadays.

'Yes, well. You joined up to a chastity club, didn't you? I remember your mother telling me you'd taken a pledge and joined a group while you were in America. No sex before marriage.' He glances at me and manages a small smile. 'But I think you are allowed a kiss or two. It's natural at your age. I don't think you should feel guilty about it.' He frowns suddenly. 'You mustn't think that it's your fault that you're ill and beat yourself up about it.'

I stare at him. He is looking down at his diary. His face is suddenly blank as if he has forgotten I am here with him.

'I'm not ill,' I say. He's making me sound like some poor creature from the Brontë era—as if I am in a decline and about to fade away. I'm not quite sure how we got into this conversation but I suddenly want to be out of it.

'I'm not ill, really,' I say, my voice a bit louder.

He looks at me as if he doesn't know who I am. He's been miles away in some far off place and he shakes his head slightly as if to bring himself back to the present. 'You're not ill,' he repeats. 'Well, that's good, Emily. You know, you don't look as if you are ill. Quite the opposite—in fact you look . . . ' He can't seem to get his head around the next word.

'I'm not ill. I'm pregnant,' I say firmly.

He looks at me with an expression of total shock on his face. I don't think I have ever seen anyone look so surprised—and at the same time he makes this noise. It's awful. Like the sound an animal makes when it is hurt. It's just a tiny cry, and then his mouth jams shut to swallow down the pain; but even so that little exclamation echoes around and around in my head, until the hairs on the back of my neck lift and the skin on my arms turns goose-fleshy.

'Pregnant?' he whispers. 'Are you sure?' Then his eyes rake over me, as I sit there, all curves and bumps, and suddenly his eyes flash like blue water and I realize they are full of tears.

'I'm sorry,' I say, and I stand up so quickly my coat slips down onto the floor between us. 'Mr Anthony, I'm so sorry.' I'm not really sure why I am apologizing. I just feel as if I have done something awful and that telling him I am pregnant has hurt him terribly.

He turns away from me—back to the window and the gulps of cold air. I sit down wondering bleakly how I've managed to make such a mess of this interview. Eventually he speaks to me and his voice is very matter of fact, as if we are discussing the weather.

'My wife has just lost another baby—it's our third miscarriage. This one happened at home, in our bed. I'm a bit raw . . . It's very hard for both of us. Are you going to . . . ? Will you . . . ? I suppose your parents want you to be sensible . . . ' He turns to face me. 'Are you going to have an abortion?' he asks very gently. 'I've told you this because, if you are going to have an abortion, you must make sure you have counselling and proper help . . . I'd never realized, not until my wife . . . how difficult it can be for . . . ' His voice fades away. His face is like one of the masks I made from paper and flour paste when I was in junior school—it is white and rigid and without expression.

'Have you talked it over with the father?' he says at last. 'It can be difficult for partners . . . '

'No! I haven't talked it over with "the father". He's not my partner or even my boyfriend. He doesn't know anything about the baby and, if I have my way, he never will.'

Mr Anthony cannot hide the anguish on his face now. 'Emily!' he says. 'This is terrible. How on earth! I know it's none of my business but how did you get yourself into a mess like this? What will your parents make of it? They've always been so proud of you. Your mother must be heartbroken. She's so . . . ' He stops.

'Emily, you have told them? They do know?' he adds in alarm.

'Yes, they know, sort of. My mother is in denial at the moment, I think.' I stop and then say slowly, 'My mother has always wanted the perfect life. We've always had to be the ideal family with the immaculate home. And now it's all gone wrong. I don't really know what I can do about it. I'm not perfect. I never have been. I've always tried so hard to be what they wanted me to be, and now I've let them down . . . But I will talk to them again, I promise,' I add, because he looks so upset.

'That's good. They'll want to be involved. And I'll help you all I can, you know that,' he says. 'But I'm not on best form today. I've had very little sleep and I really need to get to the hospital to see my wife.'

He reaches down to pick up my coat at the same time as I stand up and reach over it. We kind of collide and his face skims my stomach. He looks up into my face and I have the weirdest sensation—like a vision, only more real. I suddenly see him as a child: his face rounded with skin soft as velvet, his mouth a cupid's bow, and his hair fine as yellow silk. And then, bizarrely, I see him as an old man, his eyes haunted and red-rimmed, his face lined and sagging with the torment of the years, his hair thin and colourless. I shake my head and find my arms are around his neck and my face is pressing against his. 'I'm so, so sorry about your baby,' I say. And I hold him as if I will never let him go—until I feel wetness on my face. Then a shudder runs right through him and he pulls away from me.

'I should have had the door open,' he says bleakly, scrubbing his fists over his eyes. 'And I shouldn't have told you about . . . '

'It's OK,' I say. I am so embarrassed I can't look at him. 'I won't tell anyone or anything like that. It really is OK, honestly.'

'You will come to me if you need help, won't you?' he asks anxiously.

'You will be the first person I will find if I need help, I promise,' I say soothingly. I suddenly feel as if I am in charge. As if I am the grown-up and he is the child. I pick up my coat. Out of the tail of my eye I can see him staring at me with a haunted look as if his eyes are drawn against his will.

'You look absolutely wonderful,' he says. 'You're not ill, are you?'

'No. I'm fit as a flea and eating for England. And the best thing of all is that my brain has turned to mush so I can't worry about anything.'

He bites hard at his lower lip and then says, 'Gabby is sick all the time, day and night. I wonder sometimes if that is what causes her to miscarry but the doctors say no. You're very lucky,' he says, and then he shakes his head. 'Sorry,' he says brokenly. 'I shouldn't have said that.'

'No. It's fine. I know what you mean. And thanks for everything, you know, all the good advice. I will think about what you've said, really I will.'

I open the door quickly, because I am desperate to get away. I look over my shoulder and say: 'Bye, sir.' Then, when I turn back, I find I am face to face with Miss Zoller. I have practically walked into her so she must have been lurking right outside the door.

Miss Zoller is the bitchiest teacher in the school, even though she's quite young. She could actually be passably good looking if she didn't have such a hateful aura and such a witchy expression on her face all the time. I've sometimes wondered if her bad attitude is down to her name. It must have been traumatic growing up and always being the last on the register— but for whatever reason she's a nasty pasty all right. She has just been promoted to Head of something or other and has been on the warpath since the beginning of the year. Now she's eyeing me with a look that could freeze the entire oceans of the world.

'Now, Emma . . . ' she begins.

I fix her with a steely look: 'Emily Sutton,' I say calmly.

'What are you doing here, Emily?' she snaps.

'Discussing my mentoring with Mr Anthony,' I retort.

I am aware of Mr Anthony standing next to me. I can see he's holding his coat and his briefcase and looks edgy. No, worse than that. He looks as if he might start crying again at any moment.

'I'd assumed the block was clear of students. I was just about to lock the main doors,' she says very deliberately. And she looks from him to me and back to the door of his office again with an evil glance.

'Emily's been ill. We were discussing it. The first years were charging out. I couldn't hear myself think . . . ' Mr Anthony says apologetically. I want to scream at him not to act guilty with her but to tell her we were having a private discussion and that was why the door was closed.

Instead I close my eyes for a second to shut out his face and the misery etched there. I know as well as he does what the rules are. I can't believe the horrendous ill-luck that Piggy Zoller should be on the prowl at the precise moment I am leaving his office. And that she should be talking to him now as if he is a Year Seven caught smoking in the toilets.

Miss Zoller's face is a sneer (this passes as a smile from her) as she says: 'I won't hold you up now, Emily. I shall catch up with you later on in the week.'

I know the exact moment when she realizes I am pregnant. I turn to leave but I can't help one more glance at Mr Anthony. I want to reassure him, or make him feel better in some way.

'Bye, sir. Bye, miss,' I say cheerfully. And then in a flash I see her green eyes move across me, focusing on my stomach, and then her eyes harden until they are like pebbles on a sea shore. And I see a momentary expression of incredulity and shock flash across her face. I see her look from him to me and back again and the air seems thick with the thoughts that she is thinking. A moment of dizziness hits me. It's as if she's creating a voodoo curse or something. I feel as if the earth is spinning too fast.

70

I pull my duffle coat on and fasten the middle toggle—the one that covers my stomach—with shaking fingers. Then I turn on my heel and walk off. I feel their eyes on me. Mr Anthony's compassionate and anxious and Miss Zoller's full of spite. And not for the first time I wonder if she took up teaching because she actually hates children . . .

# CHAPTER SIX

Avoiding Corey Thomas does me no good at all because the following Saturday morning he comes to our house. I am looking particularly gruesome in a horrible tight T-shirt and cardigan and some hipster trousers that show the massive curve of my stomach. I am really embarrassed when I open the door and realize who it is. He appears to be really embarrassed by the sight of me (or the fact that I am a sight) and he stares fixedly into my eyes (I suppose to avoid looking at the rest of me).

He has the golden retriever with him. It sits obediently at his feet and gives me the doggy equivalent of a grin. I scowl back in reply.

'Yes?' I say by way of a greeting.

'I wondered if you would like to come out for a walk. If you wanted to bring the pooch I'd keep Kizzy on her lead.' He says it as if he is a robot or has been practising saying the words in front of a mirror. His face is always a bit blank but now it is wiped clear of all expression. And as he is now looking down at the dog I can't even get a glimpse of his dark eyes.

I look right past him—out into the brightness of the

day—and breathe in the thin-cold air that is streaming into the house. There was a frost in the night and the branches of the cherry tree in our front garden are laced in delicate white. The sun is breaking through and everything is sparkling.

I think of how good it would be to get out of the house and away from the toxic atmosphere that my parents are generating. And it would also be good to have some company (even if it is Corey Thomas). I haven't seen the twins since the fraught meeting in the kitchen. I suppose they are waiting for me to phone up and be conciliatory. But I'm not going to do it. I just don't seem to have the energy to talk to anyone any more. When I do make it into school I just seem to walk around in a dream and I have ignored notes from Miss Zoller and Mr Anthony asking to see me. I have taken to spending time in the library in town. I sit in the warmth of the reading room hiding historical romance novels behind *The Times*. And at intervals I wander off to a café to fill myself up on tea cakes and cheese on toast.

After a week of mooching around on my own going out for a walk in the country with someone for company seems like the ultimate treat.

'All right, thanks, I'd love to come for a walk,' I say with enthusiasm. Corey gives me a startled look. Maybe he thinks I'm taking the mick. 'I'll just get my coat.'

I leave the door open—it seems rude to close it in his face. I grab my coat from the rack and call into the kitchen: 'I won't be long. It's such a lovely day. I'm just going for a walk.'

My mother shoots out through the door talking as she does so. 'What a good idea, Emily. A walk! How lovely. Walking is wonderful exercise. Make sure you walk fast though—you need to get breathless for it to equal an aerobic session . . . ' She stops short at the sight of Corey and the hell hound. 'Are you going for a walk with a dog? That will be nice.'

'Yes. And I'll collect Peaches from Mrs Patton and take her for a little toot. I'll be home in time for lunch,' I say, as I pull on my duffle coat.

Corey and I don't speak or discuss where we will go. I collect Peaches and, without a word, we make for the path by the side of the river that leads up to Nell Acre. When we get into the open space of the moor my mood lightens. The effort of walking and looking at the scenery takes up all my thoughts and energy and I am at peace for the first time in days.

The air up here is so cold that every time I breathe it is like eating ice cream. The heather and bilberry bushes are coated in spiky filigrees of frost and the whole world is whitened as if it has been etched out in chalk. We walk fast to keep warm, with me clutching Peaches to my chest like a hot-water bottle, until Corey finally says:

'I'm sure the dogs will be all right together. Let them run around and get to know each other. If Kiz is a nuisance I'll put her on the lead.'

I take off Peaches's coat and diamanté collar and

store them in my pocket. 'Now, sweetheart,' I whisper, 'just be a brave girl.'

But as soon as Peaches is on the ground Kizzy races up to her and starts bouncing around like a great golden lion and barking. Peaches squeals in terror and I squeal in sympathy and rush forward to pick her up.

Corey grabs hold of my arm: 'Cool it. Just let them get on with it,' he says. 'Kizzy's not touching her.'

I pull away from him. Tears are prickling my eyes because I hate to see Peaches squirming and screaming. I want to pick her up and say I've changed my mind and I don't want to walk with them.

Corey crouches down and touches Peaches's head gently. With his other hand he holds Kizzy at bay. Then he starts talking to Peaches and Kizzy as if they are a couple of little kids and he is a kindly teacher getting them to be friends. It's kind of nonsense stuff—but not as crazy as the fantasy world that I have constructed for Peaches. Still, I am pretty impressed that he's prepared to do it in front of me. I didn't think boys did that sort of thing.

Gradually Kizzy settles down—she stops leaping about and barking. And Peaches manages to stand up and look a bit more like a dog instead of a lamb that is dying. 'There—what good dogs,' he says encouragingly. Then he reaches into his pocket and produces some dog treats: little choc drops for Peaches and a big bone biscuit for Kizzy. He takes it in turns to feed them and praise them. When they have finished eating he stands up and says to me, 'Now, just walk on and ignore them.'

'Whatever you say. But do tell—when did you get to be such an ace dog trainer?' I ask.

'I'm doing psychology for A level. I'm interested in behaviour patterns,' he says. 'It's a bit of an experiment, but I think it might work.' He reaches into his pocket and produces two muesli bars and hands one to me. 'I thought you might need a snack,' he says.

'Thanks,' I mutter. I feel a bit like a zoo animal with a kindly keeper. I am faintly disturbed that he has observed me so accurately and remembered that I am hungry all the time. I would like to say 'No' to his muesli bar and keep my pride. But I am peckish—and it is covered in chocolate—so I eat the bar while watching Peaches and Kizzy.

'You'll be a very over-protective mother,' Corey says suddenly. 'You'll have to watch it. How will you manage when you have to leave the baby at nursery and school?'

'What?' I say.

'You haven't taken your eyes off that pooch. And she's fine. They're ignoring each other. By the end of the walk they'll be friends. You wait and see.'

'Oh, will they?' I ask. I am stung that he is such a know-it-all—and seems to think he understands dogs better than I do when I have been walking Peaches for ages. I am also put out that he has referred to the baby. And I have to admit that what he has said sends a shock wave through me. I find I am reeling from the thought of nursery and school and of the fact that I will be a MOTHER. I'd only just got my head around the idea of a baby . . . Now I have to project into the next five years and it's really scary. I will be someone's mum. I will be called 'Mummy'. Oh-my-god-it-hardly-seems-possible.

'You're very sure that I'll keep it,' I mutter. 'The twins are busy sorting out all kinds of other solutions. And my mother thinks I need to go to a slimming club.'

'You will keep it, though, won't you?' he says.

'I don't know,' I say quietly. 'I'm still trying to get used to the idea. It's something I shall have to think about.'

We walk in silence and then he says, 'I've got some news. We're moving. The house and the land are on the market.'

'No!' I say with astonishment. 'But why? Your dad loves that house.' I don't add that Mr Thomas also loves being 'Lord of the Manor'. Nell Acre is the biggest house in the village and Mr Thomas also owns all the fields that surround the main street and the school. He has always really enjoyed allowing the village fete and the school sports to be held in his fields. Not only would he give them free of charge but he would also provide posh portable loos and refreshments. Because of this generosity he was always asked to give out the prizes and was talked about in speeches as 'our kind benefactor'. He lapped it up.

'What has happened?' I ask bluntly.

'Dad's fallen on hard times,' Corey says. 'He's run out of money.'

'How on earth can he have run out of money? He won the lottery! And he owns that big garage in Leeds.'

The whole village knew the story of how the dysfunctional family from inner-city Leeds had won the lottery and bought up the Nell Acre estate. We had talked of nothing else for months. There had been photos and stories in the newspapers about them. So, even before the family arrived, we knew all about their lives: that Mr Thomas worked as a mechanic in a garage and had two sons by two different wives—both of whom had run off and left their children to be brought up by him. Everyone had been really impressed by this story—apart from my mother. She had sniffed and said, 'Well, there must be something wrong with him if two women have walked out on him.'

'Maybe he's not a good judge of character. Or maybe it's just plain bad luck?' my father, always charitable, had suggested. But my mother had never changed her mind. I think she thought the Thomases 'common' because they came from Belle Isle, which I always thought a bit mean. Especially as she and my dad had both been born and brought up in the scruffy end of Leeds.

And anyway the Thomases aren't common or rough or anything like that—just very ordinary. And I always thought it a bit sad really because Mr Thomas obviously loved being rich and loved splashing his money about. He was like a big kid about it. He would always pay for a party for the children from the village school

78

at Christmas and organize discos in the Church Hall when it was Brett's and Corey's birthdays and everyone was invited—even if they spent the rest of the year ignoring Corey. And the party bags we came away with after these bashes were incredible! They gave my mother something else to moan about.

'It's ridiculous giving children expensive presents like radios and CD players in party bags. It makes it awkward for other parents who can't afford to do the same,' she said.

'No it doesn't!' I had retorted. 'No one expects anyone else to give presents like that. Mr Thomas does it because he's won the lottery. He wants everyone to be happy like him.' I thought having the smallest radio in the world was amazing and that Mr Thomas was like Father Christmas. Especially as my parents always seemed worried that I would grow up 'spoilt'—either that or they had trouble making ends meet because, in the main, I got really boring presents for Christmas and birthday: usefully unexciting stuff like new clothes and shoes and duvet covers. My ruby ring was a rare fit of extravagance from them.

Then one year Mr Thomas chartered a plane and flew everyone down to Alton Towers for the day and my mother wouldn't let me go. I was furious and sulked for weeks. Whenever the twins talked about it my eyes filled with angry tears, especially as Brett Thomas had (evidently) made a real fuss of them and gone on loads of rides to keep them company. I was nearly insane with jealousy.

Remembering Mr Thomas's generosity to everyone in the village makes me feel really sad. 'I'm so sorry. That's terrible news. Your dad must be gutted,' I say.

'It's all right. He's OK really. I mean, it wasn't a huge win in the first place and he's made lots of investments that haven't worked out. He knew he was taking a gamble. He could have put all the money in the bank and eked it out. But he's not that kind of a person. Having money burns a hole in his pocket. It sounds weird but he's been really poor at times in his life so the prospect of doing without doesn't really worry him. He's very philosophical about it. Obviously he'd rather the money had lasted but he just says he enjoyed spending it all. It's Brett who's taken it hard. Dad has bought him a flat at Brewery Wharf, so he's hardly on the breadline. He and Lara are moving in together which must have sweetened the pill a bit. But being rich has always been really important to Brett and he minds a lot now it is over.'

'And what about you—how do you feel about it?' I ask. I find it intriguing that he talks as if he is an adult and his father and Brett are less experienced and mature than him.

He shrugs. 'Dad's been able to give me enough to get through university. Then I shall have to look after myself. But it's only what everyone else does. I don't mind. I often wondered if I would have been happier if we had never won the money and stayed in Leeds. I like living out here but . . . '

He stops and a whole lifetime seems to be contained

in that 'but . . . ' There are no boys the same age as him in the village and we girls would never have anything to do with him. I wonder if he has been lonely, living up in the big house.

We walk in silence. I notice that Peaches is trotting along next to Kizzy and they look rather sweet together.

'You were right,' I say, kindly. 'Look! Kizzy and Peach are getting on fine together.'

'Yeah,' he says with a grin. And I am very grateful that he doesn't say, 'I told you so.'

We are out for ages because I love the cool crispness of the day and walk really slowly. And being out with Corey is fine because he doesn't talk unless I ask him a question—and so we are silent most of the time, which suits my bovine brain.

'Would you like to . . . ' he mumbles when we get to Mrs Patton's gate. 'I mean . . . they really enjoyed . . . '

'Yes. Peaches and I would love to go out with you again,' I say.

'Right. See you,' he says, as he heads off.

I am ravenous and I drop Peaches off and head home at top speed. I open the front door and breathe in deeply, hoping for a scent of lunch. I am fantasizing about something comforting and warm to eat: hot bacon and avocado salad with garlic bread, or a deep-pan pizza with anchovy and peppers, or maybe a vegetable curry with wild rice and mango chutney. I don't really mind what it is as long as it is ready NOW and there is lots of it.

I wash my hands and head for the kitchen: 'Hi. Is lunch ready?' I ask as I open the door. I know immediately that something is wrong. For a start the table is laid only for two. Also, my mother is sitting at the table waiting for me with a face that would be more suitable for a funeral than a cosy lunch party.

I slide into my seat and look at what is spread out waiting for me. I instantly recognize a Slim Zeal asparagus drink in a glass. Apart from that there is beetroot salad and some low calorie rye biscuits that remind me of cattle nuts.

'Where's Dad?' I ask uncertainly, picking up the glass and making a great pretence of taking a sip. I am actually praying that he might appear at any moment with fish and chips or a takeaway chicken tikka masala and save me from this slimmer's special.

'He's gone to visit Granny and Grandpa Sutton,' she says.

'Oh! I wish he'd told me. I would have liked to have gone to see them.' I feel myself pouting. Granny Sutton, Dad's mum, makes the world's best fruit cake which she serves with great wedges of cheese and giant mugs of strong tea. The mere thought of Granny Sutton's amazing cake makes my taste buds tingle. And the prospect of cold beetroot and an asparagus drink never seemed less enticing.

Also I am fond of my grandparents and would have been glad to see them—even if Granny Sutton's culinary skills had been the same as my other grandmother, Granny Blake.

Granny Blake is Mum's mum and she is totally different to Granny Sutton. I've never known Granny Blake cook anything unless it was in a plastic tray and could go in a microwave. I've sometimes been tempted to ask my mother what Granny Blake did before microwaves were invented. But we only go to visit her about once a year (generally at Christmas for a fleeting pit stop to exchange presents) and my mother never talks about her childhood the way my father does. Consequently bringing Granny Blake up in conversation—even to make a joke—isn't easy. Also, I have always had the impression that Granny Blake's habits and foibles aren't a laughing matter for my mother, even though Dad and I have a snigger about her when we are alone.

I reach for the salad. A wave of nausea is starting and I need to eat something fast. 'Could I have some bread, please?' I ask in a faint voice.

'I've lost five pounds,' my mother says.

I stuff some beetroot into my mouth and start chewing hard. I look at my mother's plate. She has laid out her food neatly and chopped everything up so that it looks like a miniature mosaic made by a dutiful Roman stonemason. But she hasn't started eating. She is carefully breaking up one of the slimming biscuits into bite-size pieces that would suit Peaches's little mouth.

'That's good. Five pounds is a lot,' I say encouragingly, as I stuff some lettuce and half a tomato into my mouth. The acidic taste of the beetroot isn't doing anything for my nausea. 'Do we have any bread?' I ask again, wistfully.

'I don't think you've lost any weight at all. And you haven't kept the chart I left by the scales in the bathroom. You're going to have to work on it, Emily.'

There is something brittle in her voice that makes me tear my attention away from the food and study her. She looks terrible. Her face is pale and she has double bags under her eyes. Worse than that—I can see from the narrow line of her mouth that she is just about to lose her temper with me. My mother doesn't lose her cool very often—thank goodness—but when she does it's like an atom bomb detonating and Dad and I generally make ourselves scarce until the mushroom cloud has dispersed.

# CHAPTER SEVEN

I quickly scrabble some more lettuce into my mouth. I am starting to feel really sick and I don't want to end up vomiting in the kitchen sink. My mother is very fussy about things like that.

To my astonishment and relief my mother doesn't lose her temper, although in a way what happens is more terrifying because she sort of crumbles in front of me.

'I don't know what your father and I have done to deserve this,' she says brokenly. 'We've tried so hard to give you everything . . . to give you the best possible start in life . . . and now . . . it's as if you are a stranger. And you seem to take delight in doing things which you know will upset us.'

'Is Dad really bothered about my weight? I don't think so,' I say. I must have something starchy to eat or I am going to upchuck all over my plate. I lumber up onto my feet and make for the bread bin. I start pushing a slice of lovely soft white sliced bread into my mouth while making my way back to the table. In my hand I have two more slices. I will make a sandwich . . . I can only think about that . . . But at the back of my mind is a little wriggling worm of resentment. If Corey has the gumption to realize that I am pregnant then why is my mother still persisting in the belief that I am eating myself into terminal obesity? I have after all told her the truth—well, sort of.

'Mum, I'm sorry,' I say eventually, looking up from my sandwich. I have been half listening to her tirade. She's not been angry, just kind of sorrowful and broken. A long list of accusations: I've become scruffy, my clothes don't fit, I haven't been to the hairdresser's—even though I get an allowance for looking after myself and keeping myself looking good.

'What will people think? You slopping around in that horrible old duffle coat with your hair all straggly . . . You look terrible . . . '

'And fat . . . ' I say grimly.

She looks away from me. I can see her mouth working oddly. I swallow my mouthful of sandwich and pray that she doesn't start crying until I've finished eating. If I eat when I am stressed or bolt my food then it gives me heartburn.

'I understand about your weight. I put on a lot of weight when I was a teenager . . . I had a lot of problems with food and dieting. I spent all my time losing weight and then bingeing and putting it all on again . . . It was only when I met your father at university that I got it under control.'

I stare at her, bemused and taken aback by this information. I suddenly think back to how good it felt when Corey and I talked about the baby. And I realize that however ugly the truth maybe it is better than lies.

'I'm sorry,' I say again. 'Mum, the way I look hasn't got anything to do with weight. The truth is I am pregnant—and it wasn't by an angel,' I add grimly.

My mother looks at me and gags. Honestly, for a horrible moment I think she's the one who is going to be puking. 'Emily, you can't be!' she says. She is blinking too fast and underneath her make-up I can see that her face is on fire.

I stand up, my plate in hand. I still have half a sandwich to eat. 'I think I'm going to go up to my room and eat this, if that's OK with you.'

She doesn't reply. I leave the room. I suddenly feel very tired. When I've finished my sandwich I might take a nap. My bed seems like a haven of peace and warmth. I want to curl up under the duvet like a cat and sleep away my troubles.

But before I can get to my room I have to walk up the stairs and today, more so than ever before, I am aware of the series of pictures which my parents had framed and mounted. They are paintings and drawings that have been done by me since I joined the Kissing Club. And they all have the same theme and I am in all of them—with my name written in my neat childish hand that has finally evolved into my current neat writing. Art has always been my best subject and for some of the pictures I used paints: soft water-colour or brash primary-hued acrylic. Others are in bold black pencil, ink, crayon or colour pencil. There is a particularly beautiful one in pastels. Despite these differences, and the years that divided their creation, they are in essence all the same. They are me—Emily—in a wedding dress. The design of the dress changes according to the fashion I was interested in. One is pink (how daring) but it is always me, looking like a princess—in some I am even wearing a tiara.

I make it to the safety of my room. I sit at my desk and eat my sandwich, chewing each mouthful slowly and carefully, taking comfort from the food, such as it is . . . When I have finished eating I kick off my shoes, curl up under the duvet, and go to sleep.

When I wake up it's dark and my room is full of shadows. There is a soft tapping at my door—it is this that has woken me. I know immediately who it is. 'Come in,' I say with relief.

It's Dad, with a mug of tea, and most wonderfully of all there are a couple of digestive biscuits in the saucer. He puts the mug down on my bedside table. Then he perches on the edge of the bed and looks down at me.

'Are you OK?' he asks. 'I peeked in earlier but you were fast asleep.'

I sit up and reach greedily for the biscuits and then slurp the tea down gratefully. He sits and watches me. He doesn't speak until I've finished munching.

'Both your grannies and your grandad sent their love to you.'

'Why didn't you tell me you were going to see Granny and Grandad? I would have come with you. We could have had fish and chips.'

'It wasn't really a social call. Not entirely. I only

called in to see them for a moment. I actually went over to Leeds because I wanted to see Granny Blake.'

'Really?' I say surprised.

'We had a phone call from her neighbours. Mum didn't want to say anything to you . . . didn't want to worry you. But things aren't looking too good there with GB and I wanted to find out how the land lies.'

'Why didn't Mum go with you?'

'Mum is a bit on edge at the moment. Em, you know she's very worried about your weight. So don't keep on winding her up about it. And please don't keep on making jokes about being pregnant. It really doesn't help. It may make your friends laugh, but it just upsets Mum. She's always been so proud of you . . . Proud of the way you look and the kind of person you are. And the things you believe in and the direction you want your life to go in. You've always been so focused . . . ' He gives me a worried look.

I stare down into the bottom of my empty mug. When we go to visit Granny Blake she makes tea in a huge brown pot using weird, old-fashioned loose tea. She says she can tell fortunes from the tea leaves. It's a kind of ritual that after you've finished drinking she swirls the dregs around, drains what is left into the saucer, and then peers at the patterns in the bottom of the cup.

She's like an old witch—telling stories of dark strangers, dates with destiny, treacherous friends, and unexpected money. She says she's been right loads of times and seems to believe absolutely in her own powers. The story is that generations back there was a union between a beautiful, flame-haired gypsy girl, who had the rare gift of second sight, and a great-great-grandfather who was a farmer. Just the mention of any of these ancestors or divination puts Mum in one hell of a mood—and generally means that our visit to Granny is curtailed immediately. But the idea of being able to see into the future—and Granny's knack with the tea leaves—has always amused me no end.

But now it has a darker significance. I stare into my mug and wonder if it is possible that I have inherited this gift of second sight. My mug of tea was made from a hygienic bag so there is just a rim of brownish stain and a blob of biscuit. It looks utterly depressing. And I wonder in a moment of despair if this foretells a miserable future full of woe.

To take my mind off these crazy thoughts I ask, 'What's happened to GB?'

'Well, she's lost her job . . . Do you remember it was in the news that the clothing factory in Bradford where she worked was laying people off and we wondered if it would affect her? Well, unfortunately, it has.'

'But she's worked there forever . . . isn't it usually "last in, first out"? I can't believe they would do that to her! She's worked at that factory all her life.'

'Yes, well, in normal circumstances they probably would have kept her on—she's not far off her pension—but Granny Blake has a few other problems which has meant they made her redundant.'

'What other problems?' I ask.

Dad hesitates and then says carefully, 'Well, you know she likes a smoke and a drink . . . ' Then he adds quickly, 'Anyway . . . she's not working and it is very difficult for her . . . I said I'd pop over again soon.'

'I'll come with you,' I say. I feel a sudden bolt of sympathy for GB. I don't really see why liking a smoke and a drink constitutes grounds for making someone redundant—especially when they have given a lifetime of service. It doesn't seem fair somehow.

'I'm sure she'd like to see you. But she's not on grand form, I have to warn you.'

'I'm not a fair-weather friend,' I say a bit defensively. 'I can cope when people are down. And she is my grandmother, after all.' I can't help thinking about the twins. Apart from a few text messages I haven't seen or heard from them for ages.

'It's very kind of you to suggest it. Thanks. I will take you up on the offer. It would certainly be easier for me to have someone else there when I go to see her.' He smiles at me and adds, 'And just be a bit easier on your mum, OK? She doesn't share our sense of humour, Em, you know that,' he adds gently.

This is a complete understatement because my mother doesn't have any kind of sense of humour. She doesn't understand jokes, she hates all comedy programmes, and stand-up comedians make her cringe. I can't believe that my father seriously thinks I am telling my mother I am pregnant as a joke! Doing that would be totally bizarre and cruel.

I conclude sadly that they are both in denial and I have a hard path ahead. And it is not one that I am looking forward to treading. They have been miserable and stressed out when they thought that my pregnancy was a joke and I am simply fat. I am filled with a deep dread of how they will react to the truth. I have broken my vow. I have had casual, unprotected sex. And now I am pregnant. The enormity of what I have done suddenly hits me. And just thinking about the size and complexity of my problems makes me feel really, really hungry. I must escape to the kitchen and find some food.

The twins ring me before I can get there. 'Can you come over now?' Flo asks. 'We've been desperate to see you! Life has been impossible over here! Our parents are like the Gestapo . . . They know there is something up and it's been like living in a boot camp.'

'I need to have something to eat and quickly,' I whine.

'We've got loads of food here,' she says. 'They've got a dinner party tonight. They've gone off to buy wine. Get over here fast before they come back!'

The twins take me up to their bedroom. They provide me with a bowl of crisps, bread sticks, avocado dip, and taramasalata. I sit cross-legged on Flo's bed and tuck in. The bread sticks are coated in pepper and parmesan cheese. I crunch them appreciatively.

'We've been on the phone all week,' Flo says briskly. 'And we've got it all arranged for next weekend. Everything is planned like a military operation. I've

92

had to pretend to be you, but I knew you wouldn't mind. All you need to do is to get away on the Friday. You've a counselling appointment booked in the afternoon. Then you can go into the clinic on the Saturday. Sunday you can travel home. We'll be with you all the time. Our auntie says it's not as bad as going to the dentist. And if you are positive about it you'll be fine. We've told the parents it's a school trip to London to see art exhibitions. You'll have to think of something similar to tell yours. We've even got the train tickets booked.'

Flo looks so pleased with herself I hardly know how to tell her it's not going to happen.

'It's very good of you, Flo. I'm sorry you've gone to all this trouble. I can't go. It's too late.'

'Why too late . . . ?' she says aghast.

'Too late because it's too far on for me to even think about an abortion—too late because I think I want to keep the baby—too late because—'

'Why didn't you tell us straight away? Why have you left it . . . It's just so crazy. Do you realize how dozy and stupid people will think you are?' Flo explodes. 'Girls like you just shouldn't get themselves into a mess like this.'

'Oh, Flo, don't be so horrible to poor Em . . . ' Si begs. She comes and sits on the bed with me and takes hold of my hand. I give her a grateful glance as I shovel some more crisps into my mouth.

'For goodness' sake stop eating and talk to us,' Flo says desperately. 'You took a vow. You wanted to wait for sex until you were married. You are the last girl in the world who should get pregnant this way. You haven't even got a boyfriend. Tell us what happened.'

Regretfully I push the bowl of crisps away and look at them both. 'I'm sorry I didn't tell you immediately. I didn't admit it to myself until I could see the baby growing and at that point I really couldn't deny it any longer. And since then I've thought about it all the time . . . And I've realized that on some deep, primitive level I must have wanted to get pregnant.'

Both the twins look startled and concerned by this. Si squeezes my hand. 'It's all right, you can tell us. We'll understand,' she says quietly.

I take a deep breath and say, 'I looked at him . . . the man . . . when we were . . . you know . . . quite close to going the whole way. And I thought to myself. "Oh-my-god-I-love-you-so-much-and-I-want-to-marry-you-and-have-your-children . . . " And it was after that it happened. And when I analysed it I thought that it was as if I had wished for it to happen. And I think maybe that is why I can't contemplate having an abortion. I think I would feel really guilty because it was as if I was willing it—almost like a prayer or an incantation. As if I had called up the spirit of a baby and it arrived. I think I'll love the baby . . . I think I love it already . . . I think I must do . . . ' I add lamely, 'because the one thing I do know is that I don't want to get rid of it.'

'So it wasn't really casual sex,' Si says gently, looking into my face. 'You really did love him, didn't you?'

I am not sure if facing that question makes me feel better or worse. I only know I am hit by a great rush of emotion that I have been keeping in check for months. And my feelings surface suddenly like a volcano erupting from the floor of the ocean in a shocking mix of fire and water. My face burns scarlet with shame and shock as hot tears trickle down my cheeks. 'I wanted him to say he loved me . . . I was mad for him to say it. I kept on thinking that if I just let him go a little bit further, did a little bit more, then he would say it . . . '

# CHAPTER EIGHT

The CD stops. We sit in silence. I wipe my eyes and manage (with superhuman effort) to cry without making a sound. At last Flo speaks. 'He never said he loved you, did he?' she asks grimly.

'No . . . ' I sob, shaking my head. 'He never even said he liked me . . . He used to tease me all the time . . . make horrible jokes. Maybe all the stuff he said was true . . . maybe he wasn't trying to be funny. Maybe he hated me . . . I don't know. Do boys have sex with girls they don't like?'

'Oh, for heaven's sake!' Flo exclaims. 'Don't be so wet. Exactly how many boys have you kissed?' she asks.

'Flo! Cool it!' Si interrupts. She stands up and flaps her hands at her sister. Flo tosses her head and looks away. I have seen this scenario played out many times by the sisters: Si not wanting anyone to be upset or hurt, while Flo is going for the jugular. I know I have little chance of getting out of this conversation without a mauling.

'Shut up, this is important,' Flo says imperiously. Si gives me a sympathetic glance and sits down. Flo turns to me and commands: 'Em, stop blubbing. And answer the question.'

'Why should I? Why does it matter?' I ask. But long experience has taught me to comply when Flo is as fierce as this. So I add a bit sulkily, 'Well, there was Hal, in America. He was the first boy I ever kissed.' The memory of snogging with Hal in a dark corner of the church garden after signing up to the Kissing Club comes back to me and I nibble at my bottom lip for a moment too mortified to continue. Then I add slowly: 'And then, at parties sometimes, you know. And then there were a couple of boys at school.' None of this is true and telling lies to the twins makes me uncomfortable. I go back to the truth with relief. 'And then there was Jake, who I met in Cornwall, the boy who taught me how to windsurf. I kissed him quite a lot,' I add defensively. I haven't kissed many boys at all. Compared to the twins I am a complete failure in the boy-attraction department. Hal and Jake are the nearest I've ever got to a boyfriend and both of them still email me—but we are only friends.

'And was it ever a problem, just keeping to the kissing?' Flo asks.

'No . . . ' I am really sulky now. 'I'd made up my mind when I joined the Kissing Club that I would keep my promise—I told Jake all about it. He used to tease me a bit and try to undo my bra—but it wasn't a problem.'

'Did you tell the man who got you pregnant—the father of your unborn child—about the Kissing Club and your promise?' Flo asks dramatically. She is standing in front of me but I refuse to look at her.

'Yes,' I say. I look down at my hands. I am crumbling a bread stick back into flour. I can't eat—I am too stressed.

'How did he react when he knew about it?' Flo is at her most steely. It is impossible not to answer. I can see now where she is leading. I sigh and give in. I suppose I do need to face up to this.

'I think it made him want to do it more,' I admit. 'I think he thought it was a challenge. He's so conceited. I think it was a turn on, the idea that I was giving up something so precious for him. Not just that he was the first . . . but also that I was going against what I believed and wanted. It was like the ultimate sacrifice. There—now you know.' I mop my eyes with the edge of Si's duvet. She fetches loo paper from their en-suite and hands it to me. I blow my nose loudly and mop my face.

'There! I hope you're satisfied now?' Si says indignantly to Flo and she puts her arms around me and gives me a hug. 'Poor Em,' she says lovingly. I lean into her for a moment.

Flo gives us a grim smile. 'Oh, yes. I'm quite satisfied. I know just what I am going to say to this scumbag, this low-life, rotten bastard, when I finally get to meet him.'

Si and I look at each other with round anxious eyes. 'Is it someone that we already know?' Si asks.

'No! It isn't!' I say. And I turn to Flo and add

quickly, 'And I don't think you'll ever meet him—so don't plan anything.'

Florence's warlike personality and sharp tongue are a legend in her lifetime. She is like a lioness: powerful, protective, and ruthless. And me and Si—and anyone who is downtrodden or oppressed—are like her cubs. She is a wonderful friend and a very bad enemy. I tremble suddenly at the thought of her knowing the truth and seeking revenge. She wants to study law— academically she is the sharpest knife in the box—and I can imagine her as a law lord dispensing justice and defending the weak, although in truth she is more like a reincarnation of Boudicca or a pagan goddess. Her spiritual home is the jungle and she would have managed fine when justice was carried out by the sword.

'You'll have to tell us about him eventually,' Flo says, giving me a dark look. 'There are some facts that always have to come out.'

'Yes, I will tell you. But not now . . . ' There is the sound of voices from downstairs and the twins' names being called.

I get up off the bed with relief and try to brush the crumbs from my black fleece top. I thought the fleece made me look thinner when I got dressed but now I am not so sure—the material seems to cling to my bump.

When I get downstairs I realize that Mrs Devereux is staring at me as if I have two heads. I imagine that with my crumpled food-stained clothes and tangled hair I look like a frowzy old she-bear that has just come out of hibernation.

'And how are you, Emily?' she asks. She is smiling, but her eyes are cold and she keeps on glancing at my bump—her gaze tracing over me like a searchlight.

'I'm fine, thank you very much,' I say politely. 'I'm just leaving,' I add.

'We're having friends for dinner,' she says in reply. I stop myself from making the obvious joke and saying I hope they will be tasty. She doesn't look in the mood for my sense of humour. I am acutely aware that at one time I would have been invited to stay and help with the dinner party. It is something that Si, Flo, and I have done regularly over the years. Unlike my parents, who are rather antisocial and have few friends, the twins' parents entertain regularly. They do it in style with swanky dinners and expensive lunch parties where they serve champagne and amazing stuff like quails' eggs and truffles.

The twins and I have always loved these events. We would help with all the preparation: folding napkins and polishing silver. We would then lay out all the food, do the clearing up, load the dishwasher and wash the crystal glasses by hand. It was like running a restaurant! And in return for this help we would be allowed to eat leftovers and have champagne mixed with orange juice. It was really good fun and I was always invited. Mrs Devereux used to say I was the best at washing up and the twins could learn a few lessons from me. I was always a bit of a favourite with her.

But not any more it seems . . . I don't know whether Mrs Devereux has worked out I am pregnant or disapproves of my new scruffy image. Whatever, I am definitely getting the impression that I am surplus to requirements.

'I'll get going,' I say, edging to the door. I am aware of Si and Flo staring at me with sympathetic eyes as I leave.

Because my mind is made up, kind of, about the baby—or at least the one thing I know for sure is that I will *not* be going to London to stay with the kind auntie and have an abortion—I decide I will go to see Mr Anthony. I try to work out when would be the safest time, when I am unlikely to see any other teachers, and decide on an early morning visit because I know he always starts work before anyone else.

I plan it like a military operation. I leave Dad a note telling him I need to get an early bus. And I make myself up a picnic breakfast of two hardboiled eggs, bread and butter, and half a dozen small cox apples. I put all this food in a Tupperware box and leave it ready in the fridge. Then I get all my clothes ready and have a bath and wash my hair. It seems ages since I got myself organized like this and I feel better for it. I go to bed feeling far more cheerful than I have for ages.

In the morning I am unprepared for the fact that it is still dark when I leave the house and feels like the middle of the night and my good spirits dip. The bus is deserted (which is a relief) but is also freezing cold (not so good). There is nothing to see out of the windows but grimy darkness (the windows are very dirty) and as bad luck would have it I have forgotten my iPod. I am so bored I eat all the food I have with me (and a whole packet of fruit pastilles) during the journey. As I have only a bottle of water with me I find myself craving a mug of tea or a hot chocolate. I find a rather squashed KitKat in my coat pocket and eat that slowly as a consolation.

I am so early that the cleaners are still working in school. The main doors are locked and I wander around for a while, looking in through the windows at the empty brightness of rooms that are lit but unoccupied. The rooms are all unnaturally tidy: the desks are in straight lines with the chairs pushed underneath and there are no piles of graffiti-marked bags heaped on the floors or tottering piles of dog-eared books cluttering the tables. This rare order, and the brilliance of the lighting, makes the school look like an abandoned film set.

Finally a few of the keen teachers start to arrive and I follow one through an open fire door and make my way up to Mr Anthony's room. The door is ajar—I tap and open the door at the same time. Mr Anthony is sitting at the desk in his shirtsleeves, writing report cards. Most of the teachers write only a line or two on report cards—generally something vague that fits all pupils apart from the very brightest or troublemakers. I know all about this kind of teachers' bullshit because for years I've got report cards that were full of stupid remarks like: 'Has worked well this year but could do better with more effort.' But Mr Anthony doesn't write stuff like that—he does a little essay all about the kid and what he or she has really been up to.

The early rising seems to have made me extra observant. I feel like an alien who is taking in a strange environment, or an actor on a stage. This means that I immediately notice that his cuffs are grubby, his fingers ink-stained, and he doesn't look as if he's been home to bed. He looks as if he's been sitting there all night and could do with a hot breakfast and a shower.

He looks up at me with a little jump—as if I have startled him from a deep reverie—and he gazes at me for a moment as if he doesn't know who I am or he thinks I am a ghost.

'Emily—this is such a coincidence. I was just thinking about writing you a note when I've finished these. Come in and sit down.' He moves a chair forward. 'I've got a flask of tea, would you like a cup? The stuff from the machine is horrible. I always bring my own . . . '

He is nervous. He is talking too fast and his movements are jerky.

'Tea would be great. Why were you writing to me?' I take off my duffle coat and sit down in the proffered chair.

Mr Anthony doesn't reply, instead he pours the tea from the flask into a small metal cup and says, 'It's black I'm afraid, but I do have some sugar . . . '

'Black is fine, no sugar thanks. I'm watching my waistline . . . '

He stares at me with a hurt, rather puzzled expression as he hands me the tea. I gulp it gratefully.

'Why were you writing to me?' I ask again. He blinks and looks away from me.

'Miss Zoller is very upset that you haven't replied to her notes or gone to see her. She's told me I have to report to her if I see you in school . . . ' He keeps his head turned away from me as if he is scared to look at me.

'Oh dear.' I sip the tea, which is blisteringly hot, and giggle a bit. 'Will she send out a search party for me? It sounds as if she's on the warpath. I better watch out!'

He finally turns and looks at me. His eyes are anxious. I am reminded of Sienna. These days everyone seems to look at me like that: 'You really need to arrange a meeting with Miss Zoller or Mr Rickards and your parents and sort out your unauthorized absences and the assignments you've not completed. I can't get involved. I'm not one of your tutors. I only organize your mentoring duties. I can't get involved,' he repeats. He looks down at his report cards and sighs. 'I will try to help you, Emily, but my hands are tied rather. I can't really do very much. I'm sorry.'

'It doesn't matter. I haven't come here to ask you for help.' I'm actually a bit hurt that he should think that I've come to dump on him or cry on his shoulder. 'I just thought I would tell you what I've decided to do.

You seemed as if you wanted to know . . . ' I stop suddenly, wondering maybe if it was a really stupid thing to do to come and see him like this. Maybe he doesn't care two hoots what I do or what happens to me. His mind is full of his wife and his poor little lost babies. And then, here at school, he has his needy parade of pupils with their sad lives and myriad disorders and problems. Everyone he deals with is in some kind of trouble. He obviously doesn't need any extra to carry. I am a healthy, fully functioning, sixth-former (who had been predicted to get straight As and go to a good university). I'm not one of his lost lambs.

'I'm sorry, maybe I shouldn't have bothered you. It's just you asked me to tell you. I just wanted you to know that I made up my mind that I'm not going to have an abortion. I don't know any more than that at the moment. That is as far as I've got in thinking about my future . . . ' I stop and wish I hadn't come to see him or said anything more about the baby because it all sounds a bit limp and lame now. So what if I am going to have the baby? Lots of girls do . . . not from this school maybe . . . but across the country . . . hundreds, thousands of them. Some a lot younger than me . . . Why should he be bothered anyway? As he said: he's not one of my tutors—it's really nothing to do with him.

But the effect on him is weird. He closes his eyes and leans back for a moment, as if he is very tired or praying. Then his eyes jerk open and he says urgently, 'I need to talk to you. But not here . . . Can I meet you after school?'

'OK,' I say bemused.

'Where? Where can we meet? It has to be somewhere private where we can talk. Please, Emily,' he adds a bit desperately. And then he looks at me as if I have the solution to this problem.

My mind is blank. I run through the options of where I normally meet people after school and discard them all because they are too public or will be full of people who know me (and him).

'How about we meet at the back entrance to the reading room in the public library?' I say eventually. 'Where the wheelchair ramp is . . . I'll wait there.'

'Yes, yes, that's fine . . . Say about four thirty,' he says with relief.

I gulp the last of the scalding tea and hand him the cup. I am suddenly desperate to get out of the room. I wish I hadn't come. I don't know why I feel I am really stupid and have done something wrong. I make up my mind I won't meet him.

'Is four thirty OK for you?' he asks. His eyes lock with mine. I almost feel as if he can read my thoughts—that he knows that I am full of regrets and uncertainties. 'You will be there, won't you, Emily? It is important.'

'Yes, I'll be there. Promise,' I say. I sound like a six year old. I hurry out of school, blundering along deserted corridors, stumbling like someone half-sighted, my eyes full of tears. I don't know why I am upset . . . I just am.

# Chapter Nine

The rear entrance to the Library Reading Room is a horrible place to hang around. The back of the library gets no sunlight: at this time of the year the walls are green and dripping like a dungeon. To add to the gloom, the narrow pathway and disabled ramp are surrounded by dark laurel bushes and—as the public loos are right next door—there is always a really gross pong.

It is not a venue in which to loiter, unless you are a mugger or a flasher. So why do I see so many people I know as I lurk about trying not to breathe too deeply in case I get a whiff from the toilets? It is totally unreal and the most tremendous bad luck.

First I meet a group of four girls who were in Year Seven last year and also in Mr Anthony's care. They race up the ramp, screaming with delight to see me.

'Hey! What are you lot doing here?' I ask, trying to unravel myself from their arms and hugs. Seeing them makes me feel really bad. I was meant to be their helper this year. And they are so made up to see me that they can't stop gabbling, all talking at once. They keep asking when I am going to be back in their class, if I am OK and questioning endlessly why they haven't seen me.

'I'm fine. I'll be coming to see you soon. I've just been really busy,' I lie helplessly. 'Now, tell me what are you doing here?' I repeat. I have to get rid of them before Mr Anthony arrives. I can hear the Christ Church clock chiming the half hour. He is late, thank goodness.

They are telling me about a project they are working on about local history—they have been told to come to the reference library to look at maps. Freya Morrison is taking their group now and this project was her idea. She's a history geek. Just the thought of looking at old maps and going to museums turns my brain into a fossil. Goodness knows what these kids, most of whom can hardly read, will make of it.

'Freya's not as good as you, she's always telling us off,' Sheena (who is the ringleader of the group) says, as she swings on my arm. Little Beatrice Brown has her arms around my waist. She is the sweetest little child with long plaits and a delicate pale face like a china doll. Now she looks up at me and her large brown eyes are troubled. 'Em'ly, can I ask you a personal question?' she says very seriously.

'Yes, of course you can, Beatrice. Anything you like,' I say, trying not to show my unease.

'Polly Graves said you can't come back to school because you are going to have a baby. And your stomach is *really* big.' (She's had her face pressed right up against it so she should know!) 'Are you having a baby?' she asks.

'No, Beatrice, I'm having triplets—that's why I'm good and fat. You tell Polly Graves the next time you see her and put her right,' I say lightly, and they all laugh.

'I shall be coming into the reference room in a minute and I'll help you find some maps and stuff for your project,' I say. 'Go on in, and get started,' I add, shooing them away from me, because if they don't disappear before Mr Anthony arrives I may well start to cry. The combination of stress and the nasty smell from the loos is making me feel dizzy. 'Did you know that Bilton was built on the site of an extinct volcano?' I say desperately. 'I wonder if there's a map that shows that? Ask the library lady to help you. You go and look and I'll be in soon.'

'A volcano, wow! I live in Bilton. Maybe it's near my house!' Sheena says. And they all race off.

My heart has been racing with panic. It has just started to slow down when I hear my name being called. I spin around so quickly I have to clutch at the railings to stop myself from toppling over.

'Emily! Hello there! How are you?' It's Joanne from the village with her double buggy. She has two little boys and I babysit for her sometimes.

'I'm fine. Just waiting for a friend . . .' I lie seamlessly. He is bound to arrive at any minute. So how else do I explain it? But what is she going to make of the fact that I am meeting a man who is a worn-out-twenty-something who has 'married' and 'teacher' written all over him like lettering through a stick of rock. I say a quick prayer that he really is late (or better still doesn't come at all).

'Are you going for the five o'clock bus?' Joanne asks. She has to raise her voice to be heard. Tyron, her eldest, is grizzling away under the plastic hood, and Tyler is sucking mournfully on an empty chocolate buttons packet. He will probably start caterwauling too any minute.

'Maybe . . . if not it'll be the five thirty,' I shout in reply.

'I'm just getting some more books for my mum. She's in hospital.'

'Look, if I get finished quickly I'll meet you at the bus station and we'll go for a cup of tea,' I say.

'Fine, see you then,' she replies.

'Let me give you a hand,' I add quickly. And I grab the buggy handles and start to heave it through the doors.

When I turn round he's waiting for me, standing in the dark shadow of the laurel bushes. I walk down the ramp to meet him and the damp, putrid air surrounds me like a veil.

'There're loads of people I know here. We can't go inside . . . ' I say desperately. 'And I need to get the bus home soon,' I add ungraciously.

'This won't take long. But I do need to talk to you,' he says quickly. I have no option but to join him in the shadows and despite my thick coat a shiver runs down my back because of the coldness and the unreal horror of meeting him in a place like this.

110

He moves so he is in front of me and I am shielded from view. 'It's very important what I'm going to ask you . . . I promised Gabby I would speak to you about it. We're concerned for you and the baby. You do know that you need to be very careful . . . '

'It's not being careful meeting here . . . ' I interrupt a bit sulkily. 'There're lots of people from school in the reading room,' I add. I expect him to react to that and to be concerned. I can just imagine what Miss Zoller would say if she found out we'd been meeting after school. Surely he realizes how seedy it looks?

But he carries on talking like a robot. He is lost in his own anxiety. It's scary because normally Mr Anthony is so sensitive to other people and focused on them. I've never seen him like this before.

'Have you taken any prescription or over-the-counter medicines since you got pregnant?' he fires at me. I just have time to shake my head before he rattles on with the next question. 'You must make sure that you don't take anything . . . even herbal remedies . . . And are you eating properly? Folic acid . . . if not there is the risk of spina bifida . . . You really need to go for a full ante-natal check. And a scan . . . A scan is very important. You haven't been for a scan, have you?'

Again I shake my head. And he looks at me with eyes full of concern and anxiety. 'You need to know if the baby is all right. There are lots of conditions which can be picked up by a scan . . . You have to take it all very seriously, Emily: your health and the baby's

111

development go together. It's very important. You need to get under the care of a midwife and a consultant as soon as possible to get ready for the birth. Gabby says she will go with you to the hospital if you would like her to. I told her all about you . . . she wants to help and so do I. You need to be relaxed and happy . . . and healthy . . . it's very important for the welfare of the baby . . . Gabby says that stressed mothers have stressed children. You do understand how important it is to look after yourself, don't you?'

I am dumbstruck. I just nod and splutter. I can't think of what to say. 'Thanks for the vote of confidence . . . ' or 'Mind your own business . . . ' or 'Don't talk to me as if I am a moron . . . ' spring to mind but none seems entirely appropriate or fair. I try to tell myself that it is very kind of him and Gabby to be so concerned about me and my bump. But nice feelings won't come. Instead I feel patronized and in some way insulted. OK, so I haven't rushed off to the doctor or found a midwife, but I've been eating loads and listening to my body; sleeping when I am tired and indulging myself in rest and relaxation to the point where I have done no school work at all, or taxed my brain, or stressed myself out. You would think, by the way he's going on, that instead I have been sitting in hot baths and drinking gin or throwing myself downstairs. So what on earth is he getting at?

But before I can get my head around it all he starts again. 'Forgive me for asking this . . . I told Gabby I didn't think you would for a minute . . . but one never knows. Tell me the truth, please, Emily. Have you smoked cannabis or taken hard drugs while you are pregnant? And the father . . . he's not into crack or anything bad like that, is he? I told Gabby it was more than likely one of the boys at school . . . And I do know there is quite a bit of smoking weed among some sixth formers . . . I'm not talking about that sort of thing. You know the type of boy I mean: the sort who will be in serious trouble in a few years' time. You've not got in with the wrong crowd have you, Emily?'

'I'm not in any crowd, wrong or otherwise,' I say, stung. 'And I don't really know what that has to do with anything . . . I wish I hadn't told you about the baby . . . ' I add. Tears bubble up and I cover my mouth with my hand to stop myself sobbing.

'I'm sorry. I don't want you to think I'm criticizing you . . . ' He pats my shoulder awkwardly. 'I told Gabby you are a sensible girl. But I do need to know these things . . . '

'I've got to go . . . ' I say, pulling away from his hand. It's as if he's not thinking about me and he doesn't really care if I am crying. It's because he's still wrapped up in his stupid questions. I don't recognize him when he's like this. It's as if he is a completely different person to the one I have known before. One thing is for sure—I don't like him any more.

'Emily, please . . . ' he sounds quite desperate. 'I need to talk to you. It's important!'

'Look, this isn't the time or the place . . . ' I say. My mood swings are as fickle as spring tides and suddenly the tears dry and I am angry. 'I've got people to meet and a bus to catch . . . ' I add abruptly, as I turn away. My brain is very slow at the moment but all the stuff he's said about drugs and the wrong sort of boy has just started to trickle down into my consciousness. I am really insulted. I suppose he thinks that I've gone off the rails and become a delinquent-drug-taking-hopeless-case just because I'm pregnant. Next he'll be asking me if I sniff glue!

He follows me up the ramp to the door, trying to catch at my arm, talking to me in a desperate whisper. 'Can we meet sometime soon? And not here . . . somewhere we can talk . . . somewhere private.'

I stop and shake my head. 'I don't need you or your advice. Just leave me alone.'

'Emily, please!' There is something like terror in his voice. 'Just give me a chance to explain things to you. Just say you'll meet me tomorrow.'

'No!'

'When then? When can you meet me?'

A wave of dizziness comes over me. I need a mug of tea and a KitKat. I need to be somewhere warm and safe. His voice is incessant and his hand is still on my arm. I want to go into the library and get away from him. He's made me feel angry and sick.

'All right, I'll meet you here next week,' I say in a monotone. It's the only way I can think of to get rid of him.

'Same time,' he says anxiously.

'Same time,' I echo like a dutiful child.

114

To my relief he turns and leaves, walking quickly down the ramp, buttoning his raincoat and turning up the collar. It has started to rain and the afternoon is so cold that it's a sharp sleety drizzle that hurts your skin. I had been too caught up in our conversation to notice that my face is stinging and wet and my hands feel like ice.

# CHAPTER TEN

By the time I get home I am exhausted. I have been squashed in a café with two screaming toddlers, then I helped Joanne get on the bus with a million shopping bags and a tank-sized buggy. After that I played incy-wincy-spider and this-little-piggy-goes-to-market with Tyron and Tyler, while Joanne dozed and the bus crawled through the rush hour traffic. Now all I want is hot food, a bath, and long lie in bed with a novel and soothing music.

The house is in darkness and, worse than that, there is no smell of home cooking, no meal ready, no comfort at all. I check my mobile and the house phone. And, sure enough, there are two messages from Dad. I hear his voice, rather tense, saying there is a problem with Granny Blake and that he and Mum have gone over to a hospital in Leeds to try to sort everything out. He doesn't say what has happened or what they have to sort out. It all sounds very mysterious and worrying.

I freak out and burst into tears. This seems like the worst possible end to a rubbish day and I am completely stressed. It seems so totally unreal, because Granny Blake isn't seriously old and she has never had a day's illness as far as I know. For as long as I can remember she's looked the same, with her curly auburn hair, loads of eye make-up and skinny little arms and hands weighed down with a ton of gaudy jewellery.

She's never really seemed like a granny . . . and she's never done granny-type things. (Unlike Granny Sutton who, over the years, has always baked special birthday cakes for me and knitted jumpers with kittens on the front.) And because GB's always been so un-granny-like I've never thought of her as being old or in danger of dying.

Now my brain is in overdrive. I imagine emergency ambulances and resuscitation teams. I see GB being wheeled down for critical, open-heart surgery with Mum running alongside crying . . .

Eventually, worn out with stress and hunger, I make a pile of toast and a mug of tea and eat it while lying on the sofa in the sitting room and watching TV. I must have dozed off because I wake up suddenly when the house phone rings. It is quite late and I assume that it's Dad or Mum phoning with news. I am breathless with panic. I lift the receiver and just about manage to gasp out: 'Hello.' But it's neither of my parents. It's Corey Thomas.

'Hi, Emily!' he says cheerfully. 'I came along by your house and saw all the lights were still on. I thought I'd let you know that I've passed my driving test today. If you want a lift—you know—to go into town or anything anytime. I've got a car.'

'Thanks,' I say, and I have to blink back new tears of frustration. I had been so sure it was Mum or Dad calling with news and instead it's him! I don't feel like talking to anyone or being congratulatory.

'Are you OK, Emily?' he asks quietly.

'Yeah,' I mumble. 'I didn't realize it was so late . . . My parents are in Leeds . . . '

'Are you all on your own? Would you like me to come over?' he asks. He sounds really anxious. For a boy he is very sensitive. But I am ashamed really that he had picked up on my distress. Honestly, it's frightening the way I spend the whole time either being aggressive or crying when I am around him.

I make a real effort to pull myself together and manage to say, 'You know, Corey, if you don't mind . . . I could do with a lift right at this very moment if it's not too late. My granny is seriously ill in hospital in Leeds and I'd like to go to see her.'

The sensible moment is over. I start crying again. Because I am suddenly filled with a terrible certainty that Granny Blake will die. And if she does I will not have had the chance to see her or say goodbye. That thought makes me so distracted I hang up without saying goodbye or anything civilized to Corey.

He turns up at the front door a few minutes later.

'I don't know which hospital she's in . . . ' I say lamely, while trying to wipe my face.

'Don't worry. We'll sort it when we get over there,' he says comfortingly. And he makes a big point of not looking at me—which is kind because I know I look a mess.

118

I calm down once we get in the car. And I explain about the lack of sustenance and how I am unable to cope with anything when I am hungry.

'No problem,' he says. And he stops en route to Leeds and buys fish and chips and mushy peas (because it's quick!) and also a can of diet Coke. I doubt whether Mr Anthony and his wife would approve of this meal but it's wonderfully filling. And once I am fed I feel a bit more able to cope and manage to talk to him reasonably coherently.

I tell him quite a bit about Granny Blake, and how I don't really know her that well, but that I don't want her to die or anything bad like that. Especially now with the baby and everything . . .

I can't really explain to him why the baby has changed everything. Maybe it is the knowledge that when the penny finally drops and my mum and dad realize they are going to be GRANDPARENTS they won't need any further hassles—like funerals or house clearances or miserable stuff like that. Thinking that makes me feel even more guilty and upset. I find myself wishing I loved GB the way I love my other granny and grandad and the tears in my eyes were solely for her and not for myself and my troubles.

'I wish I knew Granny Blake better. She and Mum aren't close . . . but she won't be around for ever, will she?'

'It's a shame not to get to know her as she lives in Leeds. If you've got a spare granny I'll adopt her,' Corey says. 'I haven't got any grandparents at all,' he adds.

'None at all! That's weird!' I say in surprise.

'Apart from Brett and Dad I don't have any family at all. I suppose the law of averages means that I must have some relations in China. But my mother always said she was an orphan so there's not much point in looking for grandparents there. And Dad's mum died very young and he didn't have a father.'

'Everyone has a father,' I say quietly.

'You know what I mean. Of course everyone has a biological father but whether they know about him, or he about them, is another matter entirely,' he says. We have stopped at traffic lights and he turns to look at me with a small smile. 'That's one reason why I think you should talk to the father of your baby . . . at least give him a chance to be involved. If he doesn't want to know, well, that's up to him—it will be his loss.'

'No . . . ' I say mulishly. 'I'm not going to tell him anything, now or ever.'

'He must have hurt you lots, Emily, for you to be so set against him. It's really bad . . . ' Corey says gently. The lights change and we move off. He is concentrating on the road, his hands at the ten to two position. And he's checking his mirror like a nodding dog. You can tell he's just passed his test!

He adds solicitously: 'Do you need something else to eat? There's a brilliant ice cream place coming up. It won't take long to stop there.'

'Ice cream! Oh, yes please . . . I'd love some!' I say gratefully.

He runs into the shop and dashes out with a family-sized tub of chocolate-cookie-dough ice cream and a packet of deluxe wafers which keeps me quiet until we reach the city centre.

When we finally get into the hospital—having negotiated a car park that must have been designed by someone who really hates ill people and their relatives—I am mega relieved that I have had plenty of food. Because the inside of the hospital is like a vision of hell and I certainly couldn't have coped with it if I was hungry.

I can only suppose we have arrived on a really unfortunate night when everyone in Leeds who is mad, bad (and dangerous to know), got wasted, had an accident and ended up in casualty. I really can't believe that the emergency ward is always this gross. If it is, then everyone who works here deserves danger money. The whole place is heaving. There are no seats so we have to stand. To make it worse there are lots of drunks—some bleeding, some shouting or swearing, all completely disgusting. There are quite a few policemen and women, an awful lot of crying babies and screaming toddlers, as well as a few elderly confused lying on trolleys looking half-dead. This sight doesn't cheer me up at all.

'It's not like this on the television, is it? Where are all the handsome doctors and glamorous nurses?' I whisper bitterly to Corey. But he is trying to get the attention of a bored looking receptionist who is shielded by a glass screen and he doesn't reply.

Eventually the woman looks up from the file she is

studying and speaks to us. I can't hear a word she is saying; the glass screen appears to be completely soundproof. But Corey, by some miracle, seems able to lip-read. After a few moments he pulls me away and says, 'I know where your granny is. She's on the fourth floor—Lister Ward. But it's emergency family visiting only.'

I have a sudden attack of childishness. 'Don't leave me,' I say, grabbing at his sleeve like a toddler. 'I don't want to go on my own . . . I'll say you're family. I'll say you're my brother.'

'Not very likely is it? We don't look remotely alike . . . '

'I'll say you're adopted,' I say wildly. 'I'll say anything . . . but please come with me.'

'Emily . . . your granny may not like some stranger turning up at her bedside. She was an emergency admission. She might be very ill . . . '

These words—and knowing they are likely to be true—make me panic even more. 'Please don't leave me, Corey,' I say desperately. 'I need you, honest. I can't go in on my own. I didn't know how much I hated hospitals until we came here . . . I think I've got a phobia about them. I'm hysterical inside. Please don't leave me . . . Please, please!' I start to sob with a suddenness which shocks me. I also find that I am clutching at him with both hands.

'All right, I'll come with you to find the ward. Stop shouting . . . And please stop crying,' he hisses urgently at me. He is looking really embarrassed and he is trying, without success, to disentangle himself from my grasp but I won't let go. Finally he gives in and puts his arm around me. When he turns me round I find that all the people sitting on the rows of plastic seats are staring at us. They must be bored with watching drunks and puking toddlers and we are just so much more interesting and dramatic—like one of the soaps on TV.

'Come on, it's this way . . . ' he says, and he hurries me off to the lifts and away from public gaze. It's just as well that he is in charge because I seem to have lost the ability to think and I would never have found my way if I'd been on my own. The hospital has sent me into panic mode. Thankfully, the hospital is quieter when we get away from the black hole of A&E and we wander in relative peace down endless corridors following a lime-green line on the floor until we reach Lister Ward.

'Here we are. This is it,' Corey says soothingly to me.

You can't just walk into the ward. You have to press a button and speak on an intercom. I wonder if it's to keep the patients in or unwanted visitors out. I press the button and speak clearly:

'This is Corey and Emily Sutton. We've come to see Mrs Blake, our grandmother. We think our parents are here waiting for us . . . ' I add firmly. And after I have spoken I shoot a glance at him, daring him to contradict me, but he just stares impassively ahead.

A nurse comes to the door and says, 'Wait here . . . ' without even looking at us.

'Sorry, you just got adopted. You are now officially my brother,' I say to Corey.

He shrugs and replies, 'I don't mind. I just don't want to upset your granny.'

'Granny Blake isn't like that. She isn't at all stuffy or conventional. I'll tell her how brilliant you've been. I bet she'll be chuffed to bits that we've come to see her.'

'I hope so . . . ' he says tentatively.

'First bed on the right and don't make any noise, please,' the nurse says as she opens the door wide for us.

The curtains are closed around the bed. And I've watched enough hospital dramas to know this is not good news and my heart sinks. I grab Corey's hand and yank him inside the curtains with me.

GB is lying in bed. She is wearing a faded blue hospital gown. Her hair is spread out like a red cloud over the white pillow and her tiny hands are folded neatly in front of her. The first thing I notice is that she has grey roots to her lovely auburn hair and that she is free from jewellery. The next thing I notice is that Mum and Dad are standing next to the bed. They are wearing outdoor clothes—as if they are just about to leave—and Mum is in charge of a large black bin bag. She is holding it well away from her as if it contains something horrid like a dead cat.

'Oh my goodness! Am I too late! Is she dead?' I ask in an agonized whisper. No wonder Mum is looking so traumatized. It must be GB's worldly effects in that bag . . . I feel so guilty. If we hadn't stopped for fish and chips and ice cream I might have got here in time.

GB's eyes snap open. She has very distinctive green eyes and they pop out like ripe gooseberries as she lifts her head off the pillow and demands loudly: 'What the hell are you going on about? Is who dead? Meg, I told you this wasn't a safe place to come to. I would have been better off in the dog pound. You can catch all sorts of nasty stuff in here. When can I go home?'

Mum and Dad both start shushing her but I am so relieved by these signs of life that I rush to the bed. I sit down and take hold of one of GB's hands.

'Oh, Granny B! Thank goodness. You are OK! Why are you here? What's the matter? I came straight away. This is Corey—my friend from the village—he gave me a lift.'

Mum and Dad are now shushing me even though I have been talking in a whisper.

Granny gives me a grin. Then she reaches out her arms and pulls me into a big bear hug. Although she is small she is surprisingly strong and her hug makes me gasp as we are crushed together. They've taken out the dangly gold earrings she normally wears and I can see the little holes in her ears. Because I am so close I also realize that she smells gross—of beer and spirits and smog-type-proportions of cigarette smoke.

It's a relief when she finally lets me go. I stand up quickly and move well away from the bed. Then I take a couple of deep breaths and pray that I don't start gagging. I'd thought the hospital smell was pretty bad but GB's pungent stale-party-odour is in another league altogether. She smells as if she's been swimming in a vat of beer while smoking cigars.

'You'll be able to come out tomorrow morning. They're just keeping you in for observation,' Dad says to her. 'Now settle down and go to sleep. I think you'll have a bit of a hangover in the morning so try to have as much rest as you can,' he adds ruefully.

'Poor Granny B,' I say smiling at her. 'Did you bang your head? You poor love.'

No one answers. 'I'll come and fetch you in the morning,' Dad says to Granny in his calm kind way. 'I'm going to take Megan home now. She's had a long day and she's worn out.'

I glance at my mother and I am shocked. Her face is set and white like an alabaster relief in a Greek temple. In contrast to this etched paleness her eyes are dark and shadowed—pained in a way which I have never seen before.

'Take care of yourself, Granny B. I'll see you soon,' I say softly to her.

She lifts her head and winks at me. 'Thanks for coming to see me, sweetheart. I think your boyfriend's lovely!' she says in the loudest of stage whispers, and then she raises her hand to her lips and blows us a kiss.

'Come along now, come along,' Dad says, and he herds us around the curtains and out of the ward like a champion sheepdog.

We walk down the corridor in silence. Dad takes the bin bag out of Mum's hand and carries it. She is walking along like a zombie and hardly seems to register this kindness.

'Is Granny B going to be OK? Why is she in here?' I ask, as we wait for the lift.

Dad shoots a glance at Corey and then says slowly, 'She was out for the evening and she had a bit of a wobble. She'll be fine. I expect they'll let her come home in the morning, all being well . . . '

Mum interrupts him. Her voice is low, but harsh as sandpaper. 'She was brought in here by the police. She's lucky they aren't going to charge her . . . '

'Charge her?' I ask, mystified.

'D and D . . . It is an offence,' Mum mutters bitterly.

'D and D?' I query.

'Drunk and disorderly . . . ' Mum snaps, as if I am deliberately being thick.

'Let's not talk it up,' Dad says wearily. 'They're not going to charge her and she's fine—apart from a slight loss of dignity. We'll have her at home for a couple of days, shall we, and try to get her straightened out.'

My mother makes a little incoherent noise— something between a mew and a sigh—which conveys extreme pain. None of us acknowledge this sound or look at her.

Instead, we troop into the lift and travel down in heavy silence. I glance once at Corey: his face is mercifully blank and he refuses to meet my eye. I try not to think about my little Granny B roaring around A&E

127

with all the other drunkards—shouting, swearing, puking, and frightening the children. I feel my face becoming rigid and pale. I am shutting out the world—shutting out the horror of it all. And I know that I look just like my mother . . .

# CHAPTER ELEVEN

The following evening GB comes to stay. My parents move out of their room so she can have their en-suite. This is a drag because it means there is likely to be a queue in the morning for the bathroom but that is the only down-side as far as I can see.

The enormous benefit of GB's arrival is that my mother is completely distracted. And when I say distracted I mean like a zombie. She doesn't appear to see or hear us apart from when the veil lifts for a moment and there is a flash of communication—like at a seance. I stand in front of her, wave my arms to get her attention, and announce that I have an upset stomach. I tell her I don't feel well enough for school (and ask her to, please, write me a note). She looks at me vacantly and agrees without a murmur. Then, incredibly, she mumbles something about me writing something suitable on the computer so she can sign it.

Any pity that I feel for her is immediately replaced by something close to euphoria. As I sit in front of the computer I feel like a master forger who has just received a shipment of Bank of England watermarked paper and a template for a new twenty-pound note. I type our address in an elaborate font and smile to myself as a whole world of possibilities opens up in front of me. I think of all the classes I have missed and the curt notes I have received from Miss Zoller (bitch-woman) requesting meetings. I remember the difficult meeting I had with Mr Anthony (pathetic-but-kind). And I recall the promise I made to see him again. And my brain goes into frenzy as I start to formulate a plan to get them both off my back.

I pen a note that explains I have 'chronic fatigue' (well, that bit is at least true—I've been exhausted and hungry since conception day). I then skirt around what is the matter with me now but ask for under-standing and help when I am finally well enough to return. I hint darkly about hospital tests and a per-sistent cough (that is a total lie but I do have a slight sore throat so I tell myself it's more of an exaggera-tion than a porky pie). When I have finished with the letter I am really pleased with it. It is the kind of note that could get you off school for a zillion days. I could have anything . . . bubonic plague . . . TB . . . insanity . . . and whatever it is it could take me years to recover.

I go down to the sitting room ready to do battle. I have the letter in one hand and my fountain pen in the other. My parents are huddled together whispering. The atmosphere in the room crackles with tension as if an electric storm is just about to start.

I hold my stomach in, smile wanly and say, 'I'm going to have a bath and an early night. I'm all in . . . I've done my note for school if you want to sign it now, Mum.'

'Good girl,' Dad says approvingly, smiling at me. 'Thanks for helping your mum,' he adds.

I place the note and pen on the coffee table in front of my mother. She leans forward and signs it without even reading it. This is unbelievable. I hold my breath for one more moment and then slowly exhale as relief floods through me.

'Emily, as you'll be at home for the next few days,' she mutters, without actually looking at me, 'could you please keep an eye on Granny? She's got a badly sprained ankle and she's not meant to walk. Under no circumstances must she go out . . . not to the shop or anywhere . . . '

'And especially not to the pub,' Dad says, giving me a rueful smile.

Mum bristles like a guard dog and gives him a sour look. 'It's not funny,' she says.

'Anyway, Ems,' Dad says quickly. 'Just keep an eye on her, will you? She really has got to rest and there is no need for her to go out anywhere. The weather forecast is terrible—we may well have snow. And Granny has got a bit of a cold as well as a crook foot.'

'What do I do if I want a breath of fresh air or to pop to see the twins?' I ask, trying not to sound sulky. I don't relish being a jailer and I certainly don't want to be imprisoned too. If I'm not going to school I want to be able to walk Peaches. I pine for her if I don't see her for a few days. The thought of snow is exciting

131

too—I bet Peaches will love gambolling about in it. And everywhere will look so pretty too!

A meaningful glance passes between my parents. Mum's face looks as if it has been hewn out of a glacier it is so white and cold. Eventually my father speaks. He says carefully: 'When you go out you should make sure to double lock the doors, don't just leave them on the Yale, and remember to take your keys with you.'

'So she is locked in?' I query, rather shocked.

'Well, she won't need to go out and we don't want someone walking into the house while she's dozing upstairs, do we?' he says in a reasonable kind of voice—but he won't meet my eyes.

'Fine, just as long as I know,' I say trying not to frown.

'Oh, and Emily, make sure you keep the doors locked while you are in the house, won't you?' he adds.

I don't repeat: 'So she is locked in?' because Mum is blinking as if she is trying not to cry. I've enough problems of my own without getting involved in an argument on the ethical implications of imprisoning your granny to stop her sneaking out to buy booze. They are looking after her and it's their house. They make the rules not me. I won't argue with them.

'I think I'm going to make some hot chocolate. Do you think Granny would like some?' I say brightly.

'You are a good girl,' Dad says giving me a grateful smile. 'Yes, do make her some.'

'I'll take her a KitKat too,' I add. Now I have got over the stress of writing the letter and getting it signed I am feeling quite peckish. I am planning some peanut butter and jam sandwiches (a fav of mine since I stayed with Augusta) and a KitKat (or two) would finish the snack off nicely.

Dad comes into the kitchen as I am loading up the tray. 'Are you and Granny having a midnight feast?' he asks.

'Yes, but I promise we won't drink cider . . . ' I say with a grin.

Dad smiles back but it's forced. 'Emily, you're not going to eat all those sandwiches yourself, are you? Please don't wind your mother up about the dieting any more. She really has got enough to deal with at the moment. She finds all this business with GB very distressing. So just make a bit of an effort.'

'I am trying,' I mutter. 'I'm trying to be helpful. I've said I'll look after Granny while I'm at home.'

'You know Mum doesn't like you to keep on snacking between meals. She's desperate for you to lose a bit of weight . . . '

'Yes, but I've been off colour. I think it's all the salad I've had. I just wanted something to settle my stomach before I go to bed.' I look down at the sandwiches. I defrosted a white loaf from the freezer and popped it into the oven so the bread is soft and warm. And I made a little tower of sarnies cut into triangles with the crusts removed. And now there is red jam and yellow peanut butter oozing from the sides and dripping

133

down. As I stare at my colourful supper-snack I have to make a real effort not to drool. 'After all, Dad, it is only a sandwich and a mug of chocolate,' I add sulkily.

'And three KitKats,' he says gently.

'Two are for Granny. She likes chocolate.' I'm not even sure if this is true. I just want this stupid conversation to be over. 'Please can I go upstairs and have my supper,' I add.

'Yes, of course, off you go. Just try to make a bit of an effort with the dieting for your mother's sake,' he says wearily.

I leave my snack in my room. The conversation with my father has killed my appetite for a moment. I knock on the door of GB's bedroom. 'Hi, Granny,' I call cheerfully. 'I've got some hot chocolate for you. Can I come in?' There isn't a proper reply, just a kind of noise. But I open the door anyway.

The room is dark apart from a crack of light from the bathroom. I set the tray down carefully on the bedside table and switch on the lamp—a pool of light illuminates my parents' bedroom. It is in a state that I have never witnessed before. It is untidy! Now, my mother is fanatical about tidiness. And I'm not surprised she's crying if she's had even a glimpse of the havoc in here. I am shocked because Granny's house isn't clean and tidy like ours but it isn't a total tip either. But this room is. There's a jumble of clothes spilling out of a suitcase and covering the floor, cosmetics clutter the dressing table, and a wet towel festers on the floor by the radiator like a giant mush-room. From the bathroom comes the ominous sound of running water. I hot-foot in there and find the plug in the washbasin, the tap half on, and water lapping over the side and flooding the floor.

Cursing, I turn off the tap, yank out the plug and hastily use all the towels to mop up the flood. Tomorrow, when Mum is at work, I shall have to play launderettes and get all the towels washed and dried. But for now I am just relieved that I have averted an unnatural disaster.

'Granny,' I say sternly to the hump in the bed. 'You left a tap on . . . it flooded the floor. What are you doing? Mum will go ape . . . '

The bundle of bed-clothes shifts and a wan sharp-etched face appears. Granny looks terrible: white as the sheet and ancient. She squints her red-rimmed eyes against the light and says uncertainly, 'Em'ly?'

'Hello, Granny. I've brought you some hot chocolate and a KitKat.'

'Thanks, love,' she whispers, but she makes no attempt to sit up. I move the tray a bit nearer to her but she sinks back into the pillows.

'Why haven't you unpacked?' I ask, looking around at the muddle of clothes. She doesn't reply, and when I glance at her I see that her eyes are closed. Much as I want to go next door and eat my sandwiches I feel bad about leaving her to Mum's wrath.

'I'll give you a hand, shall I?' I say cheerfully. 'You know Mum's motto. "A place for everything and everything in its place." You know she'll be upset if she finds your clothes on the floor.'

'Meg doesn't care about me . . . ' Granny mutters in an exhausted voice.

I begin to find hangers and pick up clothes. Some of Granny's clothes smell badly of cigarette smoke and I put those on the back of the bathroom door to air, mentally making a note to wash them in the morning. When I've sorted the clothes I tidy up the dressing table and put the empty suitcase away in the bottom of the wardrobe.

When I turn round I find that Granny has hauled herself into a sitting position and is watching me.

'Are you going to try your hot chocolate?' I ask her. 'I've put all your clothes away. I love your black velvet skirt and waistcoat,' I add kindly.

'I made that donkey's years ago,' Granny says. 'I don't know why Meg packed it . . . I don't suppose I shall be going to a dinner dance while I am here . . . '

'You made it? Really?' I say. 'Those kind of clothes are right back in fashion, you know. I wish I could fit into it. The material is beautiful and I love the way the skirt flows.'

'Yes, I made it myself and without a pattern,' Granny says defensively, as if I might be accusing her of untruth. 'When your mum was a little girl I made everything for her—even her winter coats.'

'Did you? You are clever!' I say to her. 'I'd love to actually make up my own designs but everything I want to do is always so complicated. I can make a shoe

136

bag and a wraparound skirt and that's just about all I've managed to do in textiles,' I add regretfully.

'Well, it's a start. You want to get yourself off to a proper dress-making class,' Granny says. She reaches out a trembling hand for the mug. She raises it up as if she has forgotten where her mouth is and finally takes a tentative sip. 'Thanks for the drink . . . ' she mutters as she puts the mug down.

'Would you like a cup of tea in the morning?' I ask her.

'Yes, pet, I'd love a cuppa, but not too early,' she says.

'I don't do early,' I say lightly. And as it happens the following morning I don't wake up until nearly lunchtime. The kitchen is still pristine, so I guess that Granny is still asleep. I take up tea and toast to her room but she only mutters to me from underneath the duvet.

'I'll help you get into the shower, if you like,' I offer. 'Then maybe you'd like to come downstairs and watch TV?'

Her small white face appears from behind the covers. 'Thanks, pet,' she says gruffly. 'Are you going to the shops at all?' she adds. Her eyes, sharp as emeralds in the ashy paleness of her face, are watching me closely.

'Maybe . . . ' I say.

'I need some fags and one or two other things. If I gave you a list . . . ' Her voice is breathy, wheedling.

'Yes, well, I'll see . . . ' I say, in a really sanctimonious tone. And I realize I sound just like my mother.

I go downstairs and wish I had the house to myself. It seems like the worst possible luck to have managed to wangle a few luxurious days off school and then to have a delinquent granny to look after. As a consolation for the harshness of my life I make myself a huge mug of tea and switch on the computer. I check my emails and find one from Augusta. I have been putting off the moment when I would have to tell her about the baby and so communication between us has been sparse. But I had emailed her to tell her that Corey and I are now friends and how nice he is. My life is so boring (or so confidential) that I considered this newsworthy.

Augusta has written back:

hi babe, good to hear from u!
glad to hear that you have a
b'friend at long last! ha ha!!
corey sounds cool and kinda
sweet. i luv sweet guys!!! i
have the most amazing news. i am
so excited i can hardly write
it!! you will never guess in a
million who i have been dating!!!!
I didn't dare tell you before cos
i thought it would be bad luck.
u know when i tell you about a
guy it always goes wrong!!!!! BUT
NOT THIS TIME!!!!!! i am just so
happy. it's WESLEY! and now for
the real shock! he has asked me
to marry him and i said YES YES
YES. can you believe it? u will
think i am making it up but im
not i really am going to be MRS
WESLEY DUBOIS—isnt it just the
coolest name in the world? we are
totally in love and we want to

138

get married SOON because only
kissing is driving us crazy. i
wish we were married right now!!!!
Because i just cant wait . . .
but of course we have got to . . .
nway my parents are very upset
and want us to wait and have a
long engagement but no way can
we do that. i still have to go
to school but Wes says he will
work and we will have a house. I
just want to stay home and be a mom
but I have to have a career cos
my parents are so materialistic
and they say Wes has no prospects
or schooling which is totally
mean. But they are paying for an
incredible wedding and I want you
to come and be my bridesmaid cos
we promised we would do that,
didn't we? write back and tell
me u will come. it has got to be
soon soon soon cos we are going
crazy for each other and some
nights we kiss in places that
you would not BELIEVE!!!!!!!!!!
i never knew it could be so hard
to be hot for someone . . . u
say u haven't been in luv so
maybe u won't know what I am
talking about!!!!!!!! but when
you find the right guy u will
know how hard it is!!!!!! don't
let anyone and specially not your
mom read this—cos I haven't told
anyone else but u. u r my best
friend!!! LOL GussieXXXXXXX

I swallow hard and wonder what to write back. Augusta's email brings back a whole load of memories that I would rather not face. I do know what she is talking about. And her ardent girlish prose brings back into brilliant relief my own experience. A balmy midsummer night when I was so hot for someone that I was crazy crazy crazy . . .

I too wanted to be married, to be a woman, to stay home and be a mom. I wanted to be an adult, not a schoolgirl, or a student with years and years of education rolling out before me like a life sentence. I was desperate with curiosity and desire. I wanted to get hold of life in all its richness and experience it: love, sex, sweat, the commitment between a man and a woman, the gift of procreation. I felt trapped by my childish life. I wanted to break free and be part of some wider world that was more real—I wanted to be a grown-up.

And now I am in the 'grown-up' world and there is no going back.

I write back:

```
Dearest Gussie. i agree with your
parents. i think u should wait a
while and have a relationship with
Wes before you get married. why
don't u get some contraceptives?
and then have fun together until
you have finished school? u can
have a big wedding then. i would
love to be a bridesmaid but i am
never getting married so i cant
return the favour. LOL
EmilyXXXXXXXXX
```

Augusta replies:

```
fyi what u say sucks!!!!!!! i
cant wait and i want to be a
proper bride. how can u say that?
and why arent you getting married?
u always said u wanted to marry
Brett? don't you like him any more?
what happened? u sound real sad
and kinda lonely!!!!! as soon as
school finishes why don't u come over
here for the holidays? then u can help
me find a wedding dress . . . and
we'll get something pretty for u
to wear!!!! tell me what colour
u think would be good. my mom
says pink but i want something
classy . . . pink is for
babies!!!!! we r going to be
married SOON!!!!!! LOL Gussie
xxxxxxxxxxxxxxxxxxxxx
```

She is going to be married soon and pink is for babies. I shake my head and close down the computer. I am suddenly tired and very hungry. I go into the kitchen and start to organize lunch for me and Granny B. Dealing with food takes up all my thoughts and the smell of frying onions and garlic makes me happy. Maybe this is what it is like to be an animal. All you think about is food and shelter . . . warmth and safety . . . I hum a tune as I make a vegetable curry. We can have it with chutney and nan bread . . . Who could ask for anything more?

# CHAPTER TWELVE

The smell of curry lures Granny down. I hear her hobbling down the stairs. Then she limps into the kitchen and sits down at the table.

'Good morning!' I say brightly. 'You'll feel better when you've had something to eat,' I add.

'Who says I feel bad,' she mutters irritably. And she stares down at the plate I set before her as if I have dished up a well-boiled human head.

'What's this?' she asks, poking her fork into a slice of aubergine.

'Egg plant,' I say.

'Any meat in here?'

'No, just vegetables.'

'I like a nice Bird's Eye chicken dinner myself,' she says. And then she pushes her curry around her plate while I eat everything I have dished up for myself and then polish off what is left in the frying pan. I don't bother to ask her if she wants seconds as she has only eaten about three mouthfuls.

'You've got a good appetite,' she says dourly. She watches me mop up the last of the sauce until my plate is clean and gleaming. Then she squints at me for a long moment and asks: 'Aren't you going to school?'

'I'm off at the moment. I've not been well,' I say quickly.

'You look fine to me,' she says rudely. There is a long silence in the kitchen. I clear the table and load the dishwasher. Granny sits, looking out of the window at the icy garden and the black branches of the skeleton trees swaying in the wind. The whole world is locked in the grip of winter and the countryside is grey and hard with frost.

'What a place to live. I don't know why anyone wants to be marooned out here,' Granny says mournfully. She is as forlorn as a lost cat.

'It's all right once you get used to it. It's great in the summer,' I say.

Granny looks at me and manages a thin smile. Then she says in a conciliatory tone, 'Em'ly, love, would you mind popping to the shop and getting a few bits for me?'

'What exactly is it that you want?' I ask, embarrassed.

'Just some cigs,' she says with the air of an innocent child.

'Mum won't let you smoke in the house,' I say.

'I can pop outside,' she says, and then she adds, 'Please, E'mly. Just run to the shop and get me some cigs and maybe a bottle of sherry?'

'Granny! I can't!' I say.

'Why not?' she asks, feigning surprise—then she gives me a sly half smile. 'You don't have to tell your mam, you know. It can be our little secret. Go on. Be a sport. You can get a little something for yourself, if you want.'

'NO! I can't and I won't,' I say mulishly. The thought that she might keep on wheedling makes me feel really stressed. 'Don't keep on asking me—cos I can't do it,' I add firmly.

'I suppose your mother has put you up to this,' she says angrily.

'It's against the law, if you must know.' Even to my own ears I sound like a bag.

'Right then,' she says. She hobbles out of the kitchen and slams the door. I hear her making her way up the stairs. I get the calendar down from the notice board and work out how many days are left of the school term. Christmas is nearly upon us! I can't help but wonder how long Granny will be staying.

For some reason having Granny in the house and the unpleasantness of our altercation makes me feel really low. I long for someone to talk to who will be kind and sympathetic. And because everyone else in the entire world is busy (apart from me and Granny) there is no help to be had anywhere. So I end up spending the afternoon reading and eating chocolate. Eventually I finish both my book and my secret stash of Green and Black plain with fruit and nut. As I put the book down I realize that I feel very full and a bit sick. I also feel certain that I will never want to see or smell cocoa, or any of its by-products, ever again. To take my mind off my greed, and my revolting chocolate binge, I check for emails. My luck is in! Augusta has sent me a desperate message that makes me forget about everything else. She has set me a challenge—which is just what I need!

Hi, Emily, i can't find a dress . . . pleeze help me . . . all the dresses my mother likes make me look like an exploding cake . . . or a giant meringue . . . HELP . . . i have put on loads of weight and Wesley is sooooo thin and beautiful . . . what do u want to wear??? we need to look kinda similar but u can't look slimmer than me. Wesley hates fat people he has a complex about it i think. he is really fussy about what he eats and if he gets in a mood he doesn't eat anything at all . . . kinda anorexic. But do guys get that? Can u design me a dress that will make me look wonderful, pleeze??? LOL GussieXXXXXXXXXXXXXXXXXXXXXXXXXXXXXX XXXXXXXXXXXXXXXXXXXXXXXXXXXXXXXXXXX XXXXXXXXXXXXXXXXXXXXXXXXXXXXXXXXXXX XXX

I email back:

Dearest Gussie—im on the case . . . i will design you the most bootiful dress in the world. send me your height and weight and the same for sexy boy Wes and I will do some drawings for you! LOL Emilyxxxxxxxxxxxxxxxxxxxxxxxxxxxxxxxxxxx

I can't imagine Augusta looking anything less than wonderful with her high cheekbones, dramatic colouring, and permanent tan. I get my sketchbook from my desk and start to think about what would suit her and Wes. He needs something which will make him look taller and Gussie needs to look slender and vulnerable. I play around with various ideas, tearing pages out of my book and posting them up around the room. Wedding dresses are my particular favourite and the challenge of making Gussie look slimmer is a brain teaser. I do a few sketches of bridesmaid dresses for myself. Though what I really need is a tent to hide in.

When the twins are home I ring them. 'Have you time for a chat?' I ask.

'Well, really we've got to get on with our prep,' Flo says.

'I thought you did all your homework at school?' I ask.

'Oh, that's just for the little kids,' she says dismissively. 'We have mountains of extra reading to do. We'd be there until midnight if we did it all at school.'

'I really need to see you,' I say, hating myself for being so needy and for being so unmotivated. All through school my grades have been better than Sienna's and have sometimes matched Flo's. They both have to work hard with Maths and Science which comes easily to me. And now I am dropping out while they sail ahead. Just for a moment panic overwhelms me. But I can only concentrate on one problem at a time and at the moment that problem is Granny.

'Come round here,' Flo says. 'We've got the house to ourselves.'

We settle ourselves in their kitchen. Si makes me a

huge mug of tea and plies me with biscuits. I nibble at the plain ones and try not to look at the chocolate ones for fear that my stomach will start to churn.

I tell them briefly about Granny staying. But when I open my mouth to tell them about the hospital and my role as jailer I can't find the right words. I also realize that I don't want to tell them. Something holds me back—some innate snobbery inherited from my mother. The twins would be sympathetic. They would be full of suggestions and offers of help. And I would put money on it that Flo would be more than ready to accompany Granny B to AA meetings, to encourage her to keep a diary of her achievements, and get her well and truly reformed.

For Flo and Si there are no problems in life that don't have a solution. But it's not the same for me . . . Looking back over the past I don't think I have ever had their optimism. For the first time I can sense that I have somehow inherited my mother's deeply pessimistic view of the world. I have fought against it all my life but I suppose it must be in my genes. There is some dark shadow, some echo from the past, which has tainted my view of the world, like a drop of ink in water, which means I see life through a shade.

'It's just sooooo sad about Mr Thomas losing all his money,' Si says. 'But I think it's brilliant of him to still have an enormous party in the church hall and to make it a farewell "do" so we can all say goodbye. I bet we'll all be in floods of tears by the end of the evening. It will be sad to see them go. It seems like the end of an era.' She smiles and adds, 'And none of us has ever managed to get a date with the totally gorgeous Brett . . . have we?'

Flo immediately registers the pained look on my face and asks, 'Haven't you had your invite yet?'

I shake my head. 'Ours came in the post . . . ' Si says, uncomfortable at having exposed me to such social shame. 'I expect yours will come tomorrow,' she adds quickly.

Talk turns to school. The twins talk in stereo. All I can think about is that I haven't been invited to the party that Mr Thomas has arranged. My throat is tight with the effort of not crying. Inside my chest is a hard wall of hurt. I wonder if everyone else in the village will be invited but not me—or my parents . . . I try to tell myself it is only a silly old party and my parents have never accepted invitations to Nell Acre or the church hall jamborees that Mr Thomas has thrown in the past. Maybe that is why we are not invited now? But it's never stopped us being invited before. The posh cards have fallen through our letterbox at regular intervals over the years. My father has always replied with some trumped-up excuse as to why they couldn't attend, but would sweeten the pill by sending many thanks and saying that I would love to come along with the Devereux family. But now this . . . I feel such a rush of resentment and pity for myself that I have to make an excuse and leave.

As I am opening the back door at home my phone begins to vibrate. It's Corey.

'Oh, hello,' I say, trying not to sound huffy and hurt and failing miserably.

'What's the matter?'

'Nothing.'

'Why are you crying then?' he asks, concerned.

'I'm not crying,' I say.

'You sound as if you are. Are you sure you are OK? Would you like me to come over?'

'No . . . ' I snuffle, although in truth I would like to say 'yes'.

'I've got a party invitation for you. It's a Christmas, New Year, and leaving do all rolled into one. I hope you'll come. I thought I'd give the invite to you rather than posting it.'

There is a long silence when I try to collect my thoughts and stop my emotions from see-sawing wildly. 'Thanks, that's very nice of you,' I mumble.

'I thought . . . I didn't know . . . I thought about going to the cinema this evening . . . do you want . . . would you like . . . '

As he's just put me out of my misery I am magnanimous. 'Yes, I'd love to go.'

Now it's his turn to mutter. 'That's good. I'll pick you up in an hour. Is that OK?'

'Yes, I'm babysitting Granny but the parents should be back by then.'

'Are things going OK with her?' he asks.

'Pretty crap . . . I'll tell you all about it later.'

As I go into the house I feel my mood shifting from one of deep gloom to one of happiness and surprise.

The main surprise is that after all these years Corey Thomas and I have become friends. I am actually looking forward to seeing him and, more incredibly, I know that I will be able to talk to him about Granny— a topic which I couldn't bring myself to discuss with the twins. This makes me feel very humble. For all these years I have despised and disliked him—for no good reason—and now he has turned out to be OK, more than OK . . . I like him lots . . . This is very strange—but also very true.

# Chapter Thirteen

It is only with Corey's help that I get through the following week. First problem is Granny. I had no idea that going without drink, when you have been used to drinking all you want, makes you ill. Granny is sick in the mornings, shakes all the time, and is in the temper from hell. She tries a couple of times to leave the house, but the snow is deep, the paths are icy, and she doesn't even make it to the end of the road. When she comes hobbling back from these expeditions her face is grey and twisted in pain and she appears to be incoherent with rage.

My parents are out of the house all the time. They both work in sales and Christmas is their busiest time. My mother is like a ghost: gaunt and white and getting thinner by the day. Her diet certainly seems to be working. I hear my father saying angrily one morning to her:

'You not eating won't make Emily thinner.'

I have started to notice that although she prepares elaborate meals for the rest of us she never seems to eat anything. But to be honest it is way down on my list of worries.

Living with Granny is a miserable experience. She is obviously fed up with me because I won't go to the shop—she doesn't speak to me at all apart from to mutter 'thanks' when I give her things. Most of the time I carry drinks and meals upstairs for her although it is all a waste as she eats almost nothing and seems to be getting paler and more scrawny.

I spend my days emailing Augusta and making sketches of wedding dresses for her and wonderful wedding suits for Wes. I actually get more excited about designing outfits for him because it's much harder and a real challenge. I fill my afternoons by walking Peaches and waiting for Corey to come home from college so I have someone to talk to.

Apart from Granny my other problem is Mr Anthony. He leaves a message on my phone just to check that I haven't forgotten about our meeting at the library. I talk to Corey about it and he says he thinks I should go and offers to accompany me. This is very kind of him but it seems weird to go along to see Mr Anthony with a minder. But I do arrange to meet Corey at the bus station afterwards and warn him that I will need lots of mugs of tea and food to recover if the seeing Mr Anthony is traumatic.

The day we are meeting is the last school day before the Christmas holidays. I can only hope that everyone else but me and Mr Anthony will be busy partying, shopping, swapping cards, and other festive stuff and won't go near the library.

As I have been holed up in the village for so long,

going into town is a bit of a shock. It is as if the whole world is Christmas crazy. There are lights everywhere and flashing Father Christmases and carols blaring out like some mad seasonal karaoke. It reminds me of being at the fair and getting through the crush is a lot like going on the dodgems—everyone but me seems to have huge shopping bags and to be barging around like maniacs. The whole atmosphere is very stressful and this makes my anxiety about seeing Mr Anthony worse.

Because it takes me ages to get through the shopping frenzy I am late and he is already waiting for me by the stinky laurel bushes.

'Can we go inside?' I whine. The day is harsh; there are brittle flurries of sleety snow in the wind and the back of the library seems as dank and cold as the dark side of the moon. I feel chilled to the bone.

'No, best to stay out here . . . ' He surveys me anxiously. 'Are you all right? Have you been to the hospital for a scan?'

'No.'

'Have you been to see your GP?'

'No.'

'But I told you how important it is,' he says desperately. 'I can't believe you are being so negligent, Emily!'

'I'm fine. I'm taking care of myself, I promise. I've been going for walks in the country and eating well . . . ' I stop and find I am chewing at my lower lip. I don't know why he is making me feel like a naughty child. It simply isn't fair.

'No one at school knows anything about it. I looked up your file. Your parents are going to have to . . . '

'Yes,' I interrupt. 'They are just a bit busy at the moment.'

'You haven't told them, have you?' he accuses.

'No,' I say. 'Well, I did tell them, but they thought I was mucking around. They thought it was a joke.'

'Emily, I want you to come and meet my wife, meet Gabriella. You'd like her, I promise you. We want to talk to you about the baby . . . '

His tension and distress are palpable. Maybe the darkness and the cold have made me more sensitive than usual but it seems to me that he is as highly strung as an over-tightened violin wire. I take a step back from him as if fearing contamination from all his stress. 'What is it that you want?' I ask breathlessly. 'Tell me what you want?'

His voice is no more than a desperate whisper as he replies: 'We would like to adopt the baby . . . we want to adopt your baby . . . ' He clears his throat nervously: 'You could keep in touch with us . . . even if we moved away. We'd always let you know where we were. I promise you that. We'd even tell the baby that you were the mother—if that is what you wanted. We'd play strictly to your rules. I give you my word.' His voice rises and gains strength as if he is convinced by his own argument as he continues. 'You could be the baby's godmother or just like a big sister . . . whatever way you want it. It would be your choice entirely.'

There is a long pause. Above the hum of the traffic

and the discordant jangled carols there is the sound of an emergency siren. The whole world seems chaotic. I want to put my hands over my ears and shut my eyes tight and make it all disappear. I must have moved right away without realizing it because his hand is suddenly on my arm pulling me back to him.

His voice is frantic, hoarse with emotion: 'Please, Emily. Please consider it. This could be the best solution for you. We're not just thinking about ourselves, I promise you. We are thinking about the baby and about you. You could just walk away from it all and pretend it never happened. Some girls find that is the easiest thing to do. Just walk away, forget all about it and get on with the rest of your life.'

There is a cold dark silence between us. I am too startled and distressed to speak. I just wish he would shut up. Listening to him is like having a hand inside my chest twisting away at my heart. I am so full of feelings I am brimming over. I want to put my hands over his mouth and tell him to shut up—that I don't want to hear any more. I can't bear to have him ranting at me, hear his voice full of pain and panic and see his white desperate face. It is making me feel sick.

'Emily, you have no idea what it is like to want a baby and not to be able to have one. It has done terrible things to us.' He is speaking in a rush without a pause for breath. It's scary, as if he can't stop now he has started and I will have to know everything.

'We were so arrogant. We assumed it would be

easy. We took it for granted that when we got married the babies would just arrive. We want so much to be a family—to have a child of our own. And some days that seems like the most impossible thing in the world for us. Gabby has suffered so much. We both have. And sometimes it feels as if all the pain and disappointment is eating away at us. As if we are both disappearing because of it and eventually it will destroy us and our marriage.'

'I'm sorry,' I mumble.

'Don't be sorry. It's not your fault. I just want you to know. I . . . we wouldn't have asked you if it hadn't been really important to us. And it would be a way out for you. You are a bright girl, Emily. You have a good future. You don't want to spoil your life. We can help you. Please let us . . . '

'I'm sorry,' I say again.

'Sorry?' he echoes.

'Sorry. I can't help you. I can't do it.'

'Don't make a decision. Think about it!' he cries.

'I really don't need to. I can't do it. It's very kind of you and I appreciate it. And I really, really hope you have a baby soon. But I can't give you mine.'

'But, Emily, you have no idea what you are letting yourself in for! You have nothing to offer this baby. You haven't even been able to tell your parents. How are you going to be able to give this child a good life all on your own?'

'I don't know,' I say stubbornly. 'But I can't just give it away.'

He turns away from me and puts his hands over his face. 'Oh my God!' he pleads. Then he turns back to me. He reaches out his hands but I back away from him. 'I'm so sorry, Emily. I shouldn't have asked you like this. I should have waited and let Gabby do it . . . ' He sounds broken. 'It's the wrong balance of power. You associate me with school. Don't make up your mind. Just say you will come and meet Gabby and talk to her. You might feel differently when you've met her. Please, Emily. I can't go home and tell her I've blown it. Please don't say "No" and walk away. I can't bear it. Just say you will meet her and discuss it. Why don't you ask the father to come along and meet us? We could talk it over—the four of us.'

'There is no father!' I say dully. 'I told you. He doesn't know and he wouldn't care even if he did know.'

'Emily, is he a bad person?'

'No!'

'Then how can you be so sure he doesn't care? Why don't you talk to him? Ask him what he thinks about the future of his child. If he's not a bad person what kind of a man is he?'

'He's perfect. He's everything you could wish for. The only problem is that he doesn't love me—not even a little bit.'

'Are you absolutely sure about that?' Mr Anthony asks hesitantly—then he adds in a rush, 'I find that impossible to believe. I would have thought it was very easy to love you.'

'You've never been dumped, have you?' My voice is cold as the sleet and harsh as the call of a crow. 'Of course you've never been rejected!' I add dismissively. 'I expect you've had a charmed life. No one will ever have turned you down.'

And I remember—in a wave of bitterness—how everyone at school had a monster crush on him when he arrived. And, although we were only little girls, the feelings we had for him were deep and sincere. We would have done anything for him! And how, even now, his hand on my arm is keeping me here, when I would have walked away from anyone else.

'You can have no idea how much it hurts to be told that you aren't good enough, that even though you've given everything, you are still not up to scratch. Being dumped is like failing every single exam you've ever taken . . . and the result being read out to the whole school. It's like being paraded naked in front of all your enemies, it's like having your pride and self confidence boiled in bleach and handed back to you completely colourless and in tatters. Being dumped hurts more than I would ever have believed possible.'

I burst into tears then. I don't know why I've told him all this when I haven't been able to tell anyone else, not the twins or Corey . . . or even Gussie, who writes me confidential confessional emails and who has told me more than I ever want to know about her and Wes and what they get up to.

'What happened?' Mr Anthony asks.

'It was last summer. I'd been in love with him for years. I never thought I stood a chance with him. But he had a massive row with the girl he's in love with. I think he started taking me out just to spite her—and to make himself feel better. She'd dumped him and his pride was hurt. He never promised me that it would be more than a few casual dates but I kept on dreaming. I was so confident. I'd assumed I could make him love me. But as soon as she clicked her fingers he went back to her. He was very honest with me . . . brutally honest. I can't say he didn't tell me the truth about that. He dumped me. He said, "Our relationship isn't going anywhere . . . " I knew he just wanted to get rid of me. I think I made him feel uncomfortable.' Suddenly my face heats as a host of unwanted memories flood into my mind and I mutter miserably, 'I think my unrequited adoration proved to be a huge embarrassment for him.'

'You should have been more careful,' Mr Anthony says wearily. 'It's all covered in the school syllabus for PSE, isn't it? You should have known how to avoid an unwanted pregnancy.'

I don't need him to tell me that I've messed up. 'I was out of my mind . . . ' I mutter. I don't suppose he would ever understand. I imagine that he has been adored for the whole of his life. I don't suppose he would know the first thing about unrequited love, or the pain and the madness that can overtake you when you really love someone who doesn't love you back.

'I can't dump this baby. I know how much it hurts to be rejected. And it's such a bad beginning for the start of a life, isn't it? Not to be wanted.'

'Gabby and I want it . . . ' he mutters.

'No you don't. You don't want this baby . . . not this particular baby . . . this one that is half of me and half of him. You want "a baby", preferably one of your own—one that will look like you and Gabby. You want a baby that will make your life complete and make you feel like a proper family. But that's a big responsibility for a little baby, isn't it? It sounds like a lifetime's work to me. And say it doesn't happen? Say it doesn't work out? What happens if your life doesn't feel complete or you don't feel like a proper family?'

'Well, it's a risk we run, isn't it? We have discussed it and we do want this baby. You don't want the baby, do you? And your parents are going to be really upset.' He is sulky as a child with me now.

'You don't know what I want. You haven't thought to ask me!' I say rudely.

'I . . . we are trying to help you,' he says desperately.

'Well, thanks, but I'll sort it out on my own.'

'What are you going to do?'

'I'm going to go home and tell my grandmother about the baby.'

'Your grandmother? Is she close to you and your parents? Will she help you?'

'No. I shouldn't imagine she'll be much help at all,' I say honestly. 'I think she's alcoholic, or maybe just a

160

drunk . . . whatever . . . Anyway, she'll probably be pretty hopeless at sorting out family problems. But she is sober at the moment. And she is ace at sewing. So I'm going to get her to help me do some dressmaking. There is a big party coming up and I want a new dress to wear.'

I've either really annoyed him, or he is upset, because he doesn't reply when I say goodbye. I just walk off and leave him. I'm not proud of myself and I'm not happy with what has happened but I can't dwell on it too much. I just have to think about the basics—getting to the bus station, meeting Corey, buying material for my new dress, and then having a cup of tea and a toasted teacake (all this emotion and crying has made me feel ravenous!). The rest of life's problems will have to wait.

# CHAPTER FOURTEEN

Corey waits outside the fabric shop while I buy the material I want. It is very expensive and my heart does a bit of a dip as I hand over my card. I could have gone to ASDA and bought something cheap and cheerful that would cover my bump. But I have this idea in my head of my perfect dress that has been growing since I saw the lovely black velvet skirt and waistcoat that Granny made for herself. I want a dress that has a lovely 1950s retro look about it and I also want to wear something that is comfortable. I am sick of hitching up my trousers and pulling down my tops. Nothing seems to fit me any more and nothing is comfy. I very much want to go to the Thomases' leaving party and I want to wear something which makes me look good.

'Did you get what you want?' Corey asks, holding out his hand for my bag. 'I'll carry it for you.'

'Yes, I got what I wanted but it was really expensive. I got carried away. I love new material—it always smells so good. I got metres of amazing velvet and it's an awesome colour: not black and not purple . . . but something in between—and it catches the light. I want to see if Granny will help me with it. I know what I want to make but I am terrified of cutting it out. Maybe I better buy her a bribe. I wonder if a packet of cigs would do. I daren't buy her booze—my mother would go mad if she started drinking at our house.'

I purchase a packet of twenty cigs from a racketeer from school who is hanging around the bus station and am staggered by how much they cost. 'What an expensive way to kill yourself,' I say to Corey. Then, when we are on the bus, I tell him: 'Tonight I'm going to have a full and frank discussion with my parents about the baby. I can't keep putting it off. If it's awful at home can I ring you?'

He nods. 'Sure thing,' he says. And I sit on the bus and think about what good friends we are now and how, if I am in trouble, he is my first port of call.

The house is in darkness. Granny is in bed. But she is sitting up and watching the TV which is an improvement on hiding under the duvet.

'Will you help me make a dress?' I ask, as I hold out the cigs. She looks down at the shiny white packet as if she doesn't know what they are.

'I'll have a bit of a puff first,' she says. 'Thanks, Emily, love. That's really good of you to get them for me.'

To my relief she doesn't ask about booze. Instead she gets out of bed, wraps herself in her coat, hobbles downstairs and props herself up outside the back door.

To my surprise she is out there for only a couple of minutes. I wonder if it is the cold that has driven her back in as she comes into the kitchen coughing.

'I wouldn't have believed it possible,' she says. 'I didn't enjoy that cig one bit. And it made me catch my breath.' She looks down at the partly-smoked cigarette in her hand and adds, 'What a turn up for the books. I've been smoking since I was seventeen and I've loved every one I've had up until now. But I've lost the taste for them. Must be all the fresh air out here. Anyway it's not the same without a drink . . . ' she finishes somewhat wistfully.

Then she smiles at me and adds: 'But it was kind of you to get them for me. Now show me this material and then I'll take your measurements.'

We go into the front room and I lay the material out along the length of the settee. It looks like a huge and very beautiful snake as it cascades down over the cool cream of the leather.

'It's a lovely bit of cloth,' Granny says approvingly. 'What do you want doing with it?'

'A dress,' I say excitedly. 'Something very Grace Kelly, something feminine and flattering. I want to wear high heels and my hair up. I want to look like a supermodel.'

Granny laughs. 'Well, we'll see what we can do. Get me a tape measure and we'll get started.'

She measures me everywhere: around my neck, the length from my neck to the end of my shoulders, my bust, and the length of my arms.

Then she kneels in front of me to take my waist measurement and I see her eyes widen with surprise: 'You're lovely and slim everywhere else but you are carrying a bit of weight around your middle, love,' she says kindly. 'You don't want to be an apple shape at your age. You ought to go swimming . . . or do some sit-ups.'

She is moving now to my hips, her face is so close to my bump I expect her to flinch when the baby kicks. But she is absorbed in her task, measuring me and then writing the figures down in my notebook. Her writing is small and sharp—just like her.

'Granny B, I'm fat because I'm going to have a baby,' I say slowly and clearly.

She leans back on her heels and looks up into my face. Her mouth is slack with surprise and her green eyes are round and startled. 'You never are! Don't joke, pet. Having a baby at your age when you're not wed is not a laughing matter, believe me . . . '

'I'm not joking, Granny. I'm sorry. I want you to help me tell Mum and Dad. It really is true.'

To my horror Granny bursts into tears: her eyes flood, their brilliant green turns grey under the deluge of salt tears and her mouth puckers into a nest of creases. She suddenly looks very old. 'Oh my lord . . . ' she laments, wiping the wetness from her face with the back of her hands. 'I don't know how our Megan will cope with this. How could you? How could you do this to your mum?'

Her response irritates me. 'I wasn't thinking about Mum . . . I wasn't thinking about anyone. I thought I was in love . . . I couldn't help myself . . . ' I say hotly. 'I don't see why it's worse for Mum than for Dad—or how it can possibly be worse for them than for me.

Mum isn't going to have to give birth to the baby, is she? Or miss out on going to university along with everyone else . . . ' Just for a moment I am immersed in self-pity and my voice breaks.

'She's always been so proud of you,' Granny says brokenly. Then she shakes her head and adds: 'But you're quite right. We have to think about you and the baby—that's the most important thing. Now you're not to let your parents bully you into getting married straight away. I know he's a nice young lad and all the rest of it—but it's not a good idea. Take it from me, love. I should know.'

I realize with a sinking feeling that she has assumed that Corey is my boyfriend. 'Corey—the boy who came to the hospital—he isn't the father. He isn't my boyfriend or anything like that . . . '

'Well, he's around here a lot . . . ' Granny says, giving me a searching look.

'We're just friends,' I say lamely. Then, partly to change the subject and partly because I am consumed with curiosity I ask: 'Why is getting married such a bad idea?'

'Marry in haste: repent at leisure,' Granny says, pursing her lips together. 'In my day they called it a shotgun wedding. If a lad got you into trouble your family persuaded him to do the decent thing and marry you. But I lived to rue the day . . . '

She turns away from me with a shuttered look on her face. I have never heard anything about my grandfather. Mum always says Granny B and he split up when she was little and she's not seen him since. But now I want to know more.

'Was it having to get married that stopped things working out for you?' I ask.

'Well, your mum will have told you all about it . . . ' she says vaguely. 'Let's get this finished, shall we?' she suggests. And she kneels again and continues taking measurements. While she is concentrating and writing I watch her and wait. Then, finally, she looks up at me and says: 'All done.' And I reply:

'Mum's never told me anything about her father except to say he wasn't around. I think you should tell me about him, Granny. I want to know.'

Granny gets to her feet, hobbles across to a chair and sits down. She passes a hand wearily across her face as if recall of the past has made her tired. 'There's nothing much to tell, love. His name was Phillip. He was a grammar school boy. He was working as a draughtsman at the council offices. And he and his mates drank at the Angel pub. There was always a band there on a Friday night and me and my friends went along to dance.' She gives me a small smile and adds: 'All the girls would dance together. We didn't take too much notice of the lads and they didn't take much notice of us! But one night Phillip came across and asked me if I'd like a drink, then he gave me a lift home on his scooter—he had a Lambretta—and after that we started going out. He was a real live wire. We had such fun.'

She leans back in the chair and closes her eyes.

'Yes . . . well . . . what happened then?' I prompt helpfully.

Granny glances at me and says slowly, 'He was my first boyfriend. We were young and silly. When I fell pregnant I was quite happy to settle down but he wasn't that interested. He was too good-looking, too popular, too keen on having a good time. He was a mod and really into clothes and his lifestyle. And he wanted to be a pop star . . . he played guitar with a band. Not that it ever came to anything. But, even so, he didn't want to be tied down with a baby and a wife. I was only seventeen. We couldn't afford anywhere to live after we got married so we stayed with his parents. His mother thought I wasn't good enough for him and she said I spoilt Megan. But I just wanted the best for her. She was the most beautiful baby . . . '

Granny's face softens. 'I used to knit and sew for her even then . . . I made her layette in white but, as soon as she was born, I made her peach and lemon coloured clothes. I thought pink was common!' Granny laughs for a moment and then continues more seriously. 'I suppose if Phil and I had waited, grown up together, we might have stood a chance. But it was all too much, too soon. When Megan was three he took a job in London working for the GLC—he said he would send for us when he got settled but he never did. Your mum cried for months and asked for him every day. That was the worst thing about him leaving us. I sometimes think it would have been better for her never to have had a father than to have one who broke her heart. I don't think she's ever got over it. Or that she's ever forgiven me for letting him go . . . but you can't keep someone by your side when they don't want to be there.' Granny looks down at her hands. They are small and brown, wrinkled like autumn leaves.

'Didn't he ever come back to see you?' I ask.

'No . . . we divorced and then he married again. Your mum saw him once when she was about ten or eleven. But it upset her seeing him with his new wife, so that was the end of it.'

'Didn't you ever want to get married again?' I ask.

Granny smiles and shakes her head. 'No . . . I like my freedom. I had my little house and my job . . . Anyway, the point of the tale is—don't rush into getting married.'

'Fat chance,' I mutter. 'Granny, will you help me tell Mum about the baby. Honestly, I've tried to tell her loads of times. But it's like she doesn't want to believe me.'

'Of course she doesn't want to believe you, Em'ly love,' Granny says, and she gives me a long look that makes me tremble. 'I'll tell her,' she says with a sigh.

I want to change the subject—talking about Granny is a lot easier than talking about myself. So I ask: 'Was your mum upset with you when you got pregnant?'

'I should say,' Granny says grimly. 'The rows in our house were something wicked. She blamed my dad and he blamed her. They fought like cat and dog about it—accusing each other of spoiling me and being soft. I was the youngest—and their only girl—and I was always a bit of a pet. And as for my brothers! They were ready to lynch poor Phil—which was hardly fair.'

'Did they ever get over it?' I ask.

'By the time of the wedding everything had calmed down. I think me and Phil getting divorced hurt my parents more than your mum arriving early. No one in our family had ever been divorced before. People didn't do it then. And I think they worried a lot about me being on my own.'

Granny leans back and closes her eyes. I notice that her hands are shaking slightly.

'Shall I make some sketches of the dress that I would like?' I ask.

'Yes,' she says wearily. 'And then I'll cut it out for you. Where can we put the sewing machine? Your mum won't like a mess in here,' she adds.

'We'll put it in my room. Then we'll be out of the way,' I say.

My parents come home together and start to prepare supper and do chores. I go and hide in my room. Granny is in the kitchen with them and I wait—almost too scared to breathe. Granny's descriptions are still vivid in my mind and I expect something dramatic to happen—for there to be a long scream from my mother or for my father to come pounding up the stairs demanding to know who has fathered my baby so he can go and get a shotgun.

It's all a great anticlimax. All that happens is my father comes and taps on my door. When I open it he gives me an anxious look and says, 'Supper is just about ready—come down and eat with us, please. Your mum is going to phone the doctor's surgery first thing in the morning to make an appointment for you.'

'I'm not having an abortion,' I say coldly.

He gives me a pained look. 'I don't think that is the idea at all, Emily. By the look of you it's far too late for that. And it's not what we would have wanted anyway—unless you told us expressly it was the only option open to you.' He avoids my eyes as he says, 'I'm sorry we haven't listened before when you've tried to tell us you are pregnant. We feel we've let you down in every way possible. I think we must be the worst parents in the world. Your mother is in pieces. She can't believe we've messed up so badly.'

He sighs and adds sadly, 'I don't think either of us is up to talking about it tonight. Let us sleep on it and discuss it tomorrow. In truth, I don't really know what we can do for you—apart from sorting out an appointment to see the doctor and notifying the school that you won't be returning. I think we'll have to go to see Miss Zoller and explain the situation. I don't know what else we can do. I suppose, if you'd wanted our advice or help, you would have asked for it before now . . . I don't suppose you want to tell us how it happened or the name of the boy involved?'

'No, I don't,' I mutter.

'We didn't think so . . . ' There is a long pause and then he adds uneasily, 'We'll just have to wait until you feel ready to tell us . . . and when you do we'll try not

171

to judge you or him too harshly. There is just one thing that bothers us. This boy . . . this boy . . . he didn't force you did he? I mean . . . ' He stops, clears his throat and wipes his hand across his brow. 'You would have told us . . . wouldn't you? If something bad like that had happened to you? You do understand what I am trying to say to you, don't you?'

'Yes, I understand,' I say in a dull monotone. It is so painful to listen to him. It is an effort for me to continue speaking. 'And no,' I add quietly. 'He didn't force me at all or get me drunk. It was nothing like that at all . . . ' I stop and add truthfully, 'It was quite different to that, honestly.'

'Well . . . ' he turns away from me with a sigh, 'that is one thing to be thankful for. I'll tell your mother . . . It will put her mind at rest. We'll do all we can to help, you know that, don't you?'

'Yes, I do. Thank you . . . ' I add automatically. And for the first time something close to panic starts to overwhelm me. I had expected my parents to be angry. I had prepared for them to be furious and got myself geared up to defend myself. But my father stands before me a broken man—he looks ten years older than he did this morning. And he is as heartbroken as if someone has died. I've never seen him like this before. And if he is like this . . . what kind of a state is my mother in? I can't believe that they feel that they are somehow at fault and the fact that they do is deeply shocking to me.

We have a cheerless meal. It is the first time that

Granny has come downstairs and had a meal with us and even though she talks only about the weather and Christmas shopping she is the life and soul of the party. If she hadn't been there I don't think a single word would have been uttered. I sit and eat solidly. I shovel food into my mouth while trying to ignore the fact that my mother appears to be eating only single grains of rice, and my father is drinking too much wine and staring into space.

I escape to my room and phone the twins. I manage to get hold of Sienna. I tell her about my parents' guilt trip and she says, 'I know this isn't going to make you feel any better but I understand where they are coming from. If you must know, Flo and I feel pretty bad about what has happened to you . . . '

'Bad?' I echo.

'Guilty, concerned, conscious that we've let you down . . . ' Si elaborates.

'What on earth are you talking about? This is crazy!' I say. 'I can't understand it at all. This baby was my mistake—my problem . . . no one else's.'

'Well, Flo and I talked about it and we decided that if we'd been better friends to you—If you had trusted us more—you might have told us earlier and we could have helped you sort it out. Or, if we hadn't been so wrapped up in ourselves and our summer holiday plans, you might have talked to us at the time—asked our advice about going out with this person. Because we worked out the dates and it must have happened when we were away. So we weren't around when you needed us. But, even when we came back, we weren't much help to you, were we? I mean . . . you didn't feel you could confide in us, did you? We feel bad about it. I mean friends should look out for each other—especially as we all promised we would be like sisters. We both feel very guilty and upset, if you must know. And we wish there was something we could do now . . . But we can't think of anything. Although I think Flo has a few ideas about what she would like to do to the guy, whoever he is . . . '

I groan. 'Please tell her not to bother. It won't help. You're never likely to meet him. He was a ship passing in the night,' I add dramatically.

'If you say so,' Si says kindly. But she isn't the one I have to worry about.

'Please tell Flo to forget all about it. Her going on the rampage isn't going to help now. You could start knitting! That would be a help!' I add brightly.

'Oh yes,' Si says cheerfully. 'I knitted a dishcloth from string in Year Seven and I think I can still remember how to do it. And they'll be little teeny weeny clothes so they won't take long.' She laughs and adds, 'The dishcloth was full of knots and took forever to make but I think I lost interest because it was so boring.'

'If you need any help my granny is good at knitting and sewing,' I say helpfully. 'Try to get Flo to forget all about the baby's father. You will try, won't you, Si?'

'Yes, I will, but you know what she's like,' Si says slowly. 'And the fact that she feels she has let you down has made her worse. She's been going off like Sherlock Holmes—looking for clues. I told her it really was none of our business but she says it is and that we owe it to you.'

I wince as I reply: 'You don't owe me anything. You've been fantastic friends to me. Some people would have stopped talking to me completely. Try to talk some sense into her, please, Si!' I beg.

'I'll do my best. But just promise me that, if there is anything I can do to help, you will let me know. I'll come to the hospital with you, if you like,' she offers shyly.

'But you've hated hospitals since you had your tonsils out and had such a bad time,' I say.

'Yes, I know I do. But I will come with you and hold your hand. I'd do it for you,' she adds.

'That's really kind of you,' I say gratefully, because I know what a big deal it is for her. 'I've been feeling quite phobic about hospitals myself since going to see Granny B in Leeds,' I confess.

'Well, we can look after each other, and then go and have coffee and muffins at Starbucks afterwards as a treat,' she suggests.

'That sounds great! We'll do it. And please don't beat yourself up about not being around for me. You and Flo have been the best friends ever. And tell Flo I don't want any revenge.'

'I'll do my best,' she says. But she doesn't sound very confident. And neither am I.

# CHAPTER FIFTEEN

My mother insists on coming to see the doctor with me. I know that she is stacked out with work and I feel really bad that she has to take time off when she is so busy. I keep on saying I can go on my own but every time I speak I am met by stony silence.

She looks terrible. She's put on make-up but it doesn't help, it shows up the bags under her eyes and the hollows under her cheekbones. She's lost so much weight that her smart business suits have started to hang awkwardly on her shoulders.

The doctor's surgery is in the next village so we have to drive. The silence in the car is worse than the silence in the house. I fiddle with the radio, switching stations, just for something to do.

The surgery is mercifully empty and we get in to see the doc straight away. I had dreaded sitting for ages in a stuffy room with people staring at me. The doctor is a young woman I've not seen before. Mum mutters to her, explaining why we have come. Then the doctor sends Mum out while she examines me. She is very brisk and professional and confirms that I am approximately twenty-four weeks pregnant and the baby is due some time in March. 'I'm assuming that you want this baby, because you've left it much too late for a termination,' she says.

'Yes, I want it,' I mutter. I am upset and I realize that I was totally unprepared for the shock of being examined. As I get dressed I say a little prayer of thankfulness that the doc is another woman and not a man. It's not that it was painful or anything—just embarrassing—and it made me feel like an animal, somehow naked and without dignity. It is also a huge shock to finally have my pregnancy confirmed. Even though in my heart I have known about the baby for ages, and thought that I had accepted it, I find it startling and somehow unsettling to hear it from someone else—especially a doctor. As I pull on my socks and push my feet into my shoes the carpet blurs. My eyes are full of sharp tears.

'You're sure you want this baby, aren't you?' she queries, as if taken aback by my sudden attack of blubbing.

'To be honest with you, I wasn't sure at first,' I say, wiping my eyes with my fingers. 'But now I do want it. It's just the timing isn't brilliant. I'm in the middle of my A levels. And my parents are very upset.'

She hands me a tissue, but doesn't say she's sorry or anything like that—instead she busies herself with handing me leaflets. At the same time she is rattling off instructions about what I must not eat and telling me that I mustn't drink alcohol at all.

'I haven't touched a drop—or coffee—since day one. Just the smell makes me feel sick,' I say.

'That's good,' she says encouragingly. 'Hop on the scales. I'll make you an antenatal appointment at the hospital. Your weight is fine,' she adds.

'Really? That's a surprise. I can't stop eating and I've doubled in size! I'm huge! I thought you'd be sending me off to Weight Watchers!' I exclaim.

'Before you were pregnant did you have issues with your weight?' she asks, giving me a sharp sideways glance.

'Issues? What do you mean by issues?'

'Did you diet excessively? Did you ever make yourself sick after you'd had your supper?'

'No!' I say, startled. 'Of course I didn't do that. Anyway . . . ' I add defensively, 'I've never needed to diet—my mother is like the food police. We're not allowed junk food, or anything which isn't a hundred per cent healthy, in our house. Why do you ask?'

She just shrugs and ignores me as she makes notes on the computer. Finally she looks up and says, 'You're doing very well. Keep on eating a balanced, varied diet because you'll need all your energy once the baby arrives.' She adds kindly, 'I'm going to be working here for a while so I'll see you again. Just pop in or give me a ring if there's anything you are concerned about. Will you ask your mother to come in to see me now?'

Mum is in the consulting room for ages. When she comes out her eyes are all red and I can tell she's been crying. 'What did the doctor say to you?' I ask curiously.

'She told me that babies are like buses—they rarely

arrive just when they are wanted but are very much appreciated all the same. I suppose that was meant to make me feel less of a failure as a parent,' Mum says bitterly. Then she adds, 'Oh, and she gave me some tablets to help me sleep.'

But I can tell that this is only half the story and I ask, 'Did she ask if you had issues about food? Did she tell you to stop dieting?'

Mum doesn't answer me. Instead she says stubbornly, 'I'm not dieting. I'm just eating sensibly.'

'Mum, you're not eating at all . . . '

We pull up outside our house. Mum doesn't cut the engine. She doesn't look at me as she says, 'You know I can't eat when I am stressed.' Then she adds firmly: 'I'm going in to work, see you later.'

'Shall I cook something for supper?' I say desperately, because I can't imagine a future when she's not stressed after the mess I've made of my life. 'Maybe you'd feel more like eating if you didn't prepare it . . . I could make a shepherd's pie? And I promise I won't use a real shepherd,' I add, because this is one of Dad's favourite little jokes.

'Thank you, Emily. That would be lovely,' she says. She turns to me and tries to smile, but I see that her red-rimmed eyes are once again full of tears.

'I'm sorry, Mum,' I say a bit desperately. 'I am sorry about the baby and I'm really sorry that you and Dad feel you are to blame. Because you're not . . . '

'We must have gone wrong somewhere . . . for things to have turned out so badly . . . ' she says brokenly. 'We'd always thought . . . if you had a problem . . . we would be the first people you would turn to—not the last.'

'You're not the last . . . not the very last . . . ' I say, but my voice is unconvincing even to my own ears. I lean across and aim a kiss at her cheek. I miss and graze her hair instead. 'You get off to work. I'll look after Granny. See you later,' I say, and I get out of the car quickly because I want to get away from her hurt expression and misery-etched face. Just looking at her makes me feel really sad.

I had assumed my parents would be angry with me. Since I first realized I was pregnant I'd gone over how it would be when finally they found out. I had heard their voices in my head—loud angry voices—asking why I had joined the Kissing Club and taken a vow in a church hall if I was going to fall into bed with the first boy who came along (and get myself pregnant). I thought they would ask for the ruby ring and take it away from me for ever as a punishment. I thought they would be shocked and horrified—angry and outraged. I thought they would question me, want to know all the details. But instead they are on the ropes and desperate: too upset and full of remorse to insist that I tell them the name of the baby's father, or the reasons why I'd had unprotected sex. They seem to feel that it's their entire fault—not mine . . .

Maybe the anger will come later. In a weird sort of way I hope that eventually they will be angry with me. If we had a blazing row it might be easier—then we could shout and scream about all the things which over the years have made us unhappy. They could tell me I am spoilt, and I could reply that is because I am an only child and if they hadn't been so selfish I would have had a brother or a sister (and then I wouldn't be spoilt, would I?). And they would throw back all the sacrifices they have made so we could live in the country. For them living in the country is the culmination of some kind of dream. But I might have been just as happy (maybe happier) living in Leeds. They would tell me that the reason I have always had everything I ever wanted or needed was because they both worked full time. And I could counter that by saying they have always been obsessed with their careers and making money. And consequently haven't had enough time for me . . . And that I have been lonely all my life . . .

And some of it would be true . . . but it would only be part of the story. Try as I might I can't find it in my heart to blame my parents. They have tried hard to make a good job of bringing me up—they have done the very best they could. And now they feel they have failed. That knowledge sits like a heavy burden on my shoulders. I feel weighed down by it—almost overwhelmed.

When I get into the house I find Granny in the kitchen. She looks as bad as I feel. She is slumped in a chair. There is a lump on her forehead and she has the beginnings of a black eye.

'Granny! What on earth have you done? You look as if you've been in a fight!' I say with astonishment.

She gives me a crooked grin and says, 'My ankle gave out and I took a tumble down the stairs. Will you get me some frozen peas, love, to put on my eye. I think I've the makings of a real shiner.'

I fuss over her, finding cold stuff to put on her bruises. And then I make a big pot of tea and lace her cup with lots of brown sugar.

'I could do with a drop of the hard stuff in here. It's good for you when you've had a shock,' she says longingly, as she stirs the mug of tea I have set before her.

'No! You don't want any of that,' I say briskly. 'It will be like the cigs. You'll have lost the taste for it now you've had a break.'

'Do you really think so?' she questions.

'Oh, definitely,' I say encouragingly.

Granny insists that she is well enough to do dress-making, so I spread the sketches of my dream dress out on the kitchen table and she sits and studies them. Finally she says, 'I know just what you want, love. Come on. We'll cut it out and get sewing.'

Cutting the material is a nightmare: it covers the sitting room floor like a great pool of dark water and we have to crawl around it, snipping away. It takes forever and the day is growing dark by the time we finish. Finally it is all tacked together and we are ready to sew. I help Granny up the stairs to my room where I have put the sewing machine out on my desk. But the sewing machine won't work—it just makes a horrible whirring noise and nothing happens.

'The motor has gone,' Granny says knowledgeably.

'Can we fix it?' I ask.

'No. It will have to be replaced,' she says.

My eyes fill with tears of frustration. I am desperate to get my dress ready and to make matters worse we'd had a hurried lunch and I am now very hungry.

'I suppose we could do it by hand,' Granny says doubtfully. 'But it will take time. How long is it until your party?'

'It's on December thirtieth. It's a Christmas and New Year party combined,' I mutter, trying not to sound as miserable as I feel, because it isn't Granny's fault the sewing machine won't work.

'I might get it done, but it's a bad colour, very tiring on your eyes. And I'm going home tomorrow or the day after. Depending on when your dad can give me a lift,' Granny says.

'Mrs Patton has a sewing machine!' I say. 'Maybe we could borrow it.'

I ring Mrs Patton and she says of course I can use her machine. But it is something called a 'treadle' and can't be moved, so she kindly invites Granny and me to her house to do the sewing. So we roll up the dress and pack up all the things we need. Then we make our way down to the village. It takes ages and Granny is white and shaking by the time we get there, even though I've held on to her arm and helped her along while we've been walking.

Mrs Patton and I get Granny settled at the machine and then I take Peaches for a little walk. When I get back I find that Mrs Patton has prepared a wonderful afternoon tea for us: tiny ham sandwiches, fruit scones, crumpets, three kinds of jam, a honeycomb and a farmhouse fruit cake. I am in heaven.

I have to take Granny's tea up to the spare room because she says she can't manage the stairs again.

When Mrs Patton and I are having our tea she turns to me and says, 'You know, my dear, I don't really think it can be right that your poor granny should be in such pain with that ankle after all this time. Are the hospital sure it was only a sprain? I think she really needs to go back and have it looked at again. I wouldn't be happy with it if I were her.'

'Yes, it has been a long time,' I say. I can't tell her that my parents are in too much of a stress about the baby to notice anyone else. They probably won't notice if poor old Granny B grew an extra head or turned bright green. I very much get the feeling they just want to get shot of her. Although how she will manage on her own I can't imagine as she can't walk without leaning on a wall (or holding on to me). 'I'll talk to Dad about it, promise,' I add.

'Good,' Mrs Patton says. 'I imagine she's not one to make a fuss. But she's obviously in a lot of pain, poor thing. And have you noticed how Peaches follows her around and sits down next to her? Peaches always seems to know when someone needs comfort—and she's never been wrong.'

I leave Granny busy sewing (with Peaches sitting on her lap). I make my way home and set to work to make the world's best shepherd's pie. I go to a lot of trouble: mixing carrots, courgettes, and mushrooms in with the mince and creaming the potato carefully. I set the table in the kitchen and defrost an apple crumble. I'm really enjoying myself.

Dad is home first so I send him to fetch Granny to save her walking. We are all sitting at the table waiting when Mum comes home.

'Supper is all ready,' I say. 'Come and eat.'

Mum washes her hands and sits down. I bustle around, dishing up the pie and passing around the bowls of peas and sweetcorn which I have cooked to go with it.

'How did it go at the doctor's? Was everything all right?' Dad asks in a conversational tone. He is looking at Mum a little nervously. He's trying to pretend that it's quite normal and proper to be asking your teenage daughter how her pregnancy is progressing. As if in time—if we all try very hard—it won't be a topic which can only be talked about in whispers.

'Fine,' I say, concentrating on my food.

'I'm sure Em'ly will manage all right if we all muck in and help,' Granny says brightly. Everyone but Mum is eating my lovely pie. She is moving her food around her plate and picking it over as if there might be gravel in the mince. I resist snapping at her and pointing out that it is not only perfectly edible but absolutely delicious.

Granny carries on talking. 'Megan's grannies took it in turns to look after her while I worked. She always had a lovely time with them. They would take her to the park to play on the swings and then they'd go home and bake cakes. They always made her favourite—sponge with butter-cream icing and Smarties on the top. Both her grannies were wonderful with her and had such a lot of patience . . . I never really hit it off with Phillip's mum, she gave herself such terrible airs and graces, but I do have to say she was a really lovely gran to Meggie. And—'

Before Granny B can continue with another trip down memory lane Mum interrupts her: 'They could be trusted with babysitting. They didn't drink . . . ' she says, and her voice is so sharp and cruel it cuts across the conversation like a scalpel.

There is a long painful silence in the kitchen, broken only by the sounds of the clock ticking and the clink of our knives and forks on the plates. I risk a glance at Granny. She is sitting staring at Mum with a wounded expression on her face.

'I suppose what you're trying to say is that because I like a little drink in the evenings I'm not a fit person to help look after Emily's baby,' she manages to say at last.

Mum glances up from her meal—which is still uneaten—and gives Granny a look of utter contempt: 'To be perfectly frank, when you've had a few I wouldn't trust you with a dog.'

Granny's chin quivers and her eyes fill. 'I don't know, Meg, I think that's unkind.'

'Hang on a minute,' I say heatedly. 'I think you're

being unfair, Mum. Granny made an OK job of bringing you up and she did it on her own which can't have been easy . . . '

'It's all right, love,' Granny says to me. 'Don't you go upsetting yourself on my account. If my having a drink or two means I won't be allowed to help look after my great-grandchild, even though I'm hale and hearty and have the energy of a woman half my age, I shall sign the pledge and give it up completely.'

'Sign the pledge?' I query.

'The temperance pledge. And I'll go to the doctor and ask for some tablets. They have ones that make you feel sick if you drink with them . . . or I'll go and be hypnotized. Yes! I'll do that. And then I'll join a self-help group. And while I'm at it I'll go the whole hog and give up the cigs as well. There, will that satisfy you?' she says to Mum.

'You won't do it,' Mum says dismissively, without looking up at her.

Granny looks exasperated. 'I've got iron willpower. If I say I'll give it up I will. Where do you think you got your willpower from? You inherited it from me. But you have to use it positively . . . not for starving yourself. Now get that meal eaten up,' she adds. 'You should be ashamed—sitting there picking at it when Em'ly went to such a lot of trouble to make it nice. It's delicious, pet,' she adds, looking across to me with an attempt at a smile. Mum puts her knife and fork down and stops pretending to be eating. Instead she stares at Granny with a blank expression.

'Would you really do all that for me and the baby?' I say to Granny. 'Go to the doctor and sign a pledge— and go to AA meetings and everything?' I can feel tears welling and my voice is breaking up. 'Would you really do that for me and the baby?'

'Of course I would,' Granny says firmly. 'Just you watch me. Now I'm not working I've all the time in the world. And you'll need all the help you can get. What could be more natural than looking after my own kin? I always regretted spending so much time away from Meg when she was tiny. I love babies. If I'd married the right man I would have had dozens.'

'Well, maybe not dozens, just three or four . . . ' I say, with a wobbly smile. 'You know you've told me a million times not to exaggerate.'

Granny, Dad, and I all look more cheerful—Dad even manages a bit of a grin. But Mum just gets up and empties her plate of food into the rubbish bin and starts to load the dishwasher. It seems such a waste of lovely food and I have to make a real effort not to lose my temper and tell her off.

Now the atmosphere has lightened—and Granny has made me feel more positive about everything—I really want to talk about my new dress. But Mum is in such a foul mood I don't feel I can mention it.

I look at the expression on Mum's face as she clears up the kitchen with staccato movements and the maximum amount of slamming and banging. She appears to hate everything in the world. In a moment of sharp self-pity I wonder if she will ever get over her despair with me—or if we will be locked for ever in an endless winter of disappointment. I have no idea what I could possibly do to make it all better—apart from magically turning the clock back to the time when I was a nearly perfect daughter. And as that can't be done it seems utterly impossible for us ever to be a happy family again.

# CHAPTER SIXTEEN

It is Mrs Patton who gets Granny's ankle sorted. She takes her off to the hospital and sits in A&E for hours while Granny is X-rayed. It turns out that Granny's ankle is broken not sprained. Mrs Patton takes Granny back to her cottage and gets her settled on a bed in the dining room as Granny has been told not to attempt stairs or walk too far. Mrs Patton tuts and fusses—it would drive me insane—but Granny seems to enjoy all the attention. Mrs Patton says Granny has got to stay with her and be 'looked after'. Everyone seems happy with this arrangement—especially Peaches who spends all her time curled up on Granny's lap.

My parents seem hugely relieved that Granny is out of the house but I miss her. Mrs Patton is sewing my dress and Granny is doing what they call 'finishing'. I have to go for 'fittings' (also I pop down there quite a lot just to see how it is getting on) so end up spending quite a bit of time with them both. I am actually quite jealous because Peaches loves Granny and I have to bribe her with choco drops to get her to come out for a walk with me.

I decide to keep my dress a secret so I only talk to

Corey about it. He pretends to be interested which is sweet of him. The twins are mad to know and it's lovely to have something light-hearted to kid them about. Now school is finished Corey and I fall into the habit of meeting up for lunch at my house and then taking Kizzy and Peaches for a walk before it gets dark.

Then, on the day before Christmas Eve, he arrives for our walk with red swollen eyes. I don't like to ask him if he has been crying but as it is he tells me straight away. 'Dad says Kizzy has to go to the golden retriever rescue to be re-homed. I asked if I could keep her but he said "No". He says he doesn't have time for her and I suppose he's right—and I can't very well take her to university with me, although I did think about trying it. She's going to the dog's home straight after Christmas. I feel really bad about it,' he adds a bit unnecessarily.

'Well, she's not really your dog, is she?' I say, trying to be kind. 'Now she's trained won't Lara and your brother take her back? I thought they were moving in together.'

'They are—but it's a flat and even if it was a mansion they wouldn't want her. Brett says she was an impulse buy. It seems so unfair. The one thing I hate about leaving Nell Acre is leaving her behind.'

I could get quite hurt by this comment as he doesn't sound as if he is going to miss me at all—and I shall certainly miss him! But I decide to be grown-up about it and manage to say calmly: 'I expect she'll soon get settled. You've made a wonderful job of training her.

She'll make someone a marvellous pet now, won't she?' I add brightly.

'Yeah, I suppose so. It's just I'll never see her again.' He looks away from me quickly. I don't like to say that she is only a dog because he is obviously upset. I don't mind Kizzy now—sometimes I quite like her—but I don't adore her. And I have to rationalize it by thinking about how I would feel if it was Peaches who was being sent away. It would be me who would be crying then!

'Never mind . . . ' I say, patting his shoulder awkwardly. I would like to give him a hug but I don't really know how to do it without pressing my big bump up against him.

Granny staying at Mrs Patton's saves my Christmas from being a total disaster. Mrs Patton goes to stay with her daughter and leaves me and Granny looking after Peaches (there's a new baby at the daughter's house and Peaches would be in the way). This is brilliant because it give me lots of excuses to get out of our house over the Christmas period and escape down to the cottage to visit Granny. Corey too seems to want to get away from playing Happy Families at Nell Acre with Lara, Brett, and his dad. So Corey and I spend our afternoons walking and then in the evening the two of us and Granny settle down in the sitting-room at the cottage to watch old films. We eat our way through boxes of chocolates, figs, and crystallized fruit washed down by ginger fizz.

I don't like to ask Granny if it's hard giving up the booze. Mrs Patton is a strict Methodist (she doesn't even use sherry in trifle!) and Granny can't make it out to the pub or the shop with her plaster cast so it's easy for her to be teetotal at the moment. I suppose the crunch-time will come when she is back in Leeds and in her usual routine. It's then that she'll need all the help she can get.

If it wasn't for this little oasis my Christmas would have been like a desert of distress and silence. My parents give me only money for a present. 'We thought it would be for the best. We discussed it and well . . . we decided that you'd need to buy things . . . all sorts of things for the baby . . . You know . . . ' Dad says awkwardly.

Their very generous cheque is embarrassing: firstly because it seems like a huge amount for them to give me and secondly because it takes me only a second to open it. I have bought them lots of little things to open— they each have a million parcels and it takes them ages to unwrap them all. And then afterwards the two piles of goodies sit under the tree as if abandoned. It seems impossible for them to cheer up—even for Christmas. I keep thinking about the First World War and how all the soldiers called a truce on Christmas Day and played football. I am tempted to ask my mother if we can do something similar but she is locked in such misery I am scared to speak to her in case I make it worse.

Granny on the other hand has taken the baby in her stride. She talks about it as if it is the most natural thing in the world. And, when she isn't working on

193

finishing my dress, she is busy knitting and making tiny little clothes. She says that having a beautiful layette is very important—it's like the first gift that a baby has on their very first birthday, which I think is a really lovely idea.

My dress is utterly and completely wonderful. Far more beautiful than I had imagined! I have to keep on reminding myself that it all started with a sketch in my book and now here it is. Granny cut all the material on the bias so it flows like water around me in graceful waves. She has put black beads, seed pearls, and sequins all around the neckline and bodice. It's totally flattering and the best thing of all is that my bump hardly shows. I don't look fat, or pregnant, I look glamorous.

I email Augusta and tell her all about the party in the village hall (I talk it up a bit). I also send a picture of myself in my new dress. She is wild with envy and emails back:

```
hi honey! u look amazing in ur
new dress. but what about my
wedding dress? FYI i have put on
another 6lbs. i hate my mom she
cooks all this food and force
feeds me. i think she is hoping
Wes will look at me and think I
am such a fat slob he won't
marry me after all . . .
help!!!!!!!! it is sooooooo hard
to diet when all I can think
about is SEX!!!!!!! i truly
believe i am comfort eating as a
```

```
replacement! i am so bad . . .
yesterday I had eight do'nuts—yes
eight . . . and it's all my
parents' fault . . . they are
prevaricating and keep saying we
are too young to get married &
too young to know our own minds.
I HATE THEM . . . and i know it
is wicked but i cant help it . . .
LOL your very unhappy friend,
Gussie.XXXXXXXXXXXXXXXXXX
```

Augusta sends me an email of herself in a wedding dress which she tried on in a store. It is too tight over her bust—in fact it is too tight everywhere—and makes her look about thirty. I do a few new sketches in my book and then show them and Augusta's picture to Mrs Patton and Granny.

'She has a wonderful figure, but she is large—and the guy she is marrying is very slim. He's gorgeous . . . but soooooo thin . . . ' I add. 'I thought something vaguely Edwardian would be lovely for him. A long jacket, because he needs to look manly.'

'A waistcoat . . . ' Granny suggests.

'Plump him out a bit . . . ' Mrs Patton adds. 'Let's look at the shoulders and the lapels.'

They chatter away. A lot of the things they suggest are really old-fashioned but some of them seem to make sense so I jot them all down.

'Now for the wedding dress. What do you want to do with that?' Granny says holding out her hand for my sketches. 'She wants to look demure. Your wedding day is not the time to show off your cleavage.'

They study the photo of Augusta and then they look at each other and sigh in unison. 'She looks as if she's been shoehorned into that dress,' Granny says regretfully.

'She looks as if she is gasping for breath, poor lamb,' Mrs Patton adds.

Granny holds up one of my sketches. 'This is lovely, Em'ly. She looks like Juliet on the balcony. It's so flattering.'

'Do you think it would work?' I ask, unexpectedly thrilled by her praise. 'I thought she needed something simple at the top. Her bust is enough without having anything extra. And I thought those little sleeves and the line of the neck would be better than something tight. I've used the same line on the bodice and then the real detail is in the veil and the skirt.'

I hand over more sketches. 'It is nice,' Mrs Patton says approvingly. 'Really lovely . . . it would be a joy to see it made up, wouldn't it?'

'Yes,' I say longingly. 'I'm always designing dresses and they never see the light of day.'

'I'll tell you what. I've got some old net curtains . . . and some left over taffeta from the girls' ballet skirts. We could make up the design in those—we could use the taffeta for the bodice and the nets for the skirt and veil. Then we could see exactly how the design works,' Mrs P suggests. 'We'll make it up to your friend's measurements and then she could try it on and see if she liked it. If she loved it we could offer to make the dress for her in silk.' Both she and

196

Granny laugh at this suggestion. They are like a pair of schoolgirls when they get together.

'Oh what fun!' GB says delightedly.

'I've got lots of bits of lace and sequins left over from costumes. We could use those for the decoration.' Mrs Patton is busily clearing the table as she speaks. 'Let's get started . . . ' she says.

'She's in America. I don't know if I would have time to send it to her.' I suddenly have cold feet about the whole plan. 'I don't want to waste your time,' I add.

'You're not wasting our time. We shall enjoy it. It's only a bit of old net curtaining, dear. Your granny and I like a challenge,' she adds, and they both laugh again.

'OK . . . Well, here are her measurements. But she seems to be getting larger by the day.'

'Don't worry! A good dressmaker is always kind and leaves a little bit of room for give,' Granny says. 'We'll cut it on the bias, like we did with your dress. That is very forgiving for the fuller figure.'

I leave them to it and take Peaches for a walk. By the time I get back the outline of a dress is hanging on the door and they are both busy sewing sequins.

'I felt quite sad when we finished your dress. It was such fun,' Mrs Patton says. 'It's lovely to have another project for us to work on together.'

'You should go into business,' I say. 'I expect lots of girls would love to have a hand-made wedding dress. I know I would if I was ever going to get married, which I'm not.'

197

'You don't know that for sure,' Granny says, looking at me over her glasses. 'You might change your mind.'

I send Augusta an email with a photo of the dress so far and a message.

```
Dearest Gussie—pleeze don't eat
any more do'nuts i can't believe
it is possible to eat eight
doughnuts in one day?????????
wat do u think of the dress.
Even tho' it's made out of
scraps it looks beautiful—white
and frothy like sea spray!!!!!
u will look like a princess in
it so tell me wat u think. LOL
EmilyXXXXXXXXXXXXXXXXXXXXXXXXXXXXXXXX

Hi Emily—it is possible to eat a
mountain of do'nuts if u are as unhappy
as me believe me!!!!!!!! i have
even thought about making myself
throw up which i know is a totally
gross thing to do—but i am getting
desperate . . . the only thing
which stops me is that we had a
discussion group at school about
it and, as well as being bad for
your health, it makes ur breath
smell like shit & the acid in your
vomit rots your teeth like
immediately!!!!!!!!!!!!!!!!! i keep
telling myself that if I am fat &
stink & have black stumps for
teeth then Wesley will certainly
not marry me . . . nway—the dress
```

198

looks amazing!!!!!!!!! everything
in the UK is just so classy!!!!! i
wish your granny and the other
lady could make it for me in white
silk with seed pearls and diamonds
for decoration!!!!!! i would like
a hand made lace veil as
well!!!!!! wat do u think?

GUSSIE!!!!!! do not even think
about the sick business—it is
gross and v.v. bad for u. i will
send you the mock up of the
dress when it is ready as long
as u promise not to be sick or
EAT ANY MORE DO'NUTS!!!!!! u have
to give me a promise!!!! i am
getting excited about the party
and cant wait to wear my dress!
everyone is going to be there.
L&LOL
emilyXXXXXXXXXXXXXXXXXXXXXXXXXXXXXX
XXXXXX

Everyone seems to be excited about the party and
talking about it. The really surprising thing which
happens is that my parents decide that they are going
to attend.

When I ask Dad straight out why this is he says,
'Your mother feels that we should support you.
Obviously everyone from the village will be there
and you want to go and see your friends. But we
don't want people to think that maybe we are
ashamed of you or anything negative like that. It's
family solidarity.'

'Granny is going,' I add. 'Mrs Patton has borrowed a wheelchair for her.'

Dad grimaces at me. 'Oh goodness . . . ' he says. 'Your mother is just getting her equilibrium back . . . I hope there isn't going to be a scene. Your grandmother is a bit of a party animal. I hope she won't get legless and show us all up. It's the last thing in the world your mother needs. At least she won't be able to dance,' he adds. 'I have vivid memories of one party where she did the Charleston on a table top and showed off her stockings and suspenders.'

'You poor old things,' I say. 'Can it get any worse? Talk about having the relatives from hell to look out for. A granny who can't be trusted near alcohol and a daughter in the advanced stages of pregnancy! Are you sure you don't want to stay home and watch TV?' Dad gives me this incredibly hurt look and I realize that my words have come out all wrong. I was trying to be light-hearted and witty and it hasn't worked.

'Your mother and I work very hard, as you well know. And you also know that Christmas is our busiest time. Frankly, we could do with a rest. But we thought it would be best for you if we show a united front. You do realize that everyone in the village will be tittle-tattling about you and the fact that you are pregnant, don't you? It's the down side of living somewhere small. If we still lived in Leeds no one would notice—or care two hoots if they did happen to find out. But people here are interested in each other.'

'Yes, I know . . . ' I say meekly.

'We could move back to Leeds if you would be more comfortable with that. I was saying to your mother that the commuting is getting to be more and more of a hassle because of the volume of traffic.'

'I don't want you to do anything just because of me,' I say uncomfortably. 'I know you both love living out here.'

'Well, we're very fond of this house and we've enjoyed being part of the village. But really we moved out of town for you. We wanted you to have the best childhood possible. We didn't want you playing in the back streets or in a grimy city park. We wanted you to live somewhere green and beautiful with clean air.' He gives me a crooked kind of a smile. 'You'll find out about how hard it is being a parent soon enough. I didn't know what had hit me when you were born. It was a shock to realize that I would do anything in the world for you—and would move mountains if needs be to stop you being hurt or upset. Your mother and I wanted your life to be absolutely perfect. I suppose we still do—but it gets harder when your child grows up and becomes an adult.' He sighs and turns away from me. 'Anyway, your mother has decided we are going to the party with you. She says you've got a new dress that Granny has helped you make. It's very kind of you to let her join in with your project. I shall look forward to seeing you in it.'

'It isn't a hardship to spend time with her,' I say. 'We get on fine together. She talks to me about things . . . And I couldn't have made the dress without her. She's been totally brilliant. I designed it and Granny just looked at my sketches and then cut it out. She's very clever. I think she was wasted sitting in a factory at a sewing machine every day for all those years. She should have gone in for making posh frocks. She knew exactly what I wanted and more importantly how to achieve it. I've told her and Mrs Patton they should go into a dressmaking business together making wedding dresses. They could make a fortune.'

'Well, that's an idea. Granny B certainly needs something to keep her occupied. I might have a little chat with them about it. It might be worth considering,' Dad says.

# CHAPTER SEVENTEEN

I am full of nerves before the party. It seems like light years since I went out anywhere or got dressed up. I have to keep on telling myself it's only a party at the church hall and that the only people there will be from the village. But, even so, whenever I think of walking into that hall, seeing Mr Thomas, Brett . . . the twins . . . everyone . . . I get butterflies in my tummy. I am excited and scared both at the same time. Also, it seems totally weird to be going out with my parents. I'm not sure that them coming along is such a good idea. Mr Thomas's parties are fuelled by excessive amounts of food and drink and are noisy affairs. It's not my mother's scene at all. I'm afraid that at the moment her idea of a suitable social occasion would be a meeting of Quakers or a gathering of Weight-Watchers.

I'm in an agony of indecision about whether to tell them I'd rather they didn't bother and I am just as happy to tag along with the twins. I practise what I could say that would sound sympathetic and not as if I can't bear to be seen out with them.

But, when I dare to broach the topic of how much

they hate parties, and what a drag it is going out on a cold winter's evening, Mum snaps at me: 'Your father and I have discussed it. We have decided that it is in your best interest for us to show a united family front.'

This is terrible—because now I know for sure this is another sacrifice for me! But I don't want an upset so I mutter something about how great it will be for us to spend some quality time together and drop the subject. It is only the thought of wearing my new dress that cheers me up. It is amazing. After I am dressed I stand in front of the mirror for ages, glorying in the sight of myself. I look tall, I look slim (well kind of), and what is more important I certainly don't look pregnant. The soft material gathers around me like a dark cloud and shimmers out into a graceful skirt. The colour makes my skin look pale and turns my hair from dull hamster brown to a rich honey colour.

I go down to Mrs Patton's to show her and Granny how I look.

'I've got something which will look lovely with that dress,' Granny says. And she hobbles into the dining room and gets her jewellery box. My heart sinks because Granny wears lots of beads and bangles. It's the kind of stuff my mother describes dismissively as 'hippy junk'. And I can't imagine that any of Granny's 'flower power' baubles will look right with my lovely retro dress.

Granny rifles through her jewellery box and finally

produces a string of gleaming pinkie-white pearls: 'This is what I've been looking for!' she says, holding them out to me.

'Pearls are right back in fashion!' I say delightedly, which makes her laugh.

'I know they are, pet. And do you know I haven't ever worn them. They belonged to my mum. To tell the truth, I think they were my gran's. They're good ones, which is why I've kept them safe. But I've never liked them. I always thought they were frumpy old things.'

She has earrings that match and a bracelet. It is the finishing touch and when I've put them on and preened myself in front of the mirror I am desperate to get to the party and see the twins.

My parents come to collect us and we all walk down together. Dad pushes Granny in her wheelchair.

'This will be good practice for you,' Granny tells him gaily. 'Get your muscles ready for pushing the pram.' She laughs, but there is silence from my parents and I am pleased that the darkness shields their faces.

The church hall looks nothing like it does normally. It is festooned with flowers and masses of glitzy gold Christmas decorations. It also smells wonderfully of booze and food. Inside there is loud music and people dancing.

Mr Thomas is at the door, welcoming everyone. 'Come on in! Mr and Mrs Sutton! I'm so pleased you could come!' he yells. He seems genuinely lit up to see them. And his enthusiasm is so genuine that even Mum unbends a little and murmurs that he mustn't be so formal and to please call them Megan and Stuart. And then she introduces GB and explains about her ankle.

Mr Thomas immediately bends over Granny's wheelchair to kiss her cheek. 'You poor little sweetheart,' he says to her. 'Now, what can I get you to drink? We've a full bar but there is also my very own recipe punch, which packs quite a kick! I call it "Mule Fuel".' He laughs at his own joke. 'Would you like to start off with a glass of sherry, or a mulled wine, or will you risk the punch? Go on, be brave,' he says to Granny, grinning down at her.

She beams up at him from her wheelchair and jangles her bracelets. Maybe it's because she's lower than everyone else that she feels she has to shout, or maybe it's that there really is a lull in the noise from the room, but for whatever reason her voice comes out blaring just as if she's got a megaphone: 'A soft drink for me, please, and don't slip a vodka into it whatever you do! I've gone on the wagon. I'm strictly teetotal!'

'What, at Christmas time! And at my farewell party,' Mr Thomas says regretfully. 'That's a pity.'

'There's more to life than boozing,' Granny says, grinning up at him like an imp. 'For a start I won't have a hangover tomorrow. But the real reason is, you see, I'm going to be chief babysitter when Emily's baby arrives. That's why I'm on a promise to give up booze and cigs. And I'm doing really well—can't you see my halo? I'm going to be a heavenly great-granny.'

'A great-granny! Never in the world! What's all this about Emily's baby?' Mr Thomas can't hide his astonishment. Granny's voice was loud but his is way beyond loud. It booms like a foghorn. I get the distinct impression that everyone in the hall has stopped talking and dancing and turned to listen to him. 'Emily's having a baby?' he echoes again, just to make sure that every single person (and probably the rest of the villages between here and Leeds) has heard correctly.

Then he turns and looks at me and, if it wasn't so awful, it would be funny because he looks so confused and surprised. It's as if he is a cartoon character with a big bubble over his head containing a giant question mark.

'Emily's baby?' he says again to himself in a small hurting kind of voice. He turns to Granny and adds beseechingly: 'Not your little Emily . . . surely?'

Granny seems oblivious to the fact that she has sent him into shock and possibly ruined his evening as well. She nods her head serenely and then says: 'Yes, due in March. I'll tell you what—I think Emily and I would like some orange juice, thanks.'

'Oh, yes please! Orange juice would be lovely!' I say brightly, hoping that this request will stop him gazing at me with such a sorrowful expression. He escorts us to the bar as if he is in a trance. He tells the barman what we want and then he turns to me. I can tell from the earnest expression on his face and the anxious look in his eyes that he wants to talk to me about the baby. I get this weird premonition that he is going to ask

207

me straight out who the father is. Mr Thomas is very kind and generous but he is also very blunt and speaks his mind. I gulp at my orange juice and wonder if he would be prepared to listen to a story about an angel-assisted-conception. But Christmas is a bad time for telling that story—it's far too topical. But there is no way I could ever tell Mr Thomas the truth—especially not at a party when he is drinking.

To my relief the doorway is suddenly full of new arrivals and he moves off to greet them. There are loads of people pushing through and I can see from their clothes that it is snowing hard again. Everyone is laughing and commenting on the weather, busy brushing snow from their shoulders and hair.

They move like a wave into the warmth and light of the hall. One of them is Brett Thomas—he's not the tallest but he catches my attention all the same. It's been months since I last laid eyes on him and he looks like a stranger. I stare at him as if he is an alien species. His hair is too long and his tan too intense for this time of the year when everyone else is winter-pale. As I gaze at him I wonder why I have spent the best part of my life thinking he was the only boy worth bothering with. Because now—having grown up fast—I don't think if we met for the first time I would give him a second glance.

The twins have arrived in the crush and are mobbing me, commenting on my dress, telling me how marvellous I look.

None of us really notice Brett closing in on us. It

is only when Sienna says artlessly: 'You don't look pregnant at all, Emily. In fact you look awesomely elegant. Like a model from the nineteen fifties. Do you agree, Flo?'

Then we realize that our group of three is actually a group of four and Brett Thomas is looking at me as if I am ET—only when he speaks it's his voice that sounds a bit like ET's from the shock of what he has overheard.

'What did you say?' he says, looking directly at Sienna.

Si blinks and takes a deep breath. Then she says in a rush: 'I was just commenting on the fact that Emily looks awesome. In fact I think she looks just like Audrey Hepburn! Her granny made her dress. I wish she'd make one for me. It's amazing . . . '

'No! Not that,' he interrupts her irritably. 'You said something about her being pregnant.' His gaze rakes over the three of us in an accusing manner. Just for once his charming exterior has failed miserably. He's rattled and he can't hide it.

'Did I?' Si says lamely, and she gives me an agonized look in an attempt to say she is sorry.

'Are you?' he says to me. His voice isn't loud but it is steely.

I shrug my shoulders in reply and turn away from him. I have no intention of being intimidated into answering him.

'Is she?' he says to the twins. Si is looking away into the middle distance with a vacant expression on her face—which is how she copes when things get too much for her. I can tell that she is embarrassed by her slip and by his reaction. Flo on the other hand is staring at Brett Thomas with a small tight smile and a sharp gleam in her blue eyes. I would be seriously worried if I were him. It's not nice when Flo looks at you like that.

'What's it to you if she is?' Flo says coolly.

Brett Thomas stares back at her. Over the years I'd always thought that if Brett was going to fall in love with one of us it would have to be Flo because she is the prettiest and the most lively and intelligent. She is also the wittiest and the best fun. Si and I have always been in her shadow, trailing behind her, following her lead and trying to keep up. But now, suddenly, as I see Brett and Flo eyeballing each other, I realize that, on some instinctive animal level, they don't really like each other very much. Or maybe what I am picking up on is that he is afraid of her . . . She's certainly not afraid of him. She smiles at him—only it isn't a proper smile, it's more of a contemptuous sneer.

'Could it be a guilty conscience, maybe?' she asks.

'I don't have a guilty conscience . . . ' his voice trails off. He turns to me; just for a moment I see a shocked, almost hurt, expression in his eyes. 'It's nothing to do with you, anyway, Florence-Devereux-Big-Mouth,' he adds. It's such a hopelessly childish remark that I can't help smiling briefly. Then I toss my head, conscious of the lovely pearls gleaming, and start to walk away from them. I want to find Corey and talk to him.

But Brett Thomas comes after me and puts his hands around my waist, or where my waist would be if I didn't have a great big bump hidden under the soft folds of material. 'Come and dance with me,' he says.

I wriggle away from him: 'No thanks. I want to talk to Corey.'

'What do you want to talk to Corey about?' He is frowning now and he moves quickly and slides his arms around me. He presses his body right up against mine and I know the exact moment he realizes that I am well and truly pregnant. I see him flushing—his face under his perma-tan turns an ugly brick colour and his mouth sags. He looks as if someone has hit him over the head with a heavy weapon.

'For crying out loud . . . Emily . . . ' he says beseechingly. 'Didn't you think to ring me?' I hear him swearing to himself under his breath. Then he shakes his head, as if trying to pull himself together, and asks, 'What are you playing at? When were you going to tell me?'

'Never . . . ' I whisper, and then I burst into tears. Immediately the twins are by my side pushing him out of the way.

'Leave her alone!' Flo hisses, thrusting her face right into Brett's in an act of outright aggression. 'Haven't you done her enough harm?' she adds furiously.

'It's none of your business, you mouthy cow,' he hisses back. 'This is between me and Emily,' he adds furiously, and then he reaches out and tries to get hold of one of my hands—but Flo and Si are like jailers, one on each of my shoulders, and he can't get near.

'Do you want to speak to him?' Si asks me in a whisper. I shake my head and then they move me off in the direction of the Ladies, leaving him stranded in the crush of people.

By some miracle the Ladies is deserted, but we all know that this is a state of affairs that won't last for long.

'Emily, just tell me one thing. Did he pressurize you into it?' Flo says, her voice low and urgent.

I shake my head.

'How on earth then . . . ?' she asks.

Si has her arm around me and is handing me tissues. I answer Flo because I know it's pointless not to. She will get the information out of me somehow. So I blurt out: 'It was last summer. I was really lonely and fed up because everyone was on holiday but me. I got a job at the strawberry farm and Brett came down one afternoon. Once he knew I was there he came down quite a lot. I was flattered that he was hanging around me. I didn't mind that he teased me. You know what he's like. It was just so hard to be cool about it. And when he actually asked me out I thought I was going to die from happiness. But it was all very casual . . . he never made out it was going to be a love affair. In my heart I think I knew I was just an amusement until he got back with Lara. But I was out of my head. I wasn't thinking straight,' I finish lamely.

'If only we'd been around . . . ' Flo says through gritted teeth. 'He took advantage of you . . . the bastard,' she adds.

'Flo . . . ' I say brokenly, 'I wish I could tell you that was how it was. I wish I could tell you that he got me drunk, or persuaded me, or make out that I have got some excuse for my appalling behaviour. But I can't pretend . . . It really was all my fault.'

'That's nonsense!' Flo says dismissively. 'He's just made you feel like that to get himself off the hook. He is older than you. He should have been more responsible.'

'It's not his fault that girls find him irresistible . . . ' I say bitterly.

'Shut up!' Flo says fiercely. 'You are NOT to keep putting yourself down. He's eroded your self-respect. You are worth ten of him. He's nothing but a conceited, over-sexed tom cat. He needs neutering. I'm going to get him if it's the last thing I do!' she adds. Her blue eyes are flashing like electric sparks and her body is tense as if she is going to run in a race.

I grab at her arm in a moment of panic. 'Flo, please leave it alone. It won't help. If he was fifty per cent to blame the other fifty per cent is fair and square on my shoulders. I got completely carried away emotionally and physically. I thought he was falling in love with me. I thought if I went all the way it would make him love me. But he didn't love me at all—not one little bit. I really was just a plaything—a distraction. But he didn't lie to me or anything. And when he dumped me he told me the truth: that I was coming on too strong.'

'Well, he's going to find out that it's me that's

coming on too strong now!' Flo says angrily, twisting away from me.

'What are you going to do?' I ask, grabbing at her and missing.

'I'm going to tell his father!' she says triumphantly. 'I'm going to tell Mr Thomas what a no-good toerag he's got for a son. He'll go ballistic—you know he will. I shan't have to do anything more . . . and neither will you . . . ' Her face is very calm, but her eyes are flickering with emotion. It's like watching lightning. She is seriously scary and utterly determined.

'Flo, please. I don't want him paid back. I don't want any trouble,' I beg. 'You don't know what you are doing . . . '

'Oh, I know all right,' she says. 'It is very simple: it's the basic rule of the jungle—dog eat dog. Just stand back and watch. He's got to pay for what he's done, it's only right: an eye for an eye and all that.'

'FLO! NO!' I say in panic. But it is no use. The door of the Ladies opens and three large women come in: Mrs Ives, Mrs English, and Mrs Martin. Flo ducks and dives around them like a pickpocket on the run and gets out. But Si and I are trapped against the washbasins by the human equivalent of hippos in floral print and polyester.

'Sorry, lovey, are you wanting to leave? I thought you were queuing,' Mrs English says kindly to us, as she heaves herself out of the way of the exit. 'By heck, it's warm. We've come in here to cool off . . . It's like a sauna out there,' she adds, fanning herself with a hanky.

'We're not queuing, thanks. We're leaving,' Si says, and I take a deep breath as we squeeze past them. But we have lost valuable minutes and we both know there is no chance of catching Flo. I make a real effort to compose my face as we go out to face the music and the fall-out from Flo's revenge.

# Chapter Eighteen

Everything is happening in slow motion. Maybe it is the heat in the hall. Mrs English was right—it is like a sauna, as hot and humid as a rainforest from people and their sweat. Or maybe it is stress that makes me feel as if I am wading through treacle. The lights are too bright and my head is spinning. The scene before me is playing out as if I am trapped in a cinema and the projector is running at half speed.

Flo has cornered Mr Thomas by the entrance. I see his head bending down to catch her words. Then she turns and points to the stage. Brett and Corey are both up there. There is no music. Something is wrong with the sound system and they are trying to sort it out. I see Mr Thomas look across at his sons and his face contorts with emotion. His face goes red and stays red so that even his blue eyes are hot. He looks like a cornered bull whose nose ring is being twisted hard. I wonder in a moment of panic if his blood pressure is very high and Flo has sparked off a heart-attack.

'She'll end up with blood on her hands,' I moan to Si, who is holding on to my arm and supporting me as if I am in danger of collapse.

'Oh, jeez . . . ' Si groans. 'What is happening now?'

Mr Thomas is thundering through the party crowd—dodging around groups as if he is escaping from a rugby scrum. I see shocked faces, I see people staring. I see him at the edge of the stage and at that moment I close my eyes. When I open them I realize that Brett is still on the stage, staring down at the sound system, and Mr Thomas and Corey are disappearing out of the doorway into the darkness beyond.

'Why? What?' I say to Si.

'Come on,' she says urgently. She takes hold of my arm—and now we are following Mr Thomas's lead and dodging through the crowds until we get to the edge of the stage and grab hold of Flo.

She is busy snarling up at Brett: 'If you are trying to deny it . . . '

'He just said he wanted to speak to Corey—not to me,' Brett says in an irritatingly cool voice.

I grab hold of Flo's shoulder and pull her round. She is swearing in a low furious voice about Brett. 'Shut up, Flo! And tell me what you said to Mr Thomas?' I demand.

'I told him that I thought he might want to know that he was going to be a grandfather. And that I hoped he could find it in his heart to be happy about it. And what a shame it was that his son didn't want to tell him the news. He didn't let me say any more. He went off the deep end—almost foaming at the mouth. I knew he would be furious,' she adds with a degree of satisfaction.

217

'Did you tell him it was Brett? Did you say his name?' I ask.

'Nooooo . . . I don't think so. I don't think he gave me time,' she says. 'Why?'

'Well, don't you think it's odd that he's taken Corey outside?' I ask desperately. 'Oh, Flo! What have you done?'

'I haven't done anything. Why on earth would he think it was anything to do with Corey?' she asks in a mystified tone.

'I don't know,' I say. 'I've just got a bad feeling about it.' I look up at Brett. He is changing a fuse with utter concentration, as if he is a cardiac surgeon working on a transplant. I get the feeling that he knows that most of the women in the hall are watching him—noticing how his blond hair curls damply against his neck and his silk shirt clings to his shoulders. He is such a poser—and so much in love with himself—that I feel an unreasonable urge to slap him.

'Brett!' I call imperiously. 'What did your father say to you?'

He looks up slowly and shrugs. Then he says casually, 'Just said he wanted to see Corey outside. That was all. What have you got your knickers in a twist about?'

Flo mouths something incredibly rude at him but it's such a jumble of obscenities that it just makes him laugh.

'Don't bother with him,' I say, and my voice sounds small and scared—which is just how I feel. 'Flo, help me. I need to speak to Corey. NOW!'

I turn and look at the throng of people and my eyes fill because I don't feel as if I have the energy or will to move through them. But Flo looks at my teary face and says, 'Well, come on then, let's find him and get this sorted.' And then she takes hold of my arm and starts shoulder-barging her way through the crowd saying loudly, 'Excuse me!' in the rudest voice imaginable. She moves through the wall of people like an icebreaker navigating the Arctic, while Si and I flutter along in her wake like a pair of lost seabirds.

As we stagger out into the dark night I hear Mr Thomas yelling although I can't see either him or Corey. The noise is coming from the car park at the side of the church hall. Mr Thomas's voice is loud and thunderous: 'If you don't tell me the truth, you damned, arrogant little sod, I'll beat the living daylights out of you, so help me God! Don't tell me you don't know what I'm talking about. She's up the duff, lad! And I didn't need her granny to tell me that! You can see by the size of her belly that she's podding. And it wasn't the bleeding Christmas Fairy that put it there. To think after all we've been through with your mum and Brett's mum. How I've told you over and over that there's nothing more important in the world than your kids. Nothing! And I've lived it, lad,' he raves. 'I've lived it. I've done everything I ever could for you and Brett. I've worked my nuts off for you two. You've always come first . . . because in my book you never, ever turn your back on your kids. And you're not going to do it either, boy. Not in my lifetime. Now what are you going to do about this baby? That's what I want to know?'

I start to cry. I want to scream but shock and the cold air have driven the breath from my lungs. I try to run but the pavement is covered in snow and ice and my high heels are dangerous—Si and Flo take hold of my arms to stop me falling. I don't understand why Corey doesn't say something to his father: something, anything, to shut him up.

Arm in arm, we stagger like three puppets with tangled strings through the snow and into the car park. The moon is full and reflects off all the gleaming whiteness on the ground so Corey and his dad are silhouette figures on a brilliant stage. And then I see why Corey isn't speaking. He is leaning up against a car and there is a dark stain gushing from his nose.

'Jud gib bee a chance to heplain . . . ' he is mumbling. But his dad is too busy dancing with rage and ranting to even hear this. It is only my scream of total despair that stops him in mid-flight as if I've severed his vocal cords by the ferocity of my anguish.

'Corey!' I yell, and I jerk away from Flo and Si and catapult into his arms.

'Don't geb ip on ore dreth . . . ' he says.

'I don't care about my dress,' I weep. 'What has he done to you?' I have no handbag. I have no tissues. I have nothing to help him with. I put my hands around his face and wish I could kiss his busted nose and make it stop it bleeding.

Mr Thomas is suddenly at my shoulder, his face

creased with concern. 'Are you bleeding, son?' he asks brokenly.

'Of course he's fucking bleeding!' I screech at him. 'What have you done to him, you great bully . . . you brute . . . you apology for a father. You great useless heap of pig shit!'

Flo is next to me. Ever cool in a crisis she has run into the back of the hall and got clean tea towels from the kitchen. She wraps a chunk of snow in one and hands it to Corey. 'Hold that on your nose and tilt your head back,' she commands. 'It's only a nose bleed. Calm down,' she says to me.

'I didn't mean to hit him hard. But he wouldn't talk to me!' Mr Thomas says. 'He shouldn't play mind games with me. He knows I've got a short fuse . . . ' he adds lamely.

'Short fuse? Short on brains, don't you mean,' I mutter angrily.

'I'm sorry, son . . . ' he says. 'I'm sorry, Emily,' he adds to me. 'We should have been civilized about this and sat around a table and talked it out. It's just I was that taken aback and shocked. I just don't know why you kids couldn't have trusted me. I've always thought you would come to me if you were in a pickle. Not keep it hidden. After all—a baby—it's nothing to be ashamed of really, is it? I'll be chuffed to bits to be a grandad whatever the circumstances,' he adds, and his voice is gruff with emotion as if tears are gathering in his throat. My anger seesaws to pity and then back again.

'Why did you have to hit him?' I ask.

'He refused to talk to me about it. I can't stand being lied to.'

'He's not lying to you. It's nothing to do with him,' I say.

'Nothing to do with him? But she said . . . ' Mr Thomas blusters.

We all turn and look at Flo. Her face is calm but she is blinking too fast. I can almost see her complex, computer-like brain trying to work out what is going on. There is only a beat of silence before Flo says in her most conciliatory and sincere voice, 'I am really sorry. I shouldn't have spoken. I was in the wrong. It would be better for you to talk to Emily yourself and get the whole story from her. I was seriously out of order . . . Me and my big mouth! I'm really most terribly sorry.'

'That's all right, love, I suppose you were trying to help,' Mr Thomas responds. But he is looking at me with a worried frown.

I know I should say something to him, but I can't think about anything but Corey. I can't speak because I don't know what to say that won't hurt Corey dreadfully. And that is the last thing in the world I want. I can't stop thinking about how Corey has been my friend for all these weeks, and how he has never questioned me. Instead he has always been on my side and ready to help me. I've learnt to respect and like him and I realize with a terrible lurch of emotion that it is very, very important to me that he should like and respect me in return. But what hope have I of achieving that? I've never told him the truth. I haven't trusted him. He will probably never forgive me when he knows the truth about me and about how I got pregnant. And now—as if all that wasn't bad enough—he's got his nose broken into the bargain.

I would like to speak but the only noise I can manage is a whimper of despair. It's Corey who saves me (once again). He puts his arm around me and says, 'Bore cold. Bore ivering. Ou bust go inthide. Ib boing home . . . '

'Hop in the Range Rover. I'll take you up to Nell Acre. Maybe when you're cleaned up you'll come back to the party and forgive your old dad for being a complete arsehole . . . ' Mr Thomas says.

'I'm going with Corey,' I say to Flo and Si. 'I want to make sure he's OK.'

'It's a nose bleed for heaven's sake!' Flo says in disbelief.

But Si gives me a knowing, kindly smile and says, 'I'll tell your parents you'll be back in a little while.'

None of us speak on the short trip back to the Thomases' house. 'Have you got your key, son?' Mr Thomas says, as he pulls up at the front door. 'I suppose I better get back. Not that I feel in the mood for partying any more,' he adds. 'You know I'm sorry about landing one on you, don't you?' he finishes anxiously.

'Yeb . . . ' Corey says. He takes the tea towel from his nose and adds: 'Don't worry, Dad,' in a nearly normal voice.

'I'll make him a cup of tea and help him get cleaned up,' I say.

'You're not to walk back down in this snow, not in your condition,' Mr Thomas says anxiously. 'Give me a call on my mobile and I'll come and fetch you.'

'OK, thanks,' I say. Although returning to the party is not on my agenda at the moment. What I really want is to talk to Corey and make my peace with him.

The house is very quiet and orderly after the noise and heat of the party. Corey sits down in a chair next to the Aga and leans his head back. The tea towel Flo gave him is red and soiled. I wash my hands at the kitchen sink and then find lots of clean tea towels in a drawer and some ice cubes from the freezer. I gingerly sponge all the blood off Corey's face with a wet tea towel and then make him a fresh ice pack. 'There, keep leaning your head back and keep the ice on the bridge of your nose,' I instruct him bossily.

'It's stobbing . . . I fink . . . ' he says.

'I think you need to change your shirt. You sit still. I'll go up and find you a clean shirt and a jumper. You're shivering. I think it's shock.'

'By roob is the second . . . '

'I know . . . ' I say. Thankfully he's not in any state to ask me how I know the layout of the bedrooms at Nell Acre. But my face flames anyway at memories of visits I made here when Brett was alone in the house.

I make myself think about the job in hand, looking after Corey and then telling him the truth, as I run up the stairs. Then I rummage in his wardrobe until I find what I want: a denim shirt and a sweater. I return to the kitchen.

'Here we are,' I say with a cheerfulness I do not feel. 'Let me help you. Keep your head back. Don't wriggle. I'll undo the buttons for you.' I unfasten his shirt with fumbling fingers. He is as rigid and unyielding as a wooden post as I peel the shirt from his chest and pull it down over his arms and hands. He doesn't make a sound or move. It's as if he's pretending it's not happening. I pause for a moment, staring down at him. Undressed he looks thin and suddenly vulnerable.

'I can manage now . . . ' he says abruptly. And he drops the icepack and reaches for his clean shirt, carefully avoiding my eyes.

There is a moment of sharp silence between us. I look away quickly from his partial nakedness, his angular bones and the creamy ivory of his skin, and chew at my bottom lip until I find the courage to speak: 'I want to tell you the truth. I've wanted to tell you for ages, but it never seemed like the right time. I suppose I was scared. This baby, my baby . . . Well, it's Brett's baby too . . . That is what Flo was trying to tell your dad. It was Brett who . . . you know . . . got me pregnant.'

'I KNOW!' Corey says, and his voice is too loud. The words seem to echo around the kitchen like unwanted visitors. 'I've always known,' he adds more softly.

'So it wasn't Flo telling your dad this evening . . . ?' I'm not really sure what I am asking. Then I say with a puzzled frown, 'How can you have known?'

225

'Because Brett told me.'

'What!' I can't help gasping with astonishment. 'Brett told you? What do you mean, Brett told you?'

Corey pulls on the sweater and huddles down in the chair as if he would like to disappear. 'When I got back from holiday last summer . . . he told me. I think it was just about the first thing he said to me. That he'd been seeing you and . . . all the rest . . . He couldn't wait to tell me all the details and rub my nose in it,' he adds bitterly.

I am crying, sudden hot tears of temper and disbelief. 'Why would he tell you? Why? And why haven't you ever told me that you knew?'

'He told me because . . . well—he may come over as the boy who has it all but he's really quite insecure. He can't help competing with everyone over everything. And he knew he'd finally got one over on me. And the reason I didn't tell you was because it really wasn't that important.' He stops and then adds, 'Though I suppose I'd hoped that one day you might trust me enough to tell me yourself—but if you didn't want to tell me then that was fine as well.'

'I don't understand . . . ' I sob.

'For crying out loud, Emily!' he says, and his voice is suddenly really angry. Not loud angry but quiet and weary angry. 'Please don't act dim. You must know how I've always felt about you.'

'I don't know what you mean.'

'What do you mean, you don't know? You must have known that you have always been my favourite person in the whole world. I've always thought the twins were cool, but you—you are something else. I've been crazy about you since we moved here. Dad and Brett have taken the rip out of me for years because of it. That is why Dad immediately assumed the baby is mine. He must have thought I'd got lucky at long last. Some chance . . . ' he adds caustically.

'Corey—believe me, I had no idea. You kept it really well hidden. I would never have guessed.' I can't meet his eyes. I am scared to look at him. Scared of how I feel and how he might feel now. Has he been talking in the past tense? Or are these feelings current? I try to get a grip on what he's been saying to me . . . but my thoughts are dipping and soaring like summer swallows fly-diving and I can't bring them down to earth.

'Well, it doesn't matter anyway,' he says in a surly voice. There is a long silence then he says in a more neutral voice: 'Dad will want Brett to stand by you, maybe even get married eventually. He's got very old-fashioned views about parenting. But don't do it. Brett is incapable of being faithful to any girl. He thinks he's madly in love with Lara. He's even had her name tattooed on his butt. But he still can't stop cheating on her. I'm afraid he'd make you incredibly unhappy.' He adds more quietly, 'I don't think I could bear it if he did that.'

I mop my eyes and say, 'I think I need to lie down. I feel dizzy . . . It's been such a weird evening.'

He takes me into the sitting room and gets me to lie down on one of the big leather settees. Then he puts a match to the log fire and asks, 'Would you like a cup of tea or something?'

'I'm meant to be looking after you,' I say, snuffling noisily into a hanky.

'It's OK. It was only a nose bleed. I'm fine. Do you want a blanket or something, are you cold?'

'Yes, I am cold . . . a bit. What I'd really like is a cuddle.'

'With me?' he asks—and there is astonishment in his eyes.

'Yes, with you. But you'll have to watch out for my bump,' I say apologetically.

'That's OK, it's not huge, is it?' He stretches out on the settee next to me and puts his arms around me. For ages we just lie holding each other and then I mumble something about kissing his nose better and plant an awkward kiss on his top lip.

'You're not doing this because you feel sorry for me are you?' he asks gently.

'No. Neither am I doing it because I feel sorry for myself. I'm doing it because I feel confident enough to.'

We kiss each other solemnly and slowly. It feels very nice and very right.

We might have stayed there for ever but his phone rings. It is only then that I realize that we have been kissing for absolutely ages, and yet it seemed like only minutes.

'Yeah, yeah. We'll come back now. No . . . we're fine—Emily was a bit tired. Yeah, yeah, see you in five.' He turns to me. 'That's Brett. Dad's busy so he's coming to fetch us. Evidently people have started to ask where we are,' he adds, with a mocking half smile.

He gives me one more kiss and helps me up from the settee. Then we make our way to the front door. 'Emily,' he says, 'if we started going out . . . do you think people would think it was weird?'

'No. But I expect they'd assume you are the baby's dad though—which would seem kind of logical but a bit unfair on you.'

'Would that worry you, if people thought that?' he asks.

'No. Why should it worry me? Would it worry you—that's more to the point?'

'No, it wouldn't worry me. Not in the slightest.'

'Well, that's all right then.'

'Yes, it is, isn't it?' he says and we both laugh. Then he says more seriously, 'There's just one thing. I've never . . . I mean, there's never been anyone but you . . . ' He bites hard on his lip and looks away from me.

'It isn't a problem. I just wish I could say the same. Augusta says some girls in the Kissing Club take a vow of chastity after they've had sex but it seems a bit strange to me. I mean you either are a virgin or not.' I take hold of his arm and pull him round to face me. 'If I could turn the clock back I would, you know that, don't you?' I add.

'The world isn't perfect, Emily. Never has been, never will be. I can live with that.' He smiles to take the sting from his words. But even so I find myself wondering how he got to be the most grown-up member of his family even though he is actually the youngest. I suspect it will be part of a sad story and I hope one day he will tell it all to me so I will understand.

# Chapter Nineteen

I have a shock when I walk into the party because most people have left. The hall has that jaded look which signals the end of a massive booze-up. The buffet table is loaded with used glasses, dirty plates, and half-gnawed chicken legs. There are a few sad sandwiches abandoned on plates and some wilting salad in the bottom of bowls. The air is heavy with the stench of alcohol, stale food, and hot bodies.

I look at my watch and realize with amazement that Corey and I left early and have come back late. Who would believe that kissing could take up so much time?

Corey touches my hand and mutters something about sorting out the sound system. I am relieved when he moves away. I feel that when we are together it is impossible for people to look at us and not to see that we are in love. Brett didn't say a single word to us on the way down, even though we were careful not to hold hands or sit too close together.

Only a few diehards are left in the hall, propping up the bar and finishing the night with a glass or three of liqueur. To my surprise my parents are still here. My next shock is that my mother is dancing—and with Mr Thomas. They are doing the salsa and are totally engrossed in it. My father is sitting at the bar nursing a bottle of Tia Maria and watching them. I have never seen my mother dance before and I am amazed by how good she is.

'I didn't know Mum could dance. When did she learn to salsa?' I say to Dad. He gives me a weary smile.

'She couldn't salsa until tonight. But she's a fast learner. She's a natural where dancing is concerned. And she's invincible when she's had a few . . . She's on the "Mule Fuel". I think it must have happy pills in it. It's certainly cheered her up. I just need to get her home while she's still in a good mood. By the way, your friend is here. She's just in the Ladies freshening up.'

'Friend?' I query.

'You know, the lassie you were at school with,' he says.

'School?' I echo again, trying not to sound irritable. It's difficult because I am tired now I am away from Corey and Dad isn't making any kind of sense at all.

He slops some more Tia Maria and ice into his glass and says vaguely: 'She's come specially to see you. Go and say "hello". She's been here for ages and asking for you. Brett's been looking after her but to be honest I think she found him a bit boring. She kept on leaving him and coming over to talk to me.'

The music stops and my mother and Mr Thomas come to a halt. But within the beat of a moment a new rhythm begins and seamlessly they begin to dance again.

'They're really good at it, aren't they?' I say admiringly to Dad.

'They should be—they've been practising for hours. I'm ready for my bed.' He stifles a monster yawn and adds, 'Go and say "hello" to your pal. I think she'll have to stay with us tonight. Then we'll try to get your mum home. You tell her that you are tired, that might do the trick. I could have dropped down dead with exhaustion and I think they would have just salsa-ed over me,' he adds with a grin.

I turn away from him and at that moment the door to the Ladies opens and I hear a great yell: 'Emileeeeeeee.'

'Oh my goodness!' I am too startled to move. 'Gussie, heaven's above! What are you doing here?' Honestly, I couldn't be more surprised if she was an angel bringing news of the imminent birth of a baby, because Augusta is the very last person in the world I expect to see.

Augusta runs across to me and throws herself into my arms. She then bursts into a fit of weeping and wailing that is so extreme I am really concerned.

'What is it? Gussie, speak to me! Why are you here and what is wrong?' I say desperately to her.

'Oh, Emily! I need to talk to you. MY WORLD HAS ENDED!'

Her voice is really, really loud. The few people arranged along the bar, as well as the barman (who was washing glasses but has now stopped) are staring at us quite openly. The eyes and ears of everyone in the hall seem riveted on me and Augusta—apart from Mr Thomas and my mother. They are still dancing, as if they are clockwork dolls. They are oblivious to everything and everyone. Even without them there is too much of an audience for my liking.

I put my arm around Augusta and move her as swiftly as I can across the sticky floor of the hall and back to the sanctuary of the Ladies. I shut the door firmly and say: 'Calm down, Gussie. Take a deep breath! Come on, please, stop crying. Just breathe evenly for a moment. Now, try to tell me what the problem is. I'm sure it's something that can be sorted out. You're over-tired that's all. Are your parents OK?'

She nods. I am busy finding loo paper and wiping her face as if she is a little toddler.

'Wesley? He is all right, isn't he?' I probe gently. Despite my outward calm I am starting to feel panicky now. Her stress is highly contagious.

'NO!' Augusta shouts. 'Wesley isn't all right! He's over! Finished! Kaput!'

For one horrible minute I think maybe he's dead. But then I see the stubborn, angry look on Augusta's face—and it is definitely not the grieving face of a girl who would-have-been-a-widow-if-we'd-only-had-time-for-a-wedding.

'What's up with Wes?' I ask carefully.

She takes the wodge of loo paper from me and mops her cheeks. 'He's finally gotten around to telling me the truth. He's had sex!' she mutters without looking up.

'What! With you?' I say, baffled. 'How on earth did that happen? You must be a really heavy sleeper, Gus! Either that or he's completely useless at it . . . Are you sure it was sex and not something else?'

'Emily. PLEEESE! Don't be so ridiculous!' she says, and she is crying and laughing at the same time. I am beginning to wonder if she is hysterical and what the best cure would be. I reject alcohol and wonder how and where I can get hold of a cup of tea with lots of sugar in it. Come to think about it I could do with one myself. And possibly something to eat . . . I was a little peckish before, but now stress (and being parted from Corey) has left me feeling ravenous.

'Start at the beginning . . . I don't understand,' I say, hoping she will get it all over with fairly quickly.

I am mentally going through what there will be in the fridge at home, because I really don't fancy what is left in the buffet here. The idea of a fried egg sandwich, with a dollop of tomato ketchup, on wholemeal bread, followed by a slice of Christmas cake and a mug of tea arrives in my head like a vision—and my stomach gurgles in anticipation of such delight.

'Tell me everything!' I command Augusta. 'Now!' I add more forcefully.

Augusta sniffs a bit but then she blurts out dramatically: 'He said he was going to wait until our wedding night and then confess everything. I'm sure as hell glad he didn't! If he had waited until our wedding night in Paris to tell me he'd been a whore boy I think I would have killed him with my bare hands and then thrown myself in the Seine.' She begins to sob again as she asks, 'Do they have the death penalty in France? Or do you think it would be considered a crime of passion?'

'Augusta,' I say firmly, 'we don't have the death penalty in Europe. And if you had thrown yourself in the Seine you wouldn't have been around to find out, would you?' My tone becomes stern as I add: 'Now, cut out the bad movie scenarios, and tell me the facts. First of all, what exactly is a whore boy?'

Augusta looks tragic and her chin wobbles dangerously as she says, 'A whore boy—you know . . . a boy who sells himself.'

'Wes did that?' I gasp. I am beyond shock. I can't believe what I am hearing. If this is in any way true no wonder Augusta is crying. 'Are you quite sure?' I add.

'YES! OF COURSE I'M SURE!' she shouts at me. 'He told me himself! He says he's told me everything. He went with one of his mother's employers because she was rich and old and she spoilt him. And he's had girls too . . . '

'And how old was this woman—the rich one?' I ask.

'Oh, like real old. Thirty or something . . . '

'Well, not quite drawing her old age pension, but I know what you mean. Did he love her?'

'I don't know,' Augusta admits. 'I was just appalled that he slept with her, and let her buy him things and pay for him to study at college. And then she dumped him because he wasn't doing anything when he was away except drinking and running around with girls. It sounds like he was having sex with everyone and anyone.'

She gives a monster sigh and then adds pathetically: 'And then he went on to become a member of the Kissing Club. And he didn't just join and become a born again virgin, he become a mentor. And now he tells everyone that Jesus has chosen him. I thought he was truly wonderful, like a modern day saint. I really couldn't believe he was ever going to be truly mine . . . I thought the Lord had sent him to me because I had been such a good girl.'

Her chin begins to wobble and her lovely dark eyes fill with huge tears that spill down over her black lashes and splash onto her cheeks. She looks the picture of misery. I don't know what to say to make things better, so I give her a big hug.

'It's all spoilt, Emily,' she wails. 'He seems like such a fraud. I mean not having sex with him has been hell for me . . . and all the time he knew what sex was like and he kept on telling me that our pure love, and taking our vows in church, was much more important. But FYI it didn't feel good to me. Not at all! Sometimes I think the stuff we did was worse than sex . . . Although I don't know . . . having never done it properly . . . ' She stops, blows her nose and looks at me hopelessly. 'I don't suppose you know either, do you, Emily?' She squints at me as she blows her nose.

'You know, honey, you look kind of different . . . ' she says in a puzzled voice. 'That's a real pretty dress,' she adds kindly.

'Augusta, I look different because I am different. I'm pregnant. And before you ask, FYI it was casual sex and it was totally unsatisfactory—and the fall-out from it hurts like hell. The one thing I do know now is that there is an awful lot more to a relationship and loving someone than sex. I don't know what the answer is. I don't know if the Kissing Club is a good idea or not. I always thought it was brilliant and my life would follow the map that I had drawn up. But life is full of surprises, not all of them pleasant. I suppose the first big surprise for me was that I could lose everything—my self-respect, my virginity, my plans for the future, all gone in a moment of insanity. I suppose none of us are really sure what we are capable of until we are tested. Well, Gussie, I was tested, and I failed miserably. I just gave in . . . and not just once, several times. And I lied and said I was on the pill when the packet was lying unopened in my drawer at home. And now I have to make the best of it, because a baby is special. And I want to be the best mother I possibly can be. But it is hard. Knowing that I've let everyone down.'

'Oh, honey . . . ' Augusta wraps me in a giant hug and sobs damply into my neck. 'A baby . . . ohhhhh-hhhhhhhhhhhhhh I can't believe it.'

She cries for a while. Then she manages to stop and says, 'One thing for sure, Emily. We are way too young for this kind of trouble. You are too young to be a mother and I think maybe I am too young to be thinking of getting married. I wish we could go back to how we were when I first took you to the Kissing Club. We were so sweet and simple, and so was our life, isn't that right?'

'Yes, and we've both been in a great rush to grow up, haven't we?' I say. 'Well, you can go back to being sweet sixteen but I'm going to be a mother and there is only one way to do that. Having a baby is a big responsibility. I'm going to have to be grown-up, Gussie.'

'And so am I,' she says. 'I'm going to be your best helper and supporter. Just you watch me . . . I'll be here for you, whatever, believe me. And I shan't care what my parents say about it.'

'That's so sweet of you! It means a lot to me,' I say. And then I get a hormone rush and burst into tears, because all of this on top of finding out all the bad stuff about Wesley is too much for me.

All this crying brings the evening to a sudden and rather damp close. Augusta takes charge and before I know it we are in Mr Thomas's Range Rover with my parents and being driven home by Corey.

I try to take careful note of my mother, as I have never seen her the worse for drink before. She isn't stupid drunk or vomiting drunk, just rather dizzy and smiling.

'We had such a lovely party,' she says to Augusta. 'It's a shame you arrived so late. I haven't enjoyed myself so much for ages. And everyone has been so kind and supportive about Emily's baby. Mr Thomas— Danny, I should say—told everyone about it and it seemed as if everyone in the hall made a point of speaking to us and wishing us well. Mr Thomas is looking forward to being a grandfather. Of course it's different for men, isn't it? I could have postponed being a granny for a good few years but I shall make the best of it. And of course my mother will be a great-granny . . . she had me very young. I wasn't planned either . . . And I turned out OK, didn't I?' she turns to my father. 'I did, didn't I?'

Dad kisses her and says, 'More than OK. World class, I would say.' And her response to this is to throw her arms around his neck and kiss him back.

'I think you and Dad should take up dancing, Mum. You are really good at it,' I say quickly. Because, although I am pleased they are getting on, I don't really want to be stuck in the back of the Range Rover with them if they are snogging.

'We've never had time . . . ' she says.

'Well, we could make time, couldn't we?' Dad says. 'Work a little less and play a little more.'

'We'll have to work harder than ever now,' Mum says. 'Babies are expensive. Do you remember how fast Emily grew? She always needed new Babygros and shoes.'

'Well, we'll see,' Dad says.

'And Brett Thomas came and apologized to us,' Mum says in a rush. Drink obviously loosens her tongue!

240

'About the baby,' she adds, as if we might have thought he was apologizing for the loudness of the music or for playing too much country and western. 'I feel so much better about it now I know . . . I've been out of my mind with worry.'

There is a long silence while we all digest this piece of information. 'He said he would help. I told him that getting an education is very important for young parents. Emily will have to think about how she can carry on studying . . . we can't go off waltzing when she needs to do her A levels.'

It seems to me that Mum is rambling slightly. My education is just one problem that I will have to address—but not until I have had something to eat. There are also Augusta's problems which need to be thought about. I am unsure what to advise her. Should she give Wesley another chance? Or should she cut and run? I don't know the answer . . . all I do know is that I would hate to be in her shoes.

# CHAPTER TWENTY

Our house is like the morgue in the morning. While I am in the kitchen having breakfast Dad comes downstairs and makes strong coffee for Mum and tea for himself. 'Your mother's got the hangover from hell. And I'm not much better,' he confesses. 'Remind me never to touch Tia Maria or coffee ever again,' he adds. Then he looks down at my plate of scrambled eggs and crispy bacon and pulls a wry face. 'And to think we were worried about your Granny B drinking too much and dancing the night away. She went home early like a little cherub. I am reminded of the saying about people who live in glass houses—what do you think?'

I look at him a bit blankly, as I haven't a clue what he is going on about.

He manages a smile and adds: 'Anyway, you are a good advert for not drinking. You look very bright-eyed and full of beans this morning. And how is your friend . . . ?'

'Augusta . . . ' I prompt. 'I've taken her some coffee but she's got terrible jet lag. Also she's been very upset about her boyfriend. She's gone back to sleep so I think I'll leave her for a while. I'm just going to pop up to Nell Acre. There's something I need to sort out.'

I text Corey and ask if Brett is around because I need to speak to him.

Corey texts back to say that he is going to the hall with his dad and Brett is just getting out of bed. He finishes with 'c u l8ter'. He doesn't ask why I feel the need to speak to Brett which is a relief because there is no way I could start to explain it all to him in a text.

I leave the house and walk quickly through the snow, ignoring an icy wind that whips under the hood of my duffle coat and stings my face. By the time I get up to Nell Acre I am really quite warm, apart from my fingers which are like frozen sausages because I have forgotten my gloves. I am also starving hungry, despite my huge breakfast.

I ring the bell and nothing happens. I ring again. I wait for a while and then lean on the bell for ages. No one appears. My face begins to burn—it's partly from the cold but mainly because of embarrassment. I am here to see Brett and he is ignoring me—it is totally humiliating. I am just about to turn away, because my eyes are starting to ache and I am close to tears, when the front door opens and Brett stands before me. He is the kind of guy who is aware of how he looks, even when he goes to bed on his own. So he is wearing low cut pyjama bottoms and a wife-beater, his feet are bare, his hair tousled, and his cheeks gleam with golden stubble. He's gorgeous—and he knows it.

The embarrassment which started while I was waiting

now overwhelms me like a river in flood. I am horribly aware of the last time I saw him when he had just rolled out of bed. And I wish I hadn't decided to come to see him in the morning. It's just if I left it for too long I was worried I would lose my nerve and never say what is on my mind.

'Hey, good morning, Emily! We must have a psychic link.' His smile widens. 'I was just about to ring you. Come on in. I'm brewing coffee—want some?' He is at his most charming. I step inside and busy myself with taking off my boots and coat. Then I pad along to the kitchen in my socks.

He motions to the table. A mug of coffee is waiting for me. 'I'm very sorry, I can't drink coffee, it makes me feel ill,' I say apologetically.

'No problem. I'll make you some tea.'

'Could I please have something to eat?' I ask politely, like a dutiful child. 'I have to eat all the time or I get nausea,' I explain.

'What the hell! Why is that?' he says in a surprised voice.

'It's not easy being pregnant, you know. I think it's the hormones,' I say. And then I bite my lip and wish I hadn't spoken.

'Yeah . . . I guess so,' he says. He goes to the fridge and finds some yogurt and a bowl of grapes and holds them out to me. 'What do you want? Would this do?' I nod and he places them on the table in front of me. 'It can't have been easy having to face it on your own. Why didn't you get in touch with me?'

I don't reply. I just start to eat the grapes and yogurt. I don't look up until I have finished. Only then do I realize that he is nursing a large mug of black coffee and staring at me.

'I haven't been on my own. The twins and Corey have helped me.'

'The twins and Corey . . . ha . . . ' he says dismissively.

'What did you tell your father?'

'The truth. There's no point in not telling him straight because he has a way of finding out whatever he wants to know. He bullies you—and then he cries, then he gives you loads of emotional bullshit, and before you know it you've cracked and told him everything. It's impossible to keep anything secret from him. And believe me, I have tried.'

'What did he say to you?'

'He was confused. He'd got you down as Corey's squeeze. But he was OK when I told him the score.'

'And what is the score?'

'Well, the score is that this is my baby as much as yours and I want to be a part of its life. There's no way Dad would ever let me walk away from a child that was mine. And I wouldn't want to either. But let's just be straight about one thing, Emily—the baby is mine, isn't it? I mean, you are sure? I don't want to be lumbered with someone else's sprog.'

He smiles in an attempt to take the sting from his words. But it's useless. I feel as if someone has got hold of my stomach and twisted it in a knot. He is still

245

talking, his voice whining into my head like a chain-saw. He is saying he is sorry to have to ask me such personal stuff and generally trying to gloss over that fact that he has just asked me if I am a whore. I feel hot—and then I feel cold. I feel dizzy. Then I feel as if I am under water and drowning in his words that are bearing down on me like a ton weight.

I stare down at the empty yogurt container and the stalks of the grapes and wish he hadn't given me a family sized carton and such a huge bunch. I also wish I hadn't eaten them all—and at such a breakneck speed—because my stomach is churning like an over-loaded washing machine.

'Excuse . . . ' I don't have time to say more. I rush into the hallway and just make it to the cloakroom toilet before I puke.

When I get back to a standing position I realize the door is open and he is standing there, looking at me with a shocked expression on his face.

'What's up?' he asks in a bemused voice.

'I can't eat and get stressed at the same time. My stomach doesn't like it,' I croak. I wash my hands and rinse my face with water. Then I go back into the kitchen and sit down. He follows me and leans against the Aga.

'Are you OK?' he asks. He is looking as if he would like to be in some other place. 'Maybe we'll talk about all this later?' he suggests. 'But before you go, just put my mind at rest. You are absolutely a hundred per cent sure that this baby is mine?'

I look out of the window and make myself concentrate on the falling snow. The flakes are huge—plump and cloud-white and floating in a mesmerizing white curtain. Eventually I feel calm enough to speak. 'Yes, the baby is yours,' I say slowly. 'You are the only one . . . I've . . . you know.'

'Well, that's fine then. Lara and I are finished so there's no problem. You can move into my flat with me. It'll be cramped with a baby but Dad says he'll sort us out with something bigger. He'll have plenty of cash when the house is sold and he thinks that all babies should have a garden, so it will be something good. It will be cool. You can find a nursery and carry on with your A levels. You can go to university if you want, although obviously it would have to be Leeds.'

'I don't understand . . . ' I mutter.

'Well, I would have thought it was pretty obvious what I am offering. What don't you understand?'

'I don't love you,' I say. 'And you don't love me.'

Brett's face creases with sudden temper. 'Look, we're talking practicalities here, not romance.'

'But it is too much responsibility for a little baby to be the glue that holds us together. We should be together because we want each other, need each other, not because of a baby.'

'I don't get you at all,' Brett says. 'Do you want me to stand by you or not? I'm not going to tell you a load of trashy stuff about how I've always thought you were the girl for me or crap like that because you'll know it's not true. But we get on OK, don't we? You like me a lot, you said as much those times when we were together. And actions speak louder than words, don't they? You could have had an abortion—but you didn't. That must mean something.' His glance towards me is sly and at the same time proud. 'I don't understand what your problem is, Emily.'

'My problem, Brett, is that I don't love you.'

'Well, you liked me well enough before. Are you playing hard to get?'

'I'm not playing anything. I have to think about myself and I have to think about the baby.'

'We could give it a try, couldn't we? I mean, before you couldn't get enough of me . . . so what has changed?' He is suddenly surly, his glance sharp and hurt. 'My dad is prepared to help us and help the baby—surely that is important to you?'

'Of course it is. But what about Lara—you are always splitting up and then getting back together. It would seem that you *are* in love with her and she *is* the girl for you. So how, exactly, does she fit in to all of this?'

'She'll be gutted,' he says. It is impossible for him to hide the pleasure on his face as he adds, 'She's pining for a baby. She's spent the last year whining on to me about how she wants to get pregnant. She'll go completely loco when she finds out.'

'Why does that make you happy?' I ask quietly.

'She dumped me. It will pay her back,' he says simply.

'Has it never occurred to you that if you really loved her you would want her to be happy wherever she was—or whoever she was with?'

'Why should I be happy that she's with some other guy? You're not making any kind of sense. Anyway, why are we talking about Lara? She isn't part of my future—but my child is. I want to be involved, Emily. You can't deny me that right.'

I shake my head. I don't have the words to explain to him. 'Can I have some more tea, please?' I ask, because I want him to stop standing there staring at me.

He makes me a mug of tea. I sip it slowly and finally I say, 'I never realized before that you should *like* someone before you fall in love with them. It seems so obvious, doesn't it? Why don't they teach us stuff like that at school? They teach us all the practical stuff and show us how to put condoms on cucumbers. But they never tell us how emotions work.'

'Are you saying you don't like me?' he asks. He is sulky now.

'I don't know, Brett, and that's the truth. I've spent my teenage years fancying you and fantasizing about you. But when we were together we weren't friends, were we? We didn't meet up because we wanted to chill and find out about each other and share our thoughts. You would tease me and I would cry. And then we'd jump on each other and wrestle. It was like we were gladiators. That was until I gave in and we had sex. But it was always as if there was a war raging and we were on different sides.'

'You're not going to tell me you didn't enjoy it!' he scoffs dismissively. 'You were keen as mustard—you couldn't get enough. I couldn't keep you away.'

'I'm not proud of the way I behaved. And I haven't got any excuses. All I will say was that it was like the scariest ride at the fair. It was like being on the biggest roller coaster in the world. I was scared and excited and out of my head—I think I must have been overdosing on desire and adrenalin. The sad thing is I thought it was for real. I thought that was what love was: that terrible needy longing, that feeling of sick excitement and the fear . . . When you kissed me I felt as if I might die from emotion. The stupid thing is, I never asked myself if I was happy or if I was enjoying it.'

'Believe me, you enjoyed it . . . you enjoyed it very much . . . ' he says slowly. His eyes are narrow and glittering—sharp as steel—and his mouth is in an angry pout. I can sense he is getting irritated by me. I blurt out what is in my head because suddenly I am desperate for him to understand.

'I never knew that when you spend time kissing someone you love you go to a wonderful dark haven. You go to a place where you feel safe and warm and protected. You don't feel scared or confused or guilty because it seems the most perfect thing to be doing—and it's totally peaceful and beautiful and right.'

'Excuse me,' he butts in rudely. 'Are you telling me you are in love with this person you've been kissing?'

'Yes, I think I am . . . ' I say slowly. 'And what we share certainly doesn't feel anything like what happened between you and me. We are best friends. If I have a problem that's where I turn, if I am happy I want to share it. I'm never scared, never confused by what happens between us. We like and trust each other completely.'

'I don't want my kid being brought up by a pair of lesbians,' he says grumpily.

'What?' I say in astonishment.

'Well, that big-mouthed Florence was going off like a complete loony . . . why else would she be making such a lot of trouble? You are a pair of les girls, don't tell me you're not.'

'If that's what you want to think . . . ' I say slowly. 'You don't have much of an opinion of me, do you? First you question me about other men, then you assume I like girls. Not that it would matter if I did. But it just shows that you don't know me at all. If it wasn't for the baby you wouldn't want me, would you?'

'Probably not,' he retorts coolly. 'What you've been saying about kissing doesn't make any kind of sense to me. Kissing just makes me feel horny and frustrated. Are you seriously telling me you are going to spend the rest of your life just kissing this person?'

'Maybe, maybe not,' I say lightly. 'None of us knows for certain where our life is going. All I do know—with absolute certainty—is that being friends, and the way I feel when we kiss, is a good foundation for spending time together and seeing what happens.'

'You should have kept to your precious Kissing Club vow then, shouldn't you?' he mocks.

'Yes. I suppose so,' I say. 'I will let you share the baby if that is what you really want. But you have to want to do it for the baby and for yourself, not as an

251

ego trip, or to please your father, or to spite Lara. This baby is a new life—a brand new beginning—and that seems like a very important thing to me. This baby didn't choose us for parents, and I would like he-or-she to arrive in this world without any emotional baggage waiting for them—and also for us to be the very best parents we can possibly be. I would also like the world to rejoice. I'm not asking for angels or shepherds or a star in the sky. Just for people to be pleased and happy and to celebrate. You can be on that welcoming committee or not, it's up to you. But that is all that is on offer.'

'Just tell me who the other person is?'

'Corey.'

'You're joking me!'

'Why would I do that?'

'He is . . . he is my kid brother . . . '

'Well, I'm sorry, but you can't choose who you love.'

'Does he know?'

'Know what?'

'How you feel?'

'Yes.'

'Are you sure about all this, Emily? He's still a big kid. You should see the way he blubbed about the dog when it went to the animal shelter. You would be better off with me, you know.'

'I'm sorry, Brett. I just don't feel it for you. I feel it for Corey.'

'It's maybe because you're pregnant. You might feel differently after the baby arrives,' he says a bit desperately.

I shake my head. 'I don't think so. Anyway, it's a risk I'll run. I'm going now,' I add. I make my way back into the hall and start to pull on my socks and boots.

'What shall I tell my father?' he asks.

'Tell him the truth, that's the best way, isn't it?' I say soothingly to him. I feel light and free and suddenly very hungry. I decide that I will call in at Bridge Cottage and see Mrs Patton and Granny. Mrs Patton always has a plentiful supply of scones and cakes. I feel in need of some carbohydrate and comfort food.

# CHAPTER TWENTY-ONE

Granny and Mrs Patton are having an early lunch and ask me to join them, which is very handy. I consume a jacket potato, cheese, ham, salad, and a huge slice of fruit cake—then I feel better!

The snow has stopped falling and the world outside the window looks beautiful—as white and perfectly-coated as a newly-iced Christmas cake.

After I have consumed two cups of tea and a plate of home-made vanilla fudge I start to feel sleepy. 'Shall I take Peaches for a little walk? I could see if Augusta is up. She might like some fresh air,' I add. I stifle a yawn because the cottage is very warm and I am in serious danger of nodding off. The soporific cosiness seems to have had the opposite effect on Peaches— she is really hyper and keeps on jumping up onto the chair by the window and yapping.

As soon as we are through the door Peaches starts pulling on her lead. This is a nuisance because the snow is quite deep and the pavements are slippery. I am very relieved that she is so small and fragile because if she was a Great Dane I would be in trouble.

I try to head for home but she doesn't want to go. She is pulling towards the main road and the post office. 'You know we don't walk up there, Peachy, it's boring,' I say. 'And the post office is shut so there're no titbits for you today. Come on, we'll go to see Augusta.'

Peaches won't follow me—instead she pulls on her leash and then she sits down and whines. I pick her up and put her over my shoulder and carry her up the road. She yaps in a sorrowful kind of way as if telling me in dog language that I am very stupid. It makes me smile. I love her when she's eccentric. 'Whatever is the matter with you, today?' I ask.

Augusta is still fast asleep and her coffee is untouched. I leave her a note telling her to ring my mobile when she wakes up. I think about ringing Corey to ask if he'd like a walk but he will be busy with the big clean-up at the hall and I doubt if he will skive (even for me!). So I fill my pockets with chocolates and set off for a walk on my own.

It is not a restful experience. As soon as we are out of the house Peaches is yanking me along, once again trying to drag me up to the top of the village. I decide to give in and just let her take me for a walk.

By the time we reach the church hall she is yapping with excitement. I can hear the sounds of voices and the hum of a vac through the open door but I don't have time to stop. We gallop past the post office which surprises me because I had assumed that was where she was heading. The post office staff are Peaches fans and have a special box of dog choco drops which they keep by the till. I had thought she wanted to visit there. But she doesn't seem interested in being sociable. Instead she leads me to the main road.

Breathlessly I pick her up. 'Do you want to get a bus to Leeds and have a look in the sales?' I ask, smiling. She wriggles in my arms and I set her down. She pulls and pulls on the lead and whines in a way that is pathetic. Eventually I slacken the lead and let her have her head completely because I haven't got a clue where she wants to go or why she is behaving like a bloodhound. Maybe we shouldn't have let her watch so much TV over Christmas.

To my horror she starts to pull me around to the squalid area behind the bus shelter. 'Peaches, there's nothing there you want to look at!' I say in alarm. I am remembering how a dead cat was once found behind the shelter. It's also a place where the local boys pee and where stupid people throw empty cans and takeaway rubbish. It is not a place to visit, not even on a day like this when the world is cleansed and whitened by snow.

'No!' I say firmly and I hold Peaches still. 'Come away,' I command. And then I try to walk back to the post office and the safety of the quiet village streets.

Peaches follows me. Then, when the lead is loose enough, she doubles back and slips out of her collar. I am terrified. I never knew she could do such a naughty thing. I look down at the empty collar lying in the snow and just about manage to screech her name. Fortunately there is no traffic on the road. When I come to my senses I see that she is disappearing around the back of the bus shelter.

'You bad girl . . . come here . . . ' I say, as I follow her. But my voice is weak and wavering. I am just so relieved that she isn't running around on the road and getting killed.

The back of the bus shelter is sanitized by snow that has fallen off the roof and landed in a drift. Peaches is digging in this soft heap and barking.

'Peaches! There's nothing here for you!' I say, exasperated, slipping her collar back on. Even covered in snow the rear of the bus shelter is a grim place and I am scared she will stand on broken glass or a rusty can. I don't want her to get hurt. All kinds of nasty things end up here. Once an old settee and a fridge were left for ages until some workmen from the council came and took them away. I am starting to wonder if someone has dumped the remains of their Christmas dinner and that is what she can smell because this is alarming behaviour from her—normally she is so fastidious.

Peaches is scratting away at the hump of snow and shaggy bits are showing through. She has obviously found an old mat or blanket that has caught her imagination (or her nose).

'Leave it, Peaches,' I beg. But she is digging furiously as more and more of the matted hair is uncovered. I suddenly realize that it is not a mat or a blanket but something that is (or was) alive. I am so traumatized by this realization that I have a sudden religious conversion. A theme from a junior school assembly comes into my mind and I find myself praying aloud to St Francis of Assisi that it isn't a dead cat that has been mangled on the road and crawled in here to die. If it is I shall scream.

When part of the hump moves I screech so loudly that Peaches stops digging. I suddenly realize that a half-dead cat might actually be worse than a completely dead one. My imagination goes into overdrive at the thought and a wave of nausea hits my stomach. Peaches yaps at me—as if berating me for being such a coward—as she returns to the hump. I am desperate to get her away. I don't know what is under the snow but I am getting seriously scared and stressed. I want to find Corey and get him to help me. I can't handle this alone.

It is while I am reaching for her collar that I really look at the hump of snow for the first time and realize that it isn't a cat—it is a dog. It is a golden retriever that is lying on its side and trying to raise its head.

I realize that prayers and tears are useless. I have got to cope with this. I kneel down next to the dog and use my scarf to scrape the snow away. My hands are trembling so much it takes me ages and I curse my lack of gloves and the terror that threatens to overwhelm me. Half the time I can hardly see what I am doing because my eyes are full of tears. When the dog is clear of snow I force myself to really look at it. The lower part of its body is black with mud and I can see smears of blood in the snow but apart from that it seems whole and uninjured. It is trying to move. 'Keep still, quiet now,' I say soothingly. At the sound of my voice the head raises and a pink tongue touches my hand. This dog knows me. In a sudden flash I recognize the dog and I also know why Peaches was so desperate to come here and find it. 'Oh, Kizzy . . . ' I moan. 'What has happened to you?'

Rudimentary first aid training filters through my panic. I need to keep her warm. I pull off my duffle coat and lay it over her. 'Stay! Stay, Kizzy!' I command tearfully. Then I pick up Peaches and run for the church hall calling out as I do so: 'Help, help! It's Kizzy! She's behind the bus shelter and she's hurt.'

By the time we reach the door of the church hall quite a crowd has gathered. Everyone is buzzing and talking at once. But the important information that the Thomases' dog is lying behind the bus shelter injured has got through. Someone puts a blanket around me. Another blanket is taken to make a stretcher for Kizzy. Nanette Blake, who works as a nurse for the local vet, appears like magic. I bury my face in my hands and sob and miss what happens. The next thing I know Corey is putting his arms around me and saying, 'It's a miracle. How did you find her?'

'Is she . . . ?' I ask.

'Nanette has looked her over and she thinks she's fine. We're going to get her to the vet hospital straight away so they can X-ray her and put her on a drip. She's dehydrated and her paws are bleeding but it seems likely she's just exhausted. She must have been running for days with nothing to eat . . . and not a lot to drink. By the time she got to the bus shelter she couldn't walk another step. It's lucky for her it snowed because it kept her warm. Will you be OK if I go with Nanette?'

'Yes of course,' I say. The hall is full of people and everyone is talking about Kizzy. They are also talking about me and saying how wonderful I am. People keep patting my shoulder or shaking my hand and telling me what a good job it was that I found Kizzy in time. I start to feel a bit embarrassed as it was really Peaches that did the finding.

Eventually I get sick of feeling like a complete fraud so I take Peaches back to the cottage and tell Mrs Patton and Granny everything that has happened. They also seem to think I have been a heroine; even though I tell them Peaches was the brains behind the discovery, and I was totally terrified the whole time. They just laugh at me and tell me I'm a star.

'Poor Kizzy,' Mrs Patton says. 'Maybe the Thomases will change their minds and keep her. She must be a very loyal dog and very attached to them to run away from her new owners and then come all this way to find them.'

'Corey is going to university and I don't think Mr Thomas has time for a dog. He's going to be living in Leeds city centre.'

'Well, I think I shall ask if I can keep her,' Mrs Patton says. 'She and Peaches are obviously very fond of each other. I've often thought about getting a companion for her. Then you can take them both for a walk,' she says to me with a smile. 'Do you think you will be able to manage two dogs and a baby?'

'I can certainly try,' I say. 'I think Corey would like her to stay in the village. You'll have to watch out for all your ornaments though, she's very big and bouncy.'

'I'll put the valuable things on high shelves,' Mrs Patton says. 'And the rest can go in the attic for safe keeping. We'll be fine.'

'Granny,' I ask, 'did you keep things from when Mum was a little girl? Things she made at school, paintings, stuff like that . . . ' I am thinking of the Fimo figurines, the bronzed ballet shoes, and the cheap plaster dogs that say 'Present from Brid' that will go to live in Mrs Patton's attic because they are too precious to throw away.

'Oh yes,' Granny says. 'The cupboard under the stairs is full of boxes. I did keep all her baby clothes but then I realized that they could be useful to someone else so I sent them to a jumble sale. Why do you ask?'

'I just wondered why some people keep things and other people don't.'

'I think maybe it's to do with space and how many times you move house,' Granny says. She looks at me with a little puzzled frown. 'Are you thinking about your mother—she doesn't hoard anything, does she?' she asks.

I nod and shake my head at the same time. 'It doesn't matter,' I say.

'I think your mum likes to keep all the precious things that have happened to her in her head. Maybe she feels they are safer there. Also memories in your mind never fade or fall to bits. Really, it might be a better way than keeping bits of paper and junk,' Granny says.

'I don't mind Mum not hoarding things. But I think I shall,' I say. 'I feel as if I will want to.'

Mrs Patton and Granny both laugh at this and Granny says, 'Oh, no doubt you will, traits like that often skip a generation. You'll end up just like your grannies.'

'Well, that will be fine by me,' I say, smiling, 'especially if I inherit your dressmaking skills and the cooking ability of Granny Sutton.' I yawn and add, 'I better get home and see if Augusta is awake. She's had a traumatic time and the wedding is postponed. I think she will need lots of TLC.'

Never was a truer word spoken. Augusta stays in bed for ten days. I run up and down the stairs with endless cups of coffee, lightly boiled eggs, and dainty sandwiches. Most of these sit on the bedside table to grow cold, congeal, and curl at the edges. Every so often I force her to wake up and eat something—even if it's only a bowl of cereal. After she has eaten she weeps for a while and then goes back to sleep.

I am just starting to get worried about her (and about myself because I feel like Sleeping Beauty's nursemaid) when she bounces downstairs one morning while we are having breakfast. Her hair is gleaming and there's a smile on her face. My parents seem startled to see her, as if they had forgotten she had been sleeping in the spare room since the night of the party. And they are stunned into complete silence when she announces that she intends to stay in the UK, because it feels like home and also because she wants to help me with the baby.

Augusta then spends three days on the phone non-stop—while I supply glasses of milk and peanut butter and jam sandwiches. At the end of this telecommunication-marathon she has an allowance from her parents, a car, and a provisional place at college. Wesley's name is not mentioned. It seems he is consigned to history.

Augusta then charges into action to organize my life. The twins moan about her like mad and don't understand why she doesn't drive me nuts with her bossiness and lists of things to do. But the truth is that Augusta is so sincere and kind I give in to all her demands. Also the last three months of being pregnant make me sooooooo tired. I feel as big and cumbersome as a blue whale without an ocean. And most of the time it is a relief to let Augusta take control.

Augusta gets so much information about giving birth it seems as if we are taking a degree level course in modern motherhood. I swear I could do a PhD in birthing. I have to research websites, watch DVDs and read books. Then I have to go to classes. I had felt a bit nervous about going along to these. But honestly Augusta is so loud (and so keen to know everything) that I don't think anyone even notices me. As soon as the midwife asks a question Augusta has her hand in the air and is jumping around keen to show her knowledge. What she doesn't know about giving birth and babies could be written on a postage stamp. Also she is huge (due to all the doughnuts she ate when she was unhappy about Wes) and she could easily be as pregnant as me. The people at the hospital probably think we are both having babies. After these classes Augusta makes me practise stuff that we have learnt: breathing and saying nursery rhymes backwards.

# POSTSCRIPT

Despite all Augusta's help and the endless research, *nothing* prepared me for the reality of having a baby. To begin with none of the signs which Augusta waited for so patiently appeared: the baby didn't move down, I didn't feel the urge to clean my room or want to buy new duvet covers, neither did I have a sudden craving for exotic food, or backache, or have to dash for a wee every five minutes. In fact none of the usual stuff which mothers claim told them the baby was on the way happened to me.

If I'd had the remotest idea that the baby would arrive early and completely unexpectedly I wouldn't have gone for a walk with Corey, Kizzy, and Peaches. But maybe that desire to be out in the open was a sign and I didn't spot it.

Anyway, Augusta had gone to Leeds to shop and I had gone for a walk. It was the lure of spring that tempted me. All the trees were at that wonderful stage when the buds are purple and tightly wrapped. There was an air of expectation in the soft wind that blew damply from the west. And the grass on the river banks was green and trembling. It was as if the whole world was just waiting to burst into life. I spotted snowdrops hiding in a sheltered hollow behind an oak tree and Corey picked one for my buttonhole as I was too fat to bend down.

I lumbered along, sniffing the air and enjoying myself, rather like a performing bear that has escaped from the circus and is tasting freedom for the first time. 'Are you getting tired? Shall we turn back?' Corey asked me.

'No . . . It's brilliant to be outside. It's such a lovely day: too nice to be indoors. I'm fine. I'm not tired now I'm out. Can we walk up to Nell Acre?'

'Are you sure you can make it?'

'Yes, the midwife says walking is good. Also the baby's head needs to engage. Maybe if I move around he or she will get the message and get into blast-off position. I feel as if I've been pregnant for a thousand years. I can't wait for it to be over and to be able to see my feet again.'

That was the last sensible thing I said. My waters broke and I just stood and stared at him. 'Corey!' I wailed. 'I've wet myself . . . '

'Of course you haven't,' he said soothingly. He had watched enough of Augusta's videos (without falling asleep) to know exactly what was happening. 'Now don't panic, Emily. You've got lots of time. We'll just walk slowly back and get your suitcase and go straight to the hospital.'

'I think Nell Acre is nearer,' I said.

'Maybe. Do you want to go there? And I'll drive you down.'

'Yes, I want to go to Nell Acre.'

It took ages to get to the house as the contractions hit me so hard I had to lean against trees and pant. And it's just as well that Augusta wasn't there because every single nursery rhyme I had ever known went straight out of my head and instead I just swore as loudly as I could. When all this ranting and raving was going on Kizzy and Peaches stood and stared at me with silent sympathy. And Corey held my hands and didn't mind when I crushed his fingers.

Corey half carried me the last stretch and all the time he was telling me to keep calm and it would be OK and that I had hours. Really, I don't know what was the most frightening thought—that I would have hours of contractions or that the baby would arrive before we got to the hospital. It all seemed to be happening so quickly. And by the time he had me sitting next to the Aga I had a strong premonition that time was very short. I didn't need a stopwatch to tell me the contractions were coming short and fast, melting into one furnace of pain.

'Call the doctor,' I said through gritted teeth. 'And ask if someone can come here immediately. I don't think I've got time to get to hospital.'

'But first babies take forever. Augusta said so . . . she said we would be able to read to you to pass the time.'

'CALL THE DOCTOR'S SURGERY!' I yelled. 'Just get someone, anyone, the caretaker, the caretaker's dog, anyone who knows anything about giving birth to come up ASAP!'

'What do I do?' he asked, after he had phoned. None of the books we had read had described this particular scenario.

'Put the kettle on. Get some towels. Do like they do in old films,' I said in between pants. 'I think I need to lie down.'

'Where do you want to be? Do you want to go up to my room?'

'Do you mind?' I asked.

'No, of course not! Come on. Lean on me.'

He had just got me settled on the bed when the doorbell rang. It was the young female doctor I had seen right at the beginning and a nurse. 'You were right,' I told the doctor. 'Babies are just like buses. Never on time . . . '

'My goodness, this baby is in a hurry to get into the world,' the doctor said with glee after she had examined me. 'There's very little for us to do. You just need one good push.'

And so my daughter arrived in a rush—tumbling head-first into a world of tangled sheets and laughter. And I was happy that she had chosen to arrive at Nell Acre in Corey's bed. It seemed like an auspicious omen for us all.

And it was a lovely start to be born in the village because everyone came to see her and brought gifts— she was a celebrity baby. There were times I even expected a couple of shepherds and some wise men to arrive. And I did have three wise women when Mrs Ives, Mrs English, and Mrs Martin came to offer beautiful hand-knitted baby clothes and lots of advice about latching on and feeding schedules.

Brett brought the most expensive present (an elaborate and ostentatious christening gown with a lace train that would touch the floor). And as I looked at it I knew I was truly my mother's daughter—because an anti-hoarding gene kicked in. I found myself wondering where on earth I was going to put it when the christening was over as it would take up at least half a wardrobe.

To cover such an uncharitable thought I quickly asked him if he had any thoughts about names for the baby and he looked surprised.

'Your mother's name for a middle name, maybe?' I suggested.

His face twisted for a second. Then he said, 'Like she deserves to be remembered!' And there was a long silence while we both looked down at the baby and I wished I hadn't spoken.

Then he said slowly, 'When I spoke to your parents at the party your mother was so amazing. I thought she might lose her temper with me. But she was awesome. I looked at her and I thought . . . ' He stopped for a moment as if embarrassed, then he said in a rush, 'I'm not saying Dad didn't do a great job. But I looked at your mum as she was talking about you, and I thought to myself that I might have turned out differently— better—if I'd had a mother like her. Could we . . . I mean I would really like it, if we gave the baby her name as a middle name?'

So her first name was left for me alone to choose. It came to me quickly. It was as if she knew what it was and told me. She's called Atlanta: this name is partly for Augusta and partly because it is a name like an ocean and conjures up images of boundless energy and promise. It suits her because she has fallen into our lives and changed the map of where we all are.

Julia Clarke trained as a teacher at Goldsmiths' College, London, and as an actress at the Guildford School of Acting. She worked in educational theatre until her children were born when she started writing novels, short stories, and articles. Six novels for adults have been followed by several novels for teenagers. Julia lives on a farm in North Yorkshire with her husband, son, and daughter. In 1999 she was awarded an MA(Dist.) in creative writing from the University of Leeds. *The Kissing Club* is her sixth novel for Oxford University Press.

# OTHER BOOKS BY JULIA CLARKE

ISBN 978-0-19-275415-8

It starts as a joke.
A strange girl turns up at a family party and pretends to
be an old friend of Alice's. So Alice plays along—why not?
It serves the others right for being so foul to her.

But the joke soon wears thin. The gatecrasher—*the other Alice*—
clearly wants more than just a free drink. Soon she has wormed
her way into the heart of the family. Only Alice knows that she
has no right to be there. But by then it's too late to tell the truth.

Who is *the other Alice*—and how can she be stopped?

**Chasing Rainbows**
*Julia Clarke*

ISBN 978-0-19-275326-7

*It is while I am sitting in Ash's kitchen that the idea
comes to me. An arranged marriage could be a very good thing.
For a parent, that is . . .*

It seems simple to Rose. Her mum is creative but chaotic. Ash's
dad is organized but uninspired. They say opposites attract—so it's
got to be a recipe for wedded bliss.

It seems like a perfect scheme.

But throw into the mix two unexpected cousins, a suspicious party
invitation, a transatlantic crisis, a helpful poetry professor, and an
injured dancer—and somehow it's not surprising that things don't
turn out quite as Rose has planned!

ISBN 978-0-19-275382-3

What's going on . . . between Jack and Sybil?

She's the most gorgeous girl in the school. So when she decides to make a play for Jack, who can blame him for being interested?

What's going on . . . between Jade and Jack?

Jade and Jack have never had any secrets from each other. So why is he suddenly so frightened to tell her the truth?

What's going on . . . between Jade and her parents?

Jack's not the only one with a secret. Jade's parents are acting strangely too. Now Jade's frightened that she's going to find out something that will change her life for ever . . .

You lose some,
You win some
life is never simple...

Julia Clarke

ISBN 978-0-19-275327-4

Mum's gone away.
Everyone's talking about Mum—and they all seem
to know more about it than I do . . .

Jon's come back.
I'm not sure how I feel about seeing him again.
And what has he been up to while he's been away?

I'm all over the place.
Parents, brothers, friends, boyfriend—they're all moving on.
So where does that leave me?

summertime
blues

it's going to be a crazy summer...

Julia Clarke

ISBN 978-0-19-275196-6

Two's company, three's a crowd.
At first my parents' divorce didn't make much difference
to me. Then my mother, dressed as a born-again tart, got
together with bad-tempered Seth.

The horror, the horror.
Now I'm forced to join them in their love nest—a manky
cottage in Yorkshire. It's the pits. What's a lad to do?

Could this be the summer from hell?
Me, and two girls—scruffy Louie and impossibly
perfect Faye—and a whole herd of goats. How could that
possibly turn out to be fun?